LINDA SEALY KNOWLES

To Shirley,
Have a truly wonderful day. Enjoy this sweet love story.
Linda

Where Love Happens

By

Linda Sealy Knowles

Copyright © 2024 Linda Sealy Knowles
Forget Me Not Romances, a division of Winged Publications

All rights reserved. No part of this publication may be reproduced, stored in a retrieval system, or transmitted in any form or by any means, with the exception of brief quotations in printed reviews.

This book is a work of fiction. The characters in this story are the product of the author's imagination and are completely fictitious.

Forget Me Not
Publisher
~ Where stories take flight~

ISBN: 978-1-962168-66-3

In Memory

This love story is in memory of my husband, Pete. He is always on my mind and in my heart. My one regret I have is he isn't here to enjoy my stories. Love surrounded us. I am blessed to have had him in my life for forty years.

Other Books written by Linda Sealy Knowles

The Maxwell Saga: (Six Books)
Journey to Heaven Knowles Where
Hannah's Way
The Secret
Bud's Journey Home
Always Jess
Ollie's World
~
Abby's new Life
Kathleen of Sweetwater
Sunflower Brides
Trapped by Love
The Gamble
Joy's Cowboy
A Stranger's Love
Anna, the Lawman's Problem
Forever Mine
Not for Love or Money

Social Media Contact

Website: authorlindasealyknowles.com
Email: Lindajk@cox.net
Facebook: Linda Sealy Knowles or Linda Knowles
Goodread.com

LINDA SEALY KNOWLES

Chapter 1

Lizzy Montgomery stood out in the backyard, hanging the Monday wash. She was singing, "Oh what a beautiful day," when she felt a tug on her skirt. "Lizzy!" Joshua, one of her seven- year- old twin brothers yelled, "You got to come to the front. A man is lying over his horse. I think he's dead. Come, now!"

"Oh, Joshua, I don't have time for your shenanigans. Can't you see I'm busy?" she said, picking up another piece of wet laundry. She could hear Blue, the children's dog, barking.

Joshua wasn't giving up. He ran up to her, jerked the shirt from her hands and began pulling her across the yard. "I ain't playing. His big horse is drinking water from our trough. Come on, hurry."

Lizzy sighed and gave him her full attention. She hurried to the front of the house. "Quiet, Blue, and get back under the house." Lizzy waved her apron at the dog, who was growling and barking at the strange horse. "Oh, my goodness, Joshua. Go to the barn and round up Jake. Tell him to come and help." Lizzy was surprised to see a man and horse in front of the house. He appeared to be severely hurt, maybe even dead.

Lizzy eased over to the stranger lying sideways on the giant horse, with bloody chaps and hands. "Come on, boy," she spoke softly to the horse, hoping he would allow her to lead him to the porch, which was three feet off the ground.

Blue was steadily jumping close to the horse's hoofs, growling.

Five-year-old Pearl, Lizzy's baby sister, stood in the doorway. She dropped her doll down by her side and pointed to the man. "Who's that, Mama Lizzy?"

"I don't know, Sugar, but you can help me by getting a clean sheet from the big chest. I need to spread it on the porch so we can drag this man into the house."

"But, Lizzy, you said never let a stranger in. Are you sure you want to let him come inside?"

"Please do as I asked and hurry with the sheet." Lizzy smiled at her frightened little sister as she ran back inside.

Jake came running from the barn, cow manure between his toes and hay in his hair. He stopped with wide eyes. "Who's this man, Lizzy?"

"I'm guessing he's a drifter, but he's been hurt. Wash up some so you can help me drag him off his horse and inside the house. But, first make Blue behave and stop barking. He's upsetting the stranger's horse."

"Quiet, Blue," Jake yelled. "Get under the porch, now." Blue whined, then crawled on his belly to the edge of the porch to stand guard.

Jake hurried to the water trough, rubbed his hands clean, and hurried back to his sister. "How are we going to get this big boy down from his horse onto the porch?"

Lizzy studied the man and horse. "Joshua, you hold the horse's head, as we lead him to the porch, then Jake and I'll pull him off his saddle to the porch. Then, we can roll him onto the sheet, drag him inside, and put him on my bed." She looked at her two brothers. "Are you ready?"

Joshua stood next to the horse while Jake grabbed the man's right leg and tossed it over the saddle. The stranger cried out when his shoulder landed on the porch. Joshua walked the horse and tied his reins to the hitching post. Then, rushing back to Lizzy and Jake, he helped turn the man onto his back. "Lizzy, look at all that blood. He's sure gonna ruin your sheet."

"It'll be all right. I'll soak it in cold water, but let's pull the stranger inside." Lizzy and both boys each took a corner of the sheet and dragged him into the living room. "Come on, let's take him to my room. He can't lie out here."

After a few more tugs, they had moved the stranger into Lizzy and Pearl's room. After judging the man's size, she said, "Now we need to lift him onto the bed."

Lizzy stood and looked at her three siblings. What was she thinking; there was no way they were going to be able to help her with this tall, lanky man. Just then, Jake burst out with a suggestion.

"Try to wake him, Lizzy. Maybe, he can help us."

"Good idea. He did make some noise while on the porch." Lizzy knelt and took the man's face in her hands. She slapped his sweaty cheeks softly to try to wake him. "Hey, fellow, can you hear me? I need your help." After a couple more tries, the man moaned and opened one eye. He saw a beautiful young girl with a scarf wrapped around her wild, reddish hair. He was sure she was a windblown angel.

"Help me," he mumbled.

"We're trying to, but you have to try and stand. Can you try, please?"

This time the stranger opened both eyes and groaned. "Help me up," he said, offering his arms to Lizzy. His legs wobbled as Libby and the boys pulled him to a standing position. They immediately allowed him to sit back onto the bed. Sighing big, the stranger fell unconscious again.

"Thank the good Lord," Lizzy said. "Jake, please bring me a pan of hot water and, Joshua, retrieve my medicine box and put it beside the bed. Pearl, you can remove his boots and socks. Boys, please remove his chaps and jeans, too."

All the children fell into action while Lizzy went to retrieve her scissors. After laying them on the table beside the bed, she remembered her wash and rushed outside and threw the wet clothes over the line. She didn't want to have to redo the wet things. When the wet clothes were secure on the line to dry, she returned inside to find a sheet covering the stranger from his waist down.

The children had undressed the stranger, and he was sleeping, by the time she returned. "Thank you so much. I can take it from here. Except boys, take the man's horse, unsaddle it, and put him in the barn with some oats. Poor animal could use a good rub down."

"If he dies, can we keep that fine horse?" Jake asked.

"Jake Montgomery, I won't have such talk. We all need to pray for this poor soul." Lizzy didn't get her feathers ruffled often, but she was surprised to hear her brother coveting another man's possession.

Examining the young man, she saw sweat on his bare chest. As she pulled the sheet over his body, she felt a radiating, unhealthy heat coming from his skin.

Lizzy knew she had to take care of this stranger immediately. She hurried into the kitchen, grabbed a bottle of vinegar, and poured some in the hot water that Jake had fixed for her. She preceded to sponge his face, neck, arms and chest. After straightening the sheet, she placed a cold compress on his brow to bring down his fever. Next, she needed to check where all the blood had come from.

Holding her breath, Lizzy slowly lifted the sheet. Flames of embarrassment shot through her body at the sight of his nakedness. Thank goodness the wound was just below his waistline. She gasped as she looked at the hole in his side. The bullet had penetrated all the way from the front to his back. It was a raggedy wound. After cleaning away most of the blood, she knew the wound needed a good cleaning before it could be stitched closed.

Chapter 2

After Lizzy thoroughly inspected the bullet wound, she could tell the man had been wounded a few days earlier. The injury had festered and would require more than just a cleaning. The man required a doctor to tend his wounds, but the last time she saw Doctor Hayes, the local doctor, he said he would be going to St. Louis to learn more about performing surgeries. He said he'd be out of town for several weeks but would drop by to check on them as soon as he returned.

Doctor Hayes was a dear friend who had delivered the twins and little Pearl. Several weeks after Pearls' birth, Lizzy's pa had run off, leaving the family stranded. Her mama was in poor health, and at the age of sixteen, Lizzy had to be the family's caretaker. Doctor Hayes helped by giving advice on how to care for the little ones. In addition, he stopped by often while visiting others in the area.

As she looked at the stranger's injured side, even after all the years of caring for the little ones and her poor, deceased mama, they had not prepared her for this. As she leaned over his body, she heard his stomach grumble. *Good gracious, if he got shot a few days ago, he's likely not had anything to eat. He is probably starving.*

Lizzy covered his body with the sheet, rushed into the kitchen and pulled down her string of gingerroot that she kept close to the kitchen window. She pounded a piece and placed it in a small pan of water to make wild ginger root tea. This would treat him from the inside, too.

He lay still as death when she carried the tea back to him. She blew on the tea and attempted to spoon-feed it to him. The liquid only dribbled from his lips. It rolled down the side of his face into his ear, which she quickly wiped away.

She tried again to force another spoonful, but it only made him cough.

Lizzy pressed her hand to her mouth, almost in tears. She had to find a way to get nourishment in him. Then, suddenly, she saw the tall sunflowers in a vase on the side table. The flowers made her think about the tall cattails at the river's edge. They would make great straws. Yes, she could have him sip the liquid into his mouth.

"Pearl, please sit in the padded chair at the foot of the bed and watch over our patient. You can be his little nurse. Do not touch him, understand? I'm going to the river and gather some cattails. I will tell the boys where you are, all right?"

"Yes, mama, I will be the Nightingale nurse while you're away." Lizzy smiled at Pearl, remembering the children's story written by Hans Christian Anderson that she had read many times.

As fast as she could, Lizzy tiptoed into the water at the edge of the bank. After plucking several cattails, she raced back to the house and found her little nurse and patient both sound asleep.

Taking a knitting needle, she reamed out the pith from the cattails' center, then poured water into a cup and tried using the straw to sip some. It worked. Pleased with her new tool, she lifted her patient's face and pried open his mouth with her fingers. She placed the cattail down his throat, gagging herself at what she was doing to him.

Working so close to the man, Lizzy realized her pulse was beating strangely. She had never experienced such weird sensations nor had such forbidden thoughts about any man. Giving herself a shake, she scolded herself. *Lizzy, concentrate. You need to feed this man.* She tried to wake him enough to have him sip the tea, but his eyeballs rolled back, and he closed his eyes.

Drifting in and out of consciousness, the stranger wondered if he opened his eyes would all this be a nightmare, or was all the pain that was gnawing at his body real. His body ached all over. He tried to move around, but he didn't realize what was being done for him.

Lizzy couldn't keep the liquid in the cattail, so she filled her mouth and blew the ginger tea into the straw down his throat. As she lifted the straw a little, he swallowed. Again and again, she forced him to swallow the tea. She continued to feed the cowboy, until he moaned and clapped his teeth closed, letting her know he had enough. She tried to pry open his teeth, but he bit her fingers. She held in the scream, withdrew her hand, and sucked the blood off them.

Lizzy decided she couldn't put off doing anything about his wound any longer. She had to see what she could do to help him. It was terrible, but luckily the bullet appeared to have passed through the other side. Pus was already forming, and the skin around the wound was an odd color and smelled putrid. If gangrene had already set in, he could die if she didn't do something. He seemed to be relaxed and sleeping, so this was an excellent time to doctor the injury. All she had in her cabinet were alcohol, vinegar, mineral oil, and turpentine. But then she remembered reading about an ancient treatment--maggots.

The thought made her skin crawl, but she had to do something. She knew that the insect was creepy and slimy. The slime was a great healing balm that could consume the infected tissue and leave the good tissue unscathed. Cold chills ran up and down her spine just thinking about the treatment, but what other choice did she have?

Hurrying to the front door, she called the boys to come inside. "Now listen to me, please," she said to Jake and Joshua. "I need you to scout inside the old hog pen and search for some old rotten, wet boards. Look for aboard that has some white maggots clinging to it. Don't touch the bugs, understand?

"What are you going to do with those awful things?" Jake asked. "You ain't planning on cooking them to eat, are you?

"Mercy, no. I need them to help make our patient

better. Just scoot and bring me several boards and leave them on the back porch. I'll attend to the bugs."

Lizzy stood at the front door and watched her two brothers run around to the old hog pen. They were wonderful boys who never gave her trouble and did whatever she asked. Realizing it was nearly noon, she washed her hands to prepare lunch. She headed to the side of the house and opened the cellar door. She removed eggs and potatoes that were buried deep in the straw, and reaching up on a hook, she took down a smoked ham.

While the boys were gone on their bug hunt, she fried ham, and scrambled eggs with small potatoes, one of the children's favorite meals. Lizzy sliced the bread she baked earlier that morning and covered it with yesterday's homemade butter.

Once the boys returned with a large plank that held the white maggots, she made them wash their hands until they shone.

"But Lizzy, we didn't touch anything but the boards," Joshua said. "You would never catch me touching one of those nasty creatures."

After lunch, Lizzy figured it would be best to care for her patient while the children were busy playing in the tubs of wash water. She carried a small jar to the back porch and examined the white creatures crawling on the wet board. Using her tweezers, she plucked a dozen active maggots, and put them in the container. She strode to the sink, pumped water in the jar, and shook it around. The nasty creatures had to be as clean as possible.

~

Pearl had awakened from her long morning nap. "Something smells good and I'm hungry. I think that man is hungry too, or has a bear in his tummy. I heard it growling."

"Come here, sweetheart and let me wash your face and hands. I've cooked some lunch and I want you to eat really good for me. Afterward, I may need you to help me again."

Lizzy turned to Jake. "Would you please say the blessing, so everyone can eat?" Lizzy asked.

"I guess, but why can't Joshua ask it sometimes?"

"I did," he fussed. "I said it last night at supper."

"I want to say it," begged Pearl.

"All right, Pearl, pray so we can eat." Lizzy said, watching the boys bow their heads.

"Oh, Lord, come in here," she said in a loud voice and laying her hand over her heart, "and help us not to be bad because we'll all go to hell. Amen." Pearl glanced at the family, proud of herself.

Lizzy was speechless. The boys giggled at her performance. "Pearl, what kind of blessing is that? Where did you hear such terrible talk?"

"At church last week. The Preacher--you know the old man, was standing in front of the room yelling at everybody and said we better not be bad because we'll go to . . ." Pearl raised her hand and pointed to the floor.

Lizzy shook her head in utter disgust. "Let's eat, and later you and I'll talk about prayers and blessings. I'm sorry you misunderstood what Preacher Booker said. And don't ever call Preacher Booker an old man."

Hearing some movement from her bedroom, Lizzy left the table to peek in on her patient. She gasped. Dear Lord! The stranger had turned on his injured side. She pushed and grunted against his limp weight until she managed to flip him on his back. Lizzy knew before she looked at his side what she was going to find. His wound was bleeding again.

She sighed heavily, rushed back into the kitchen to gather her medical supplies, what little she had, and returned to the stranger. She noticed the children were still eating their food.

"Boys, place your plates in the dishpan when you have finished. I have to doctor our patient, so I'll be busy. We'll have your school lessons later this afternoon. If you like, you can play in the two tubs of wash water but remember to take off your pants and shirts. Pearl, you can play too, but take off your dress. Please don't come in the bedroom, and please try to play quietly."

Chapter 3

Lizzy rushed to care for her patient while the children were busy playing outside in the tubs of wash water. She retrieved her jar of maggots, and entered the bedroom, and removed the sheet where the wound was located. Before she placed the bugs in his body, the area had to be cleaned. If she learned anything from Dr. Hayes it was a nurse had to have clean hands, and the injury must be clean. She didn't need to cause more infection.

Lizzy slipped an oilcloth beneath his right side, then, she used alcohol to wipe his side and back clean. With another alcohol cloth, she swabbed deep into both sides of the wound. The patient groaned and attempted to touch the injury. The rotting skin smelled awful. Sighing deeply, Lizzy cleansed the wound once more, before quickly putting the maggots inside the gaping hole and placing a tight bandage over it so the bugs couldn't crawl out.

"Thank you, Lord," she mumbled. Then, lifting his side, she worked a strip of cloth beneath him so she could tie it tightly across his waist. Breathing deeply, she placed her face in her hands and sat on the bed, happy that she had completed that awful task. She glanced at the stranger and was surprised to see him watching her with glassy eyes.

~

As the stranger opened his eyes and saw the red-haired angel he had seen before, he was sure he wasn't dreaming this time. The girl was beautiful even with reddish blond hair hanging wildly around her lovely face. Her wrinkled clothes made him wonder if she had been wrestling in bed with him.

"Who are you, and where am I?" His voice sounded like a frog, and he grabbed at his throat. "What's wrong with me?"

"Just relax and slow down with the questions." She patted his shoulder as she pulled the sheet over his naked chest.

He lay still for a minute, suddenly feeling an awful, raw pain in his side. The area was stinging and itched. He couldn't identify the pain because he'd never felt anything like it before. He knew this wasn't a nightmare because he'd seen a beautiful woman sitting on the bed. He closed his eyes and tried to remember where he was. The beautiful woman hadn't answered any of his questions. So, he tried again. "Where am I?"

~

Lizzy's patient hadn't moved any part of his body except opening and closing his eyes. Now, he was awake and asking more questions, which was good.

"First, tell me your name and how you got shot?" Lizzy asked, thinking about the maggots eating away the infection in his wound. Did he feel the bugs?

"Pete Peterson," he croaked, but his voice was pathetic, and pain spiraled to his toes.

"Nice to meet you, Brett Paterson."

"Pete," he moaned. His attempt to speak again shot a searing pain through his throat.

"Oh, I must have misunderstood. So, your name is Pete?"

"Yes." He shook his head. "What's happened to my throat?" He placed a hand on his neck.

"You needed nourishment, so I had to put a foreign object down your throat. I'll make some chicken broth until your throat is better.

"Where am I?" he attempted to ask, grabbing at his throat.

"This is my home. My siblings and I live on this small farm. We live about five miles from Crooksville."

"Crooksville, Texas?" he murmured.

"Yes, Texas. Are you from Texas?"

He quickly avoided answering but pointed to his side. "Who took care of this?" he motioned to the bandage on his side.

"I did the best I could. Unfortunately, you were bleeding, and infection had already set in. I'm doctoring you now, so please lie still and don't turn over onto your side. Do you know who shot you and why? Are you an outlaw?" Lizzy asked, very worried he might be an evil man.

He quickly shook his head and closed his eyes. Then, he motioned that he was hungry.

"If you promise to lie still, I will get some broth and a piece of soft toast." He waved her away.

She returned with the broth, propped up his head, and instructed him to open his mouth. She spooned broth into his mouth, and he winced when he swallowed. She continued to feed him until he felt she'd drowned him. He jerked the spoon away, and the broth flew across the room.

Lizzy gasped. "Behave yourself, Mr. Peterson. Look at the mess you've made."

He made a growling sound and closed his eyes. As she wiped the floor dry, she noticed he had fallen asleep.

She circled the bed, lifted the bandage from his side, and saw the bugs doing their job. Lizzy would remove them in a couple of hours, hoping he would never know what she'd done to him.

Leaving him to rest, Lizzy called in the children, dressed them in clean pajamas, and fed them supper. Jake and Joshua took down their second-grade readers and took turns reading. Lizzy was so proud of their progress. When the town hired a new schoolteacher, her siblings wouldn't be behind in their lessons. Pearl had learned her *ABCs* and could count to twenty. She was thankful that the children enjoyed learning.

Lizzy listened to the children say their prayers and kissed each one goodnight. Since the stranger was in her bed, she laid Pearl at the foot of Jake's bed, and she slept beside Joshua.

~

Lizzy was awakened by the sun shining down on her face from the window. She made coffee and sat on the front porch enjoying the fresh morning breeze and the aroma of her rose bushes in full bloom.

Blue came out the front door and placed his head on her leg. He whined and begged for his breakfast.

"You're sure a good dog, Blue, my boy," she said as she entered the kitchen and retrieved a pan of scraps. He gobbled his food, and then pushed the pan around on the floor. "All right, I'll give you some water."

After caring for Blue, she decided to check on her patient. He was propped up on his arm, looking all around. "Good morning," Lizzy said. "How's your throat this morning?"

"Better," he croaked but he didn't sound like a bull frog.

"Are you hungry? I'll make you some milk toast that might not hurt you to swallow."

Shaking his head, he pointed to his side. "It itches."

"Yes, I will take care of it when you nap."

"Why do I need to be asleep when you doctor me?" he tried to say, but she understood what he was asking.

"I meant to say after your nap. Let me go and get you some coffee. Do you like milk and sugar in it?"

He nodded and Lizzy brought him a fresh cup of hot coffee. "Now sip it. Don't burn your throat." After entering the kitchen, she found Pearl at the table. "Morning Pumpkin," Lizzy said, kissing her little sister on the cheek.

"Is that man awake?"

"Yes, and his name is Pete Peterson. Mr. Peterson to

you and the boys. I am going to make some pancakes. Are you ready to eat or do you want to eat with your brothers?"

"Now. I'm hungry." Pearl said as she twirled a finger around her long hair.

"Come over to the sink and let me wash your hands and the sleep out of your eyes."

"They ain't dirty. I didn't do nothing, but sleep," Pearl replied.

Lizzy laughed as she gave Pearl a dish towel to dry her hands. "Would you like pancakes or do you want some eggs?"

"Just pancakes with jam on them, not syrup. That dark stuff burns my throat."

"Cane syrup will do that sometimes." Lizzy placed milk over a piece of toast for her patient. He needed something soft to swallow. She placed the bowl on a tray and carried it to him.

~

Pete was thrilled to see the food. His stomach had been growling, and he couldn't wait to dig into the food. "What's this crap, woman? I want food, not that slop." He pushed the bowl away.

"Fine, but first you need to improve your manners."

"You cook me some decent foods and I'll think about it."

"All right. I'll try you on a small pancake." In a few minutes, she returned with a small pancake with butter. Do you want syrup or jam?"

"This's better, but it isn't much," he murmured as he forked a piece and shoved it in his mouth. Pain shot in his throat as he swallowed, but he forced the pancake down and sipped a little coffee. He took another bite and pushed the tray away. He drank the remainder of his coffee and held up his cup for more.

~

She took his cup, refilled it, and brought it to him. "More pancakes?" She asked, but already knowing the answer, she didn't want to appear like a smarty-pants. After a while Lizzy returned to the bedroom with a glass of soda water and a pan for him to spit in. "Drink this and move it around in your mouth. It will make your mouth and throat feel better."

Lizzy heard her two brothers enter the kitchen. "I'll be back soon, but I have to feed my brothers." Lizzy walked out of the bedroom, but left the door cracked.

Her brothers were already dressed and ready to do their morning chores. After preparing pancakes for them, she gave them instructions about their chores.

"Be sure to make all the cattle go to the pastures. The calves like to stay in the corral, but they need to eat the tall grass. See if you can find Starbright and feed and water her. She's been rooting a deep hole under the house. We need to build a new hog pen."

"I'll bring in the eggs. We need to build a chicken coop, too. I'm tired of stepping in chicken poop or having it fall in my hair while working in the barn," Joshua said.

"I know," Lizzy said, "but I'm not good with a hammer. One of the Johnson boys may come over and help us later. We've got to send our patient on his way before taking on any more projects."

As Lizzy stood close to the stove ironing, she heard Blue barking as a black carriage drove near the front porch. She placed the hot iron on the stove and raced outside to greet Dr. Hayes. It was good to see him, but she wondered what he would think about what she'd done to her patient's wound.

"Hello, Doc," Joshua said, as he helped Jake climb into the carriage. The doctor smiled at his greeting from the children and rubbed each boys' hair as he gave them each a peppermint stick.

"So good to see you, boys. I believe you both have grown a foot in the two weeks I've been gone. Where's that pretty sister of yours?"

"Here I am, Mr. Doctor." Pearl stood next to Lizzy on the porch. "I wish I could climb in the big carriage with my brothers."

Doctor Hayes stepped onto the porch, reached for Pearl and patted her backside. He pointed to his shirt pocket, and she dug into it and retrieved a piece of candy. "Thank you," she said as she sucked on it.

"All right kids, lets allow our guest to come inside." Lizzy watched as her children moved away from Doctor Hayes, and she followed him into the house. "I hope you had a nice trip. We have missed your weekly visits," Lizzy commented as she walked over to the stove to get the doctor a cup of fresh coffee.

"I had a grand trip but I am hoping I don't have to use any of my new procedures on anyone." He smiled and sipped his hot coffee. "Now that's a fine cup."

"We have a cowboy in Lizzy's bed," Pearl shouted as she pointed at the bedroom door.

"You don't say? Lizzy, do you have a guest?" Lizzy's face warmed up at how it must look.

"Pearl, I was going to tell Doctor Hayes about our patient. Now all three of you run outside and continue with your chores."

Pearl twisted next to the doctor. "I ain't got any, but I know you want me to get lost, so I'll go and play in the barn with the young goats." She followed the boys out the door.

"Mercy, Doctor Hayes," Lizzy sighed, "There aren't any secrets when Pearl is around," she laughed. "I do have a young man in my bedroom who arrived here hurt. He'd been shot a couple days before, but his horse managed to bring him here. I have doctored him, but I know he'll be happy to have a real doctor check his wound. I want him to leave as soon as he can ride."

"Do you know who he is?" He stood and headed to the bedroom.

"His name is Pete Peterson, and he says he's not

wanted by the law."

"Well, that's good, if it's the truth."

~

Pete was lying on the bed, listening to Lizzy talk with the town's doctor. They appeared to be friendly. He waited for them to come into the room.

Lizzy led the doctor into her bedroom. "Mr. Peterson, it's good to see you awake. Doctor Hayes is the town's doctor and my family's good friend. He's going to examine you."

Doctor Hayes walked to the bed and placed his black bag at the foot. He gave the young man a smile. "Hello young man. I can see you're doing well. I'm going to remove the bandage and see what Lizzy did to you." He unwrapped the bandage around his back and waist. "Oh my," the doctor said as he stepped back from the bed.

"What's wrong? What has she done to me? I know she did something because she wanted me to be asleep while she doctored me." Seeing the surprised look on the doctor's face, Pete knew that something was wrong. He tried to sit up and look at the hole in his side. Lizzy quickly pushed him onto his back to make him lie still.

"You're a lucky young man, if I do say so. You don't have any infection or gangrene which could have killed you." Doctor Hayes smiled at Lizzy and requested a pair of tweezers. Lizzy hurried into the kitchen.

"Listen to me, young man. You lie still, and in a few minutes, I will stitch your side up. You have a big gaping hole and it's going to take many stitches. I have some laudanum that will put you to sleep so you won't feel any pain."

Pete sighed and tried to sound tough. "I don't want to be put to sleep. Get on with it. I can take the pain."

Doctor Hayes looked at Lizzy who'd returned with a jar and gave a chuckle. "I will not stitch your side while you're awake. No medication, no stitching. Take your choice."

"All right, give me the stuff. I want to get better so I can hightail it out of here." He swallowed the liquid while

Doctor Hayes removed something black from the wound.

The doctor shuddered. "I can't believe you used this ancient procedure?"

"If you saw my medicine cabinet, you would know I had no other choice. I only have bottles of alcohol, mineral oil, and vinegar."

"With you being so young, Lizzy, how did you know about this?"

"Mama had many books, so I read a lot. I happened to read about it, and for some reason I remembered reading about maggots. I wasn't sure it would work, but I prayed. The good Lord was watching over me and this cowboy."

"Maggots? What did you do to me? Pete gasped.

"Yes, maggots. Lizzy, you did well, and like you, I call on our Father often for help and guidance. Now, Mr. Peterson, relax. Lizzy, please soak this thread and needles in alcohol while I wash my hands good, then I'll stitch his side together. He is going to be just fine, but he'll need to remain here for another week if you can put up with him. If not, I will take him into town and put him in my back room."

"He's fine here, but if he wants to leave, what should I tell him?"

The doctor shook his head. "Tell him he can cause the wound to break open and start bleeding again. He's lost enough blood, but sometimes you can't reason with some men."

Chapter 4

After Pete woke from the medicine the doctor had given him earlier, noise crashed around him like a freight train. The two boys in the next room were chasing each other and screaming foul words. A chair bounced off the floor, and several dishes crashed as they hit the hearth.

Suddenly, a woman's voice was heard over the ruckus, and then dead silence ensued. Pete leaned on his elbow to hear what was happening in the front room.

Lizzy, his sweet-spoken nurse raised her voice. "What is the meaning of this? Just look at my clean room. Jake, explain to me what brought on this fight with your brother."

The one named Jake mumbled, "Ask Joshua. He started it."

"Young man, I asked you, and I want an answer immediately." Lizzy wasn't brooking any nonsense.

"After Doctor Hayes left, Joshua said that you would marry that cowboy sleeping in your bed. I told him he was crazy, and if you married any man, it would be the Sheriff Jackson."

Joshua bellowed. "She ain't going to marry that man. He hates all of us and wants to send us to an orphanage. Ain't that right, Lizzy?"

"Lord in heaven, where do you boys get these ideas." She surveyed the room. "All right, boys. Let's get this room cleaned up . . . now. Then, we will sit down and have a family discussion about my future. I have no idea why you both are worrying about my marriage plans."

~

In less than an hour, Lizzy set the two brothers down at the kitchen table. Pearl was sitting in the rocking chair with her rag doll, probably happy that she wasn't in trouble this time.

Lizzy left the bedroom cracked. She hoped the patient couldn't hear everything that was being discussed at the kitchen table. Lizzy removed her apron and patted her hair back into place. She joined the boys at the table. "First, before we begin, I want you two to make up and say you're sorry for the ugly names that you called each other. I'm ashamed of you both for your misbehavior this afternoon. You were raised better than that."

Lizzy held her chin high as she lectured her two brothers. She waited for them to climb out of their chairs, stand before each other, and apologize. After they smiled at each other, Lizzy grunted and said, "You forgot something."

Both boys whirled around and shook hands, seeing who could squeeze the others' hand the tightest.

Lizzy rolled her eyes and waited until they were seated. "Now, I want you to listen to me. First, I have no idea where you got the idea about me marrying. Have I ever said anything about marrying and leaving you all behind? Have you seen a man coming to court me? Do you honestly believe I would marry a man that you didn't approve of?" Lizzy sat waiting for the boys to give her an answer to at least one of her questions.

Finally, Jake said, "I overheard the sheriff bragging how he was going to marry the prettiest gal in the county, that being you. I figured you must like him too."

"Jake, sweetheart, Sheriff Marvin Jackson is nice, but I'm afraid he doesn't want a ready-made family. I'm a package deal. If and when I marry, we'll still be together. I couldn't leave my three extra hearts behind."

Joshua slid out of his chair and stood beside Lizzy.

"What about marrying that cowboy who's sleeping in your bed?"

"Lizzy laughed. "Joshua, just because he's in my bed doesn't mean I love him. You see when I marry, it will be to a nice man to whom I will give my heart. I will love him like I love you three." She glanced around at Pearl and Jake. "Mr. Peterson will soon be well, and he'll be leaving. Besides, we don't know anything about him."

After the kids had gone outside, she moved quickly through the bedroom not even noticing the bed and went straight to the large chest in the corner. She removed several day dresses that needed to be ironed. With a glance at the garments, she shook them out and laid them over her arm.

"Hey you," Pete said, "have you forgotten about me. That food smells larruping good and I'm starving."

Lizzy turned to the cowboy, who was looking healthier every day. "I don't know how good it is, but there's plenty of it."

"Is it possible that I could have some? I might even walk to the table this evening. What do you think?"

"Let's wait until in the morning to start walking. Give yourself another day of total rest. I'll fix you a big bowl of dumplings and a large slice of buttered cornbread. Would you like some cold milk, coffee or tea to drink?"

"Cold milk, please. And tomorrow I will get out of this bed and try to gain my strength back."

After removing the tray from Pete's room and washing the dishes, she heard the sound of horse hooves near the front door. She told the kids to go into the bedroom with Mr. Peterson and be quiet. She didn't like for strangers to see her young brothers and sister.

Blue was barking and growling at the two strangers. "Blue, come here!" The dog jumped on the porch, and Jake opened the bedroom door and called him to come to him.

Lizzy walked to the edge of the porch and looked at the two strangers. "What do you men want?"

"Well, that doesn't sound very welcoming coming from

a pretty gal like you."

"My husband will be here in a few minutes. He's working out in the north pasture," Lizzy said, hoping to discourage the men. "You can water your horses at the trough."

"Now, that's more like it." The tall stranger got down from his horse, tossed his reins to his partner and leaped on the porch beside Lizzy.

"My partner and I are looking for a man. Have you had any visitors lately that could possibly have been shot?" The man asked as he pushed on the front door and entered the living room.

"I didn't invite you into my home." Lizzy followed the rude man into her house. "No, we haven't seen anyone in days. Please leave before my husband returns. He doesn't like strange men in our home."

"I want to look around if you don't mind. Strolling over to the boys' bedroom, he smiled. "How many youngsters do you have, pretty lady?"

When Lizzy didn't answer, he pointed at the closed door of her bedroom. "What's in that room," he asked as he moved toward it. Lizzy stepped in front of him. "It's only another bedroom where my children are taking a nap, or would be, if not for hearing you arrive."

"Move, lady," he said, pushing open the door. Blue's hair stood up around his neck, and he growled low and showed his teeth. The dog stood on all fours, ready to pounce on the stranger. Lizzy followed him into the room. A muffled voice came from under the covers and said, "Quiet, Blue."

Pearl lay at the top of the bed with her golden curls spread over the pillow. At the foot of the bed, Joshua pretended to be asleep while Jake lay on the side of the mattress, leaning up on his elbow.

"Golly, pretty lady, how many rag tails do you have?"

"Never mind." Lizzy faced the children. "Now, kids, try to rest and take a nap. Your pa will be home soon, and you can get up." Lizzy led the man out of the bedroom as she silently said a prayer of thanks for the boys' quick thinking.

Once back in the living room, the stranger glanced out the window. "I don't see no husband." He immediately grabbed Lizzy around the waist and pulled her into his arms.

Lizzy struggled with the tall stranger and tried to push him away. He kissed her neck and breathed heavily while attempting to kiss her on the mouth. She shoved and tried to kick, but her long skirt trapped he legs.

"Let's you and I go into the empty bedroom and have a little fun. I know how to please a pretty girl like you." The stranger grabbed her by the hair as he tried to lead her across the room.

Out of the corner of her eyes, she saw the twins tiptoed out of the bedroom to the fireplace. Joshua got on his knees while Jake climbed on Joshua's shoulders. Jake lifted the double-barrel shotgun down from the deer horn rack. Joshua lowered his brother to the floor. Jake straightened and pointed the heavy shotgun at the stranger.

"Let her go before I blast you into kingdom come," Jake shouted with a forceful voice.

The stranger turned to see the youngster, who held the gun in shaking hands. Then as fast as she could move, Lizzy pulled herself loose, raced to her brother, grabbed the gun from her brother, and pointed it directly at the stranger. "I know how to use this gun, and if you don't walk out of here now, you might not be able to in a second."

The stranger held both hands in the air and said, "All right, pretty lady, I'm going." He walked to the porch and jumped down the few steps.

From the window, she saw the two men climb on their horses and ride around the house. A gunshot rang out as the men rode up the trail.

Lizzy raced around the side of the house and found her precious hog, Starbright, lying on her side, dead. The twin boys joined their sister as Lizzy cried over Starbright's body. "This was so senseless. This goes to show how mean those

WHERE LOVE HAPPENS

men were."

Chapter 5

Pete crawled out of bed. The children had protected him by leaping on top of him as he lay there helpless. They had knocked the breath out of him, but they had saved his life. He didn't know how he would ever be able to repay them. Pete had heard the gunshot and then Lizzy crying. He inched slowly over to the door and peeped into the living room. Finding the room empty, limped outside on the porch. Voices came from the side of the house, so he eased down the steps and around the house. Lizzy was bending down on her knees, and the twins were crying. A giant black hog lay on its side, bleeding.

"Did those two men do this?" Pete asked.

"Yes." Lizzy shook her head but kept her eyes on the dead pig. "As they rode away, they shot her. Starbright was going to have piglets in a month or so. She gave us a couple of litters which brought in a good income. Now, I'll have to try to purchase another female hog."

"Where are you going to get the money to do that," Jake asked.

Lizzy glanced at her young brother, who was already maturing into a little man, at the age of seven. "Now, don't you fret over money because the good Lord always provide." She stood, brushed her hands on her apron and patted her twins' shoulders. "Now, we've got to find a resting place for our dear friend, Starbright. Let's go to the barn and get the shovels. We'll find some soft ground and bury her."

"Now, Mr. Peterson, let's get you back inside. I hope the children didn't hurt you when they piled on top of you earlier."

He shook his head. "You know, they saved my life. They were so brave. Your dog is something else. His growling scared the man. I was afraid he might shoot him."

"I knew those two men were up to no good, but I didn't realize they could be so cruel. I'm sure he was taking revenge because I forced him to leave."

"I'm sorry he killed your pig." Pete shook his head, disgusted. "I've got money, and I'll purchase a new one. I feel responsible since the men were looking for me."

Lizzy peered at Pete as he stood without a shirt and barefooted. "We'll discuss this later in private after we have taken care of Starbright. Please go back inside and lie down. I'll be in later and check your side."

~

After the burial, Lizzy needed some alone time. The stars, bright and twinkling, gave her comfort. At night she needed to escape from the pressure of young eyes watching her every move. She blew out a breath. What was she going to do with the handsome stranger in her house?

Lizzy walked to the corral fence and watched the small herd of cattle as they lay on the hard-packed ground. They seemed so content, something she hadn't felt in a long time.

"It's late for a pretty gal to be wandering outside," a familiar voice said close to her ear.

"Gracious, Mr. Peterson, I mean Pete, what are you doing out here? You could catch your death in this cool air."

"I saw you from the bedroom window, and I hoped you might want a little company. Unfortunately, I couldn't sleep because I slept all afternoon." He gripped the corral fence and held tight to keep from falling.

"You're still as weak as a kitten. Doctor Hayes told me that you had lost a lot of blood, and it could take weeks to regain your full strength back." Lizzy said as she watched beads of sweat form on his upper lip.

"Come, and let's get back inside before you fall." Lizzy took his arm and led him to the porch steps.

"Can't we sit in the porch swing for a while?" After waiting for Lizzy to take her seat, Pete said, "I feel so awful that one of those men killed. . . Starbright. I know I can't replace your pig, but I want to purchase another one. I have money and if I hadn't been here, those fellows wouldn't have come."

When Lizzy finally spoke, her voice was exceedingly soft. "I want nothing from you except for you to gain your strength back and be able to leave here." She looked into the distance as if she had other things on her mind. "Your kindness and consideration for us are appreciated but very surprising."

"What have I done to you to make you think that I'm an unfeeling brute?" He looked at his beautiful nurse.

She turned to face him. "Well, you haven't been the nicest patient."

He lifted his chin, "It just goes to show you that you don't know me. Maybe I was a little gruff, but dang it, I was in so much pain. I knew you were trying to save my life but woman, at the time, I thought you were trying to starve me and . . . oh no, please don't cry."

She felt Pete's hand on her shoulder as she broke down, lowered her face in her hands, and sobbed. He saw her shoulders shaking. This was out of character and disturbing for the woman he had gotten to know. He only wanted to make up for all the hurt he'd caused her while here. Before he could say anything, she leaped out of the rocking chair and raced into the house.

Lizzy was ashamed of her actions. Never in her life had she cried before a man, much less a stranger. Her feelings of the day's events had been bottled up inside. Those two men had terrorized her and she didn't want the boys to know how scared she was. The boys had been so brave and saved her from the man who had planned to do her bodily harm. Then, the awful man shot Starbright.

It was a relief to have the tension released from her body, but her breakdown in front of Pete had made her feel vulnerable. So many unpleasant thoughts rushed through her mind. All the joy of celebrating her youth had been crushed by her mama's death, taking on the responsibility of three young siblings, and then also the care of the farm without help. All the pent-up frustrations came crashing around her as she sat in her rocking chair in her bedroom. For the first time ever, she cried for all the sacrifices that she had made.

As she prepared for bed, she thanked God for his many blessings of the day. As she crawled under the covers, she promised to tell Pete that he had not caused her tears and he hadn't been a really bad patient. Of course, she would never tell him that she was enjoying his company, and she'll be disappointed to see him ride away.

Late into the night, Pete lay awake puzzling over what he had said to make Lizzy cry. First thing in the morning, he would apologize and hoped she'd accept it. He had never felt the need to apologize to any woman before, but seeing her cry made him feel like a heel. She didn't deserve his angry tone as he spoke to her.

~

Before dawn, Pete heard Lizzy walking softly in the front room. She passed his doorway, opened the front door and walked outside. He thought she must be in a better mood because he heard her humming ever so faintly. He heard Blue bark and dashed off the porch, chasing something moving in the distance. He imagined her standing on the porch waiting for the sun to peek over the trees and for the morning to begin.

"Watching the sun rise, Miss?" he asked, as he stood in the door frame in only his denims.

"Mr. Peterson, you're up mighty early, and you're practically naked. I'll iron your shirt this morning."

"Do you happen to know where my saddlebags and

bedroll are? I do have several sets of clothing wrapped in my bedroll."

"I'm sure the boys know where your things are. They took your horse to the barn and unsaddled him the first day you arrived. I know they struggled with your saddle, it being so heavy, but they placed it on a box. We have a saddle stand, but they're too small to lift your saddle."

Grateful that the boys hadn't thrown his saddlebags away, he said, "I'll ask them to show me where my things are after breakfast." He reached for a towel and wrapped it around his shoulders, covering part of his bare chest. "Listen, I need to say how sorry I am for making you cry last night. I never meant to sound so ungrateful for all you have done for me."

"Please Pete, don't feel that you have to apologize. I feel so foolish for acting like a child. I haven't cried in years. Yesterday was a very scary day with those two men barging in the house and then killing our pet pig. Let's just put yesterday behind us and start over. You're not to blame for those men killing Star Bright. They were just plain mean. I'm just happy that they didn't find you or hurt me or the children." She smiled at him and asked.

"How are you feeling this morning?"

"My side and back feel fine today. The only ache I have now is my stomach. I'm so hungry I could eat a horse."

She almost laughed out loud. "Well, come inside and I'll make coffee while I cook breakfast."

Chapter 6

It was a lovely, sunny morning, just perfect for a carriage ride to church. The children wore their best clothes with fresh haircuts and clean fingernails. But all through the service, it took a lot for Lizzy to concentrate. She tried to listen to the sermon, but as she sat silently, she couldn't stop thinking about Pete Peterson.

Thankfully, those two men had not discovered his whereabouts a few days ago. Standing to sing a hymn, she could only mouth the words as she was remembering how his simplest touch made her feel. *Please, God, don't let me make a fool out of myself when he does mount his horse and ride away.*

A tug on her sleeve told her the service was over. She glanced down at the big blue eyes looking up at her. "Were you daydreaming, Lizzy Mama? I do that a lot when that old man is screaming," Pearl said as she waited for Lizzy to move out into the aisle.

"No, honey, I was just saying an extra prayer. Sometimes we need to say something special to God, and I was doing that. Sorry you had to wait on me."

"It's all right. Can I play with Mary Jane while you visit with the Sheriff? He's coming your way, and he doesn't like me."

"Yes, but don't get your dress dirty," Lizzy said as she waited for the sheriff to approach her.

"Good day, Miss Lizzy. If it is all right, I want to ride out to your place this afternoon and sit a spell with you," Sheriff Marvin said with a shy grin.

"Well, I guess it would be fine. You may take supper with us if you like." Lizzy hoped he would refuse, but he beamed with joy and said he would be pleased to share her table.

"I will be out your way about four this afternoon." He tipped his Stetson and practically waltzed past some of the other members in the aisle.

"Is that old goat coming to our farm today?" Joshua asked as he watched the sheriff shake hands with the parson.

"Yes, he is, and he'll be having supper with us, too. I expect you to be on your best behavior." She pushed him to let her into the aisle so she could walk to the front door.

Parson Booker was waiting for Lizzy and the children. "Well, I guess congratulations are in order. The sheriff tells me that you're courting now, and it won't be long before there'll be a big wedding."

Lizzy's face flushed bright pink. "I'm sorry that the sheriff gave you the wrong impression, Parson, because I'm not courting anyone. The sheriff is a nice man and he's having supper at my home tonight. There are no wedding plans in the future."

"Oh, my goodness. I hope I haven't stirred up a hornet's nest between you. I'm sure I heard him correctly." The Parson appeared embarrassed.

"I'm sure you did, but the sheriff doesn't want a ready-made family. I'll never give up my siblings like he suggested in the past. He said I should place them in an orphanage. I'll never give up my siblings for any man. Good day, Parson."

~

"He's here, Lizzy," Pearl shouted from the front porch. She raced into Mr. Peterson's bedroom without knocking. Pete had been sitting on the side of the bed when Pearl stormed into his room.

"Mr. Peterson, the sheriff is here to see Mama Lizzy. He wants to marry her. Please don't let him." Pearl threw herself into Pete's arms and placed her face on his chest. "He doesn't like the boys or me."

He smoothed her hair. "Maybe your sister might want to marry him?"

"No way. He's too old for her. Have you ever seen him?" Pearl frown.

"No, I haven't ever been in town, and he hasn't been out here since I've been here."

She waved a dismissive hand. The sheriff's just an old fat- belly man with a loud voice. He scares me. You got to have supper with us. Please come to the table now," Pearl said, as she attempted to pull him off the bed.

Pete stood, tucking his clean shirt into his jeans, and ran his fingers through his hair. He slipped on his boots. "How do I look?"

"Good, come on now." She tugged on his hand. "You can be my man tonight."

"Well, my little princess, let's go to supper." Pete entered the living room and saw a big old burly man standing next to the counter with a glass of tea. He had a full bushy, gray mustache and bright red sunburned cheeks. The man wore a plaid western shirt tucked in his khaki pants supported by red suspenders. On his hip under a roll of fat was his Slim Jim holster that had a Colt pistol.

When the sheriff noticed Pete, he placed his glass down, removed his holster and gun, and placed them over a chair along with his Stetson.

"Mama Lizzy, Mr. Peterson is my man tonight."

Pete whispered to Pearl. "Say I'm your date."

"I mean he's my date." The twins laughed, pulled out their chairs, and sat at the table. Pete pulled out a chair for Pearl then stood waiting for Lizzy to take a seat.

The sheriff approached Lizzy and said, "You didn't tell me we were going to have company. Who is that man, and what's he doing coming out of your bedroom?"

"We don't have company, Marvin. Pearl has a date tonight." Lizzy smiled at Pearl and Pete.

When he didn't get a proper answer from Lizzy, the sheriff turned to Pete. "Who are you, young man, and what are you doing in Lizzy's house? I noticed you came out of her bedroom."

"My name is Pete Peterson, and I have been here for a week. I got hurt, and Doctor Hayes and Miss Montgomery have been caring for me." Pete extended his hand, but the sheriff ignored the handshake.

"You've been in this house with only Lizzy and the children for a week?" Not waiting for an answer from Pete, he lifted his chin. "You look well enough to me, so I expect you to leave tonight when I do."

Lizzy placed a hand on the sheriff's arm. "Please, Marvin, this is my home. Let's have supper and we'll talk about Mr. Peterson afterward. Who would like to say the blessing tonight?" When no one spoke, Pete said he would.

When Lizzy seemed surprised, Pete gave her a wink, then closed his eyes. Lizzy raised her eyebrows while she waited for Pete to speak. "Heavenly Father, we give you praise tonight for all your blessings. Bless this food and the hands that prepared it. Amen."

"Thank you, Mr. Peterson. If everyone will give me your plate, I will serve the chicken and dumplings. Marvin, please pass the bread to everyone."

The sheriff looked around the table at the twins, hoping to make conversation. "Have you boys been doing any hunting?"

"No, we can't use the gun." Joshua replied sadly.

"It's *no sir*, boy," Marvin demanded while glancing at all the children.

"Joshua, you have manners. Please use them," Lizzy said, glaring at Marvin.

"We know how to use the gun, but not for hunting. Jake and I got it down and scared two bad men away." Joshua said, lifting his own chin at the sheriff.

Lizzy glared at her brother. "Joshua, please eat and be quiet," Lizzy raised her voice at her brother.

"Yep, you sure did, but they shot Starbright, "Pearl said as she shoveled a mouth full of dumplings.

Marvin laid his fork down and glanced at Libby's red face. "So, it seems there's a story I need to hear. Who wants to start?"

"There's nothing to tell. Everything has been taking care of." Lizzy frowned at the children, daring them to open their mouths.

"No." Marvin slapped his palm on the table, causing everyone to jump. "I want to hear about these two men who came to your farm, and I want to hear it now. And who is Starbright?" When he didn't receive a reply from Lizzy or the children, he stared at Pete. "Do you, Peterson, want to tell me what went on here since Lizzy is determined to keep it a secret?"

"As Miss Montgomery said, everything is fine now. I believe she'll tell you all about it in private, if you give her a chance." Pete smiled at Lizzy.

"Yes, if you insist on knowing what happened here, you and I will talk after supper, alone. Please eat. I have apple pie for dessert."

"You bet we will and you, Peterson, start packing your things while Lizzy and I talk." Marvin spoke as if he owned the place.

"Sheriff, we don't need your help around here, because Joshua and I can take care of things," Jake said. He It was obvious he didn't like him courting his sister.

"Jake, please keep still and eat your supper," Lizzy said, embarrassed but proud that her little brother had told the sheriff how things stood at the farm.

Supper was a long, very uncomfortable affair. Once she noticed that everyone had finished eating, she leaped up and cleaned away the plates. "I'll serve the delicious apple pie."

Pete stood and took the dirty dishes out of Lizzy's hands and carried them to the dishpan while she brought smaller plates to the table. Lizzy could hardly keep her eyes on serving the pie for watching Pete. "I kept these apples in the cellar, saving them for a special occasion. We don't have company very often." Lizzy was nervous and felt herself

35

babbling.

"Sheriff, would you like a cup of fresh coffee?" Pete asked, as if he had been doing it all the time.

"Yep, coffee will be fine," he said, never taking his eyes off Pete and Lizzy.

~

Once everyone finished their dessert, Pete told Lizzy that he and the children would clean the kitchen. "You and the sheriff go out on the porch and visit."

Lizzy stared at him like he had lost his mind. Marvin jumped up from the table, took Lizzy's elbow, and led her out of the room. She continued looking over her shoulder as she left the room.

"Come on, kids, give me a hand with cleaning the table. I'll pour hot water in the dishpan and wash. One of you can dry, and the other can put them away. Pearl, you can sweep the floor and keep a watch on the porch."

"What am I looking for, Mr. Peterson?"

"Just make sure he doesn't try to kiss her. If he does, run outside and sit in Lizzy's lap."

"The sheriff might get mad at me," she said, shuffling her feet.

"Good, then maybe he'll leave." Pete gave her a big smile.

After a while, the sheriff stormed into the kitchen, retrieved his hat, holster, and gun and but he didn't say a word as he rushed out the door.

~

Lizzy came in from the porch and looked at the anxious expressions on her siblings' faces. "The sheriff has left, and he was angry. I confronted him about what he said to Parson Booker about us courting. He said he wanted to marry me, and he wasn't giving up. He intends on winning my hand and soon."

"Well, Miss Montgomery, your brothers and sister are

worn out and ready for bed. I'm sure they're happy you shared your feelings toward the sheriff, because they were worried you might want to marry him." Pete picked up a sleepy Pearl off the floor, groaned, and favored his side. The boys kissed Lizzy on the cheek and hurried to their beds.

Lizzy followed and watched as Pete carried Pearl to bed and tucked the twins under their covers. "They're ready to say their prayers," Pete said and sat down in a rocking chair in front of the fireplace. His injury ached, but it was his fault, so he relaxed while waiting for Lizzy to come and join him.

Lizzy reappeared from the children's bedroom and sat down in a rocking chair beside Pete.

"I was surprised the sheriff didn't wait for me to pack and leave with him. He acted like he wanted to arrest me," Pete said.

"Oh, he demanded that you leave with him, but I told him you weren't well enough to travel. Doctor Hayes will say when you're well enough to be on your way, so I expect a visit from the doctor tomorrow or very soon." Lizzy smiled. "I also told him this was my house, and he couldn't dictate who I let stay in my home. He didn't like that statement and he said if I didn't change my mind about marrying him, I might regret that remark. I felt like that was some kind of threat."

"It does sound like a threat. Have you ever given him a reason you might want to marry him?"

Lizzy waved a dismissive hand. "Heaven, no. When I was about sixteen, he came out and asked my pa if he could call on me for a spell, and then marry me. Pa got so mad, he ran him off. He told the sheriff he was old enough to be my pa. The sheriff was angry, but he never came back after Pa ran off. Mama was so sick. She never recovered after giving birth to Pearl. Once Mr. Jackson became sheriff of Crooksville, Marvin questioned me about what would happen to my brothers and sister after Mama died. Other than that, over the years he has stopped me on the street and asked if he could come and visit. I've always politely refused his request. Today in church, he asked if he could come out for a short visit. I said I guess it would be fine and he could share our evening meal. So, that was all there was to it."

Pete scratched his neck. "He seems to be a fast worker. The kids said he didn't like them. Where did they get that idea?"

She sighed. "After mama died and I had full responsibility of caring for them, Marvin told someone I should place the kids in an orphanage. Jake overheard him, and he questioned me about it. Of course, I told the sheriff I would never give my siblings up for adoption or have them separated."

"You said that the doctor is a good friend of yours? Maybe he will speak with the sheriff about your relationship."

Her face puckered. "We don't have a relationship of any kind. As far as I'm concerned, we aren't even friends. I don't want that man to come around me again."

Chapter 7

After the children had completed their morning chores, Pete asked the boys to show him where they had placed his saddlebags. The three of them trekked outside. Pete's horse trotted over to the corral fence, where he patted his nose and ran his hand down his long, slick neck. "You sure look good, fellow."

Jake and his brother joined him and jumped up on the fence. "Joshua and I've been riding him in the corral and giving him a good rub down every day. He loves apples."

"Well, he's been well cared for just like me. I'm lucky this big guy brought me here since I was nearly unconscious." Pete smiled at the boys.

"Go in the barn. We put your saddle on a big old trunk because we couldn't get it on the saddle stand. Your things are in there." Joshua pointed to the big black trunk. "Your gun and holster are in there, too."

Pete opened the trunk and removed his gun and holster. He hung them over the stall. Then he pulled the two saddlebags out and laid them on top of the trunk and unstrapped the buckles. Reaching inside, he pulled out a handful of paper money.

The two boys' eyes were as large as saucers. "Golly, Mr. Peterson, you're rich," uttered Jake.

Ignoring what the young man said, Pete reached into the other saddlebag and retrieved a bag of coins. He tightened his grip on the bags and looked at the two young boys. "Boys, I'm not rich, and I did not steal this money. Most of it came from home and I won some of it in a card game. That's the reason those two men were hunting for me. They were sore losers, and they were determined to steal back their losses. Please promise me you won't say anything about this money. I'll tell your sister when I feel she needs to know. Promise? Pete made eye contact with both boys, confident they'd do as he asked.

"Yes, sir, we promise to keep your secret." Joshua said, his brother nodding.

Warmth radiated throughout Pete's body. He couldn't contain his grin, no matter how hard he tried. Pete was beginning to have feelings for these young boys, and it would be hard to leave, but he knew he'd have to go soon. "Can you boys help carry my things into the house? I need to sort out my personal things and get my clothes out of my bedroll."

"Are you leaving us, Mr. Pete?" Joshua shortened 'Mr. Peterson' for the first time, and Pete liked it.

"Soon, the doctor will be coming to examine me. He'll say when I can travel. Your sister needs her bedroom back," Pete said, with a little chuckle.

Joshua kicked against the hay on the ground. "You could tell the doctor you don't feel well enough to ride a horse. We could use some help around this place. Lizzy ain't any good with a hammer and Jake and me aren't strong enough to fix some of the fence that's falling down. We are good helpers, but we can't do it by ourselves."

Pete glanced around the farm and smiled. "I'll speak with your sister about staying a while to help with some of the bigger chores you boys need help with. We'll see what she says. But, let me do the asking, all right?"

Both boys nodded and walked ahead of Pete toward the house with a saddlebag thrown over their small shoulders. Pete carried his gun, holster and bedroll.

Lizzy was lifting an apple pie from the oven when she heard Blue barking. She glanced out the kitchen window and saw Doctor Hayes' black carriage driving toward the house. Quickly, she removed her dirty apron and hurried out on the front porch.

Doctor Hayes stopped near the steps and leaped down from his carriage. "What a warm greeting, Miss Lizzy." He approached with his hands stretched out wide. She noticed a strange expression on his face. He was not only smiling, but seemed to have a spring in his step, like a young man.

Once he stepped on the porch, his outstretched arms wrapped around her shoulders, pulled her into his chest, and hugged her tight. She stood frozen as he continued to tell her how lovely she looked and how he had missed her. In all the years she had known the doctor, he had never embraced her like this.

Lizzy motioned for him to enter the house, but she was still in shock about his behavior. He acted like a husband who had been away for a while and had just returned, instead of the doctor who had been her friend since she was a child.

"Where are the children? It seems awful quiet without them, but I'm glad to have a moment alone with you." Lizzy noticed Doctor Hayes had not brought in his black bag.

"Why do you want a moment alone with me, Doctor Hayes? Do you have bad news to deliver to me?"

"Oh no, my lovely chick. I have missed you and I've a personal request I want to ask you." Lizzy stood frozen wondering what all this was about.

"Lizzy, I'd like to court you. I have always had great fondness for you, and I feel we have so much in common. We'd make a great couple. I would like you to become my wife, after you get to know me better." A flush of adrenaline rushed through his body. He could tell he had her complete attention.

A heavy feeling pressed in the pit of her stomach. She prayed she wouldn't lose her lunch. Her hands rushed to cover her mouth. Fuzzy thoughts, and the inability to think, spiraled through her mind. She didn't know what to say. How was she supposed to respond to his ridiculous proposal? For goodness sake, she thought, Doctor Hayes was old enough to be her father.

The children rushed into the house. "Hello, Doctor Hayes," Pearl said, as she held her hands up for the doctor to take her. When he only patted her on the head, she jumped at his side for him to pick her up. He smiled at the boys and reached into his shirt pocket and passed all three children a peppermint stick. "Children, your sister and I are having a private conversation. Will you go back outside and play? Later I'll visit with you." He turned the kids around and pushed them toward the front door.

Once the children were outside, Pete came from Lizzy's bedroom. "Hello, Doctor. I thought you'd be coming out today. I guess you want to examine me?"

Doctor Hayes' face reddened, but he answered Pete straightaway. "Yes, of course, but not right this minute. Can I visit with Lizzy before I examine you? We need some time alone."

Pete appeared to be s u reprised, but he gave the doctor a nod. "Certainly, I'll go outside with the children. The boys want to show me where they need a new hog pen built. Call me when you're ready for me."

~

As Pete walked out the front door, he glanced at Lizzy's pale face. What did the doctor have to talk privately to her about? Now, wasn't the time to ask her. He stepped on the porch with the boys and saw tears in Pearl's eyes. "Why the tears Princess? Come, sit in my lap and tell me what's made you cry."

"The doctor always picks me up and lets me dig in his front shirt pocket for candy." She held the peppermint stick out. "Doctor Hayes only patted my head and didn't say anything to me. He did give us the candy, but I always like to talk to him. He just pushed us out of the house."

"Well, if it will make you feel better, he pushed me out, too. Why don't you go with the boys and me to see where we'll build a new hog pen?"

The boys jumped off the steps and headed around the house toward the back side of the barn. Pete picked up Pearl and followed them. "What do you think of this place, Mr. Pete?" Jake asked.

Pete tried to concentrate on the space for the hog pen, but his thoughts were on Lizzy and the doctor. What could he be speaking to her about?

"Well, what do you think? Should we build it somewhere else?" Joshua wrinkled his brow.

Pete realized the young man was asking him for his opinion. "I think this is a perfect place. It's far enough away from the house, but not too far to check on the hogs at night."

Jake smiled and announced they had some good boards in the barn. They have been stored on the rafters for years, but they should still be good."

"Great. After the doctor leaves today, I'll climb up and bring down some of the boards. We'll need to clean out the old pig pen before we start building. Let's go back to the porch and wait until the doctor calls me to come inside." Pete placed his hands on the boys' shoulders and led them to the front of the house. His mind was clearly distracted by what was happening between Lizzy and the doctor.

~

Once Pete and the children rounded the corner of the barn, he noticed Doctor Hayes' carriage was gone. The children rushed into the house and looked all around. Lizzy was sitting in the rocking chair. "Where's the doctor?" Pearl asked.

"Where's Mr. Peterson?" Lizzy asked, ignoring Pearl's question.

"Here I am, Miss Lizzy. Why did the doctor leave before he examined me?"

She smirked. "I'm sure he'll be back another day soon.

Now boys, please get your readers out and read one or two stories. Pearl, you sit and listen to the boys read aloud today. I want to take a walk around the farm with Mr. Peterson.

"But, Lizzy, what did the doctor want to talk to you about? Why did he make us go outside? He's never done that before," Jake asked.

"I promise I'll tell you later while we're having dessert," Lizzy said taking her shawl and wrapping it across her shoulders. She followed Pete out the door, while the boys retrieved their readers from the bookshelf.

Jake and his siblings watched Lizzy and Pete walk outside. "Lizzy thinks we're dumb, but something is going on between her and the doctor," Jake whispered to his twin.

"I heard you, smarty-pants," Pearl said climbing on the sofa with her brothers.

Chapter 8

As Pete entered the barn with Lizzy, he glanced up at the boards in the rafters and thought there were enough to build a hog pen. "You can start the conversation anytime you wish. I waited for the doctor to examine me and tell me I could travel. Why didn't he call me inside for an examination? The children are disappointed he didn't visit with them."

She walked out of the barn to her rose patch, Pete tailing close behind. "To tell you the truth, I was surprised he wanted to talk privately with me. And I was even more surprised, or rather shocked, at what he wanted to speak to me about." Lizzy glanced around at her roses. "He asked me to marry him. I nearly fainted. I've known Doctor Hayes for years. He brought the twins into the world and later Pearl. Doc Hayes came to the farm pretty regular when Mama was ill." Lizzy ambled to the corral and leaned on the fence as Pete's horse trotted over to see him. "You know, Pete, the doctor and I have hardly ever had a private discussion about anything unless it was about the care of the children or Mama. I was taken back and told him he was old enough to be my father. As soon as I said that I felt bad. I'm afraid I wasn't very tactful."

Pete sidled up to her and leaned on the fence. "How did he take that remark?"

"He said age didn't matter and he was fully able to care for me and the children. I could go with him on his daily trips to see patients and we would be a great doctor-and-nurse team. I reminded him I have three children to care for, but he had everything planned out. We could sell this farm and move into town with him. His housekeeper would take charge of the kids while I was away."

He studied her face. "I can see that he had given this a lot of thought. Do you want to sell your farm and live in town?"

"Heavens, no," Lizzy said, with a change of volume in her voice. "I love my home along with my siblings. The boys and I already work hard to sell the pigs, dig the potatoes, collect and wash eggs, and make cheese. I have to collect enough money each year to pay the taxes."

"If you marry the sheriff or the doctor, you won't have to work so hard." Pete said matter-of-factly.

Lizzy appeared shocked that he would even suggest something so awful. "Ew, I would rather die than marry one of those old men. I have no idea why the doc or the sheriff proposed to me. If I can't marry for love, I'll remain an old maid," Lizzy said running her hands though her hair.

"Maybe the men think your situation on the farm has changed for the better? Maybe you've found oil on the place or you've inherited money from a long lost relative." Pete cocked his head to one side as he questioned Lizzy.

"Good grief. Oil on this place would be something," Lizzy laughed. "Both of those men have known my family for years, and they know that my folks struggled to make ends meet. They would never think I had money. My papa ran off and left me to work the farm. I collect money weekly at the dry-goods store. I've got a small bank account with fifty-seven dollars in it." Lizzy laughed. "Surely they don't want to take on me and three children for such a small amount."

~

Pete smiled at Lizzy as she joked about her wealth, but then he grew serious. "Lizzy, I want to talk to you about my plans."

"Are you planning on leaving, even though you haven't

been released by the doctor?" Lizzy asked.

"You and I know I'm well enough to travel and be on my way, but I would like to stay for a while. I want to try and repay you for saving my life. I can do this by helping with some chores around the place. The boys and I have talked about building a new hog pen. You have fences that need to be replaced and a winter crop of potatoes to plant. The barn roof leaks, and I want to replace your pig. Please agree to let me stay on awhile." Pete whispered in a husky tone.

Lizzy smiled for the first time all day. Enthusiasm waved through her as she looked at the pretty horse. "I guess it will be all right. But I think we need to make a bed for you in the barn, now that you're better. It'll look better if you aren't in the house at night."

He shrugged. "That's fine with me. The boys and I can rearrange the tack room and put in a cot." Pete gave his horse a sugar cube he'd discovered in his pocket.

~

Pete climbed into the barn loft and lowered longboards from the rafters. He instructed the boys to stand back and let them fall. Once he felt he had enough boards, they measured each side of the pen. Jake retrieved a hand saw, and they cut the timber. Pete walked to the edge of the corral and cut down two tall trees to use as posts.

After the pen area was cleared, they pounded the posts in the ground and nailed the boards on each side. The three stood back and admired their handy work. It was a nice pen for a large sow and little piglets. After the boys threw fresh hay in the bottom, the only thing left to do was make a trip to the next-door neighbor's farm to purchase a sow.

Lizzy praised the young boys and Pete for a job well done. "Tomorrow, we can take the wagon and ride over to Mr. Johnson's, and hopefully he'll have a sow for sale," Lizzy commented.

"Can we swim at the pond we'll pass on the way back?" Joshua asked.

"I'll tell you what. I'll pack a lunch, and you can swim

while I sit under the shade trees." She giggled. "Can't really guard them since I can't swim a lick."

"Don't you like the water?" Pete asked, as he repacked the saw, hammer, and extra nails. "I'll slip off my shoes and wiggle my toes in the cool water. That's enough for me," Lizzy giggled as she smiled at Pete.

She'd probably drown," Pearl whispered loud enough for Lizzy to hear.

"We might have to do something about that," he winked at Pearl as he watched the shocked expression on Lizzy's face.

~

The morning chores were done, and the kitchen was clean. Lizzy had packed a big lunch with fresh fruit. She added fresh towels and a large blanket to the pile. Pete drove the wagon to the front door and the twins jumped on the back, ensuring Pearl was safe between them.

Mr. Johnson was out in his winter garden when he noticed Miss Montgomery and her siblings coming in his drive. "Hello, Miss Montgomery. It's been a long time since you came to visit. Please get down while I call Verna to come out of the house."

"What a surprise," Verna said, wiping her hands across her apron.

"What can we do for you folks today?" Mr. Johnson hopped up on the porch wiping his hands on a rag that hung from his pocket.

"My farm needs a good breeding sow because ours met with an accident. I need to replace her, and I hoped you'd have one for sale?"

"Sure do, but who's this young man with you?" Mr. Johnson looked Pete over.

Lizzy covered her mouth. "Please forgive my manners. This is Pete Peterson. He's my hired hand for a few months."

"Mr. Johnson, nice to make your acquaintance." Pete held out his hand for a greeting.

He shook his hand. "Well, Mr. Peterson, come with me and we'll look over my stock. I'm sure you will find one to your liking."

"I believe Miss Montgomery needs to come with us. She's more of an authority when choosing a sow than I am."

Mrs. Johnson turned to the children. "I have fresh-baked cookies. You sit on the steps, and I'll bring them out."

Lizzy looked at over a dozen nice-sized pigs and finally chose a mature sow. "She'll be ready to breed soon. Bring her back over in a few weeks and I'll breed her for you. You'll have new piglets to sell before Christmas."

"I can't thank you enough." Pete reached for his wallet and gave Mr. Johnson the fee he asked. "You aren't going to squabble with me about the price?"

"No, sir. You've already made a deal with Miss Montgomery. You'll be getting the pick of the litter, and I'll be bringing over a bag of potatoes next week. If she's happy, I'm happy. Pete smiled and placed two boards on the back of the wagon to make a walkway for the sow to get into the back. He walked around and raised the two sides. The children would all sit on the front bench and on the floor.

"What a good idea." Mr. Johnson said, as he watched Pearl waving a cookie under the sow's nose as she led the animal up the two boards into the wagon. Pete locked the backboards and helped Pearl climb over the front bench of the wagon.

"Now, Pearl, give the sow the cookie," Pete said, sweetly.

"Shucks," she murmured but did as Pete instructed.

"I'm sure going to remember this morning. A man ain't never too old to learn new tricks." Mr. Johnson smiled, patted Pearl's head, and shook Pete's hand. He stepped back away from the wagon, holding his wife's hand, and waved goodbye.

As the young couple drove out of the farmyard, Mrs. Johnson commented. "That sure is a handsome young man to be living alone with Miss Montgomery."

"Now, Gertie, I don't want to hear any gossip about Miss Montgomery. That man is a hired hand and she's trying her best to give her siblings a good home."

Chapter 9

Pete drove the wagon near a few shades trees and watched the boys jump to the ground. "Don't get too close to the water until I hobble the horse in the tall grass. Boys, help your sister with the blanket and basket of food. I'm already hungry," he said laughing.

Lizzy shook her head. "You are always hungry and it's too early to eat. I did bring some cookies we can share after we get our picnic area ready." Lizzy jumped down from the wagon and placed Pearl on the ground. "Stay close to me until you're dressed to swim."

"You going to put a dress on me to go swimming?"

Lizzy smirked. "No, silly. I meant wait until I can change your clothes to play in the water."

Pete went to the water's edge. "Boys, let me look the water over and see how deep it is in certain places. You both said that you could swim, but I want to make sure you can stand in some places. Someone hung a rope swing in that tree, and it looks like fun." Pete removed his boots and rolled his jeans up to his knees. He removed his shirt and his belt from his pants. He walked to the edge of the lake and eased into the cool water. It felt so good. He scanned the whole area along the edge of the pond to make sure there weren't any snakes or other critters nearby. "Lizzy, are the boys ready to come into the water?"

"Yes, they can swim in their underwear," Lizzy watched both boys jump from the bank and swim under the water to come up next to Pete.

Pete headed to the bank and reached for Pearl. "Come with me, sweet girl, and I'll hold you tight. Don't be afraid because I won't drop you."

"Here I come, Mr. Pete!" Pearl jumped into Pete's arms, splashing water onto their faces. "Oh, this is so cold."

"You'll get used to it if you move around. I'll hold you up while you move your arms and legs."

"Hey Pete, can we use the rope and swing out over the water and drop?" Joshua yelled.

"Boys, you don't have permission to call Mr. Peterson by his first name. Please use your manners," Lizzy said.

He frowned, not wanting to interfere with her parenting, but he said it anyway. "Lizzy, I told them when we are home alone or off like this, they can call me Mr. Pete or just Pete. We're very good friends."

"Well, if you're sure they aren't being disrespectful." Lizzy smoothed the grass near the bank and took a seat.

"Would you like to come in, Lizzy? I can hold you close like I'm holding Pearl."

She waved a hand as if the idea was revolting. "Thanks, but no thanks. I love watching all of you enjoy the water. I'll serve lunch in a little while."

"The boys are wanting to swing on the rope across the water. I'd better test it first. I don't want one of them to get hurt, so, Pearl stand right here next to the bank while I check out the rope swing."

Pete took the bottom of the rope and carried it over to the bank. He shook it several times to make sure it was tied tight. Then he grabbed it and swung out over the bank, yelling like a big ape as he swung back and forth until he reached the middle of the pond and let go. He dropped into the water and they all laughed and clapped, but when Pete didn't come up, they got afraid and began to scream. "Pete, Pete, come up!"

Pearl began to cry as Lizzy bolted to her feet. Suddenly, a large gush of water splashed all around the group. Pete stood close to the bank, but when he saw Pearl crying, he grabbed her and swirled her around in the water.

"You scared us, Pete," Joshua yelled, and Jake gave him a shot of water in the face.

"Can we have a turn now?" Jake asked.

~

Mr. and Mrs. Johnson sat across the field in their wagon watching the little family enjoying themselves in the water. "That man is nearly naked. Shame on him," Mrs. Johnson murmured.

"Gertie, surely you wouldn't expect him to swim in all of his clothes. Don't you remember we'd sneak away and swim in that same pond wearing a whole lot less." Mrs. Johnson face flamed red. "Oh, you hush."

~

After a long week, Pete and the two boys worked all day to complete the new hog pen. Around the dinner table, the children tossed out names for the new sow. Starbright-two was rejected. Blackie sounded like a dog's name, but when Pearl suggested the name Princess, the boys laughed, but agreed it was a good name.

"I found red paint in the barn so I'll paint a sign with her new name on it," Pete suggested.

The fence posts were replaced, and the barn now sported new roof tiles over the leaks. For hours, Lizzy and the boys had sat on the front porch and sliced potatoes to be planted. Pete used their old mule and plowed row after row in the field to plant the vegetable.

Later that evening, Lizzy heated several buckets of hot water for Pete to soak his tired body. His injury was healed completely, but he had used muscles that he hadn't used in months. On his father's farm, a crew of men came and planted their wheat and corn. The men returned when it was time to harvest the fields. The hardest thing he did was record the date the fields were planted, each man's hours, and when they were expected to return.

Once the children were tucked in their beds, Lizzy and Pete sat on the front porch. Pete regretted what he had to tell her. It was time for him to go home. He had been on his way through Texas when he stopped in Perryville to have dinner and he decided to sit in on a card game. After he collected his winnings, the two men who had come to the farm looking for him, had not been good losers. They'd claimed he cheated, but other players at the table disputed their argument.

Pete decided to tell Lizzy about his life and family, so after she brought him iced tea he began. "Lizzy, I've got to go. I thought I would pack and start for home in the morning while you and the children are at church. I'm sure going to hate to tell them goodbye. You've done a great job of raising them."

Her head lowered, and her voice came out in a whisper. "I wish you didn't have to leave so soon, but I understand. You never intended to stop here. It was my honor to nurse you back to health, and you certainly have repaid me many times over.

"No, I never intended to get shot, but the good Lord led my horse to your farm. He gave her a cock-eyed smile. "I had been on a trip away from home. Actually, it was the first time I had been away from home since I returned from college in Dallas. My father is presently a judge for the city of Austin and has an office in the capital building. He's an advisor to congressmen who serve the state of Texas. I'm in charge of our farm while he's working at the capital, but I want to see other parts of Texas. So, I traveled around most of the state.

Our farm has many good people who work for us and Hester runs the household. She's an older woman who's has been with us for many years. A tall, lanky black man named William lives with us, too."

Pete leaned back in the rocking chair and sighed. My father is a character. He cares about his fellowman, in many ways. When the war broke out between the states, he told

William if he wanted to fight, he was free to go and join the side he believed in. A year later, William returned, and he has been with us since."

Pete looked around the room, wanting to remember every part of the house. "I have two brothers. Will and Jeff. When they married, they each built a home on the property. Both of their wives help Father. Will's wife, Marilyn does a lot of charity work. Jeff's wife, Evelyn, teaches school."

Sounds like you have a nice family to return to," Lizzy said, her voice husky.

"I'm sure our foreman is ready for my return, but I have to admit I've enjoyed being here." He tilted his head backward and covered his eyes. He opened and blinked as to catch the moonlight in his sight. Should he tell her the truth?

"You mean a lot to me, Lizzy, and the thought of not seeing you every day is tearing my insides apart. I have no right to ask anything of you, but I'd like to return after I see that I'm not needed at home. I have no right to ask you to wait on me, but I care for you and the children more than I ever believed possible."

"Please, Pete," she said softly, "I knew last week that you had to leave. People are beginning to talk about your presence in my home." Lizzy sighed and glanced at Pete. "I'm going to miss you, too. If and when you return, maybe we can talk about the future, but for now, you have to leave."

Pete reached for her hand, but Lizzy pulled back and stood. "Tomorrow will be here before we know it. Good night." Lizzy walked into the kitchen, took a dipper of water, and strolled into her bedroom.

~

Hours later, Lizzy climbed out of bed and padded to the bedroom door, shy of reaching for the doorknob. She wanted Pete's strong body lying close to hers but gave herself a shake. *Behave yourself. It's not to be tonight,* she thought. She crept back to her bed and lay looking into the darkness. Scrunching her pillow under her head, she wiped a tear that had dripped onto her pillowcase. She squeezed her eyes shut, fighting not to weep. She had fallen in love with the cowboy in the barn but he was leaving in the morning, probably never to be seen again. *"Please, God, take care of him."*

~

Pete undressed and lay down on the single cot in the barn. For the first time he thought about Lizzy's bedroom, his hospital room, for several weeks. Compared to his room at home, Lizzy's bedroom had the bare necessities. His parents' large house was decorated with beautiful draperies, four-poster beds, and lovely bed coverings with decorated pillows to match. Large fireplaces dominated each room, and beautiful tapestry rugs adorned each room's floor. Glancing around in this old barn with only a clean bed, Pete couldn't have been more comfortable.

Pete's fist punched his pillow, creating a muffled sound of loneliness. Hugging the pillow close, he'd never felt so low. He was going home, but he was leaving part of himself here.

Earlier than he planned to leave, a storm descended upon the house and barn. Rain cascaded down in sheets and pounded upon the tin roof. Thank goodness the patches on the barn roof were holding and no rain dripped inside. The cattle, pigs and chickens were very quiet.

~

Much to Lizzy's amazement, Pete unlocked the house's front door and entered the dark room. She immediately turned up the lantern next to the rocking chair where she sat watching the storm. Instant relief flooded over her as she recognized her intruder. Pete was surprised to find Lizzy sitting in the room.

"I'm sorry to disturb you, Lizzy, but I wanted to ensure you were fine. This is a bad storm with strong winds, and I was worried . . . "Pete let his words fade away.

Pulling her woolen shawl closer around herself for

modesty, she smiled at him. "Come on in and I'll make us some coffee." She stood and hurried into the kitchen.

"Did the storm awaken you?" Pete asked as he removed his raincoat and hat. He slipped off his wet boots and walked to stand in front of the fireplace, reaching down to toss another log on the fire.

"I guess so." She called from the kitchen. "I was just thinking about my future once you've gone."

"Can I help with some of your planning?" Pete asked, taking the tray of coffee from Lizzy as she entered the room.

"No, not really. The children and I'll return to our daily lives like before your arrival." She smiled and sat in the rocking chair just as lightning flashed nearby.

"I hate storms. I always worry lightning will hit the house and burn it down while we sleep."

"Yes, I can understand that, especially with you being responsible for the children."

Pete finished his coffee and listened to the storm. "I believe the storm has moved away from us. I'd better get back to the barn and rest." Pete glanced at Lizzy. "Please remember you can reach me at this address." He gave her a piece of paper. "I plan to return soon, but contact me if you need me before I get back. I'll come running." He gave her a grin and walked out the front door.

Chapter 10

Lizzy couldn't sleep after Pete left, so she got up as soon as the rain stopped. The storm had still been raging when Pete had ridden out of the barn toward town. She had hoped he would have waited for the storm to let up before leaving.

She headed out to the barn and then into the room where Pete had slept. There wasn't any sign that Pete had ever spent a night in it. She walked over to the cot and saw an envelope on the pillow. Recognizing Pete's handwriting, she read her name on the front of it. She held it to her chest, hoping it was words of endearment that she would cherish forever. It felt heavier than a mere note. Opening it, to her surprise, there was money and a short note.

"*Lizzy, I can't tell you how much I appreciate all the care you gave me. I enjoyed my stay here. Know that I will plan to return, but I can't say now when that will be. Please take this money as payment for all you did for me. I know you will use it wisely. Be sure to tell the little ones I already miss them.*

With deep devotion
Pete

Sitting down on the bed, Lizzy read the note again. He missed the children. Would he miss her, too? Taking the green bills, she counted five hundred dollars. *My goodness. So much money.* She never dreamed he was a rich man.

Holding the money close to her chest, she cried, "Oh, Pete, I wish you were still here." She closed her eyes against the regret that flowed through her heart. That's what hurt the most, knowing he had to leave. She had fallen hopelessly in love with Pete Peterson.

Wiping her eyes, she whispered to the empty room. "Pete, I will use your money wisely. I'll go to town and pay the farm's taxes that are overdue, catch up the feed bill, and pay the doctor for his visits." Actually, this amount of money would keep the farm running for two years or more.

Lizzy went back inside the house to her bedroom. Where would be a good hiding place for this large amount of money? Suddenly, she remembered the loose brick at the bottom of the hearth on the fireplace. Counting out one hundred dollars, she placed it in her apron pocket, but the rest she placed in the hole in the hearth. She would tell Jake about the hiding place, in the future, if she felt he needed to know.

The morning had cleared from the terrible storm. The children came to the breakfast table, and immediately Pearl said they had to wait for Pete to come from the barn.

Lizzy sat quietly for a moment, trying to gather her words, to explain to the children that Pete had gone. "Pete had to leave early this morning. He lives near Austin, Texas, and he wanted to catch the morning train that would take him home to his farm."

"But he didn't say goodbye." Pearl climbed down from her chair and laid her head in Lizzy's lap. "I don't want him to leave."

"I know, sweetheart. He cares deeply for each of you and it made him sad to have to leave, but we knew when he came here that he wouldn't be staying. We all nursed him back to health and he paid us back by doing some much-needed chores around the place. But he has responsibilities at his home."

"You like him a lot, don't you, Lizzy?" Jake said, looking up from his oatmeal.

"We all liked him and we're going to miss him, but we need to get back to living like we did before he came." Lizzy smiled at her siblings. "Now, let's eat and get dressed for church. You can all see your friends today."

As Lizzy drove her horse and wagon into the church's parking area, several men who always helped her and the children get down from the wagon acted as if they didn't even see her.

That's odd, she thought, but she and the children got down. Jake carried their bucket over to the well and pulled up water for the horse. Joshua saw his friend Billy and waved at him. Billy's mother grabbed the boy and pushed him forward, not allowing the young boy to wave back at Joshua. Something was wrong, thought Lizzy, but she gathered the children and entered the building and took their regular pew. She noticed that not one church member looked her in the eyes.

Pearl wiggled and turned in the pew to speak to her little friend. "An old cat got your tongue today, Mary Lou," Pearl asked her friend.

"No, I can't talk to you," she said loudly.

"Hush, young lady, sit back and be quiet," the child's mother scolded her.

"Pearl, turn around, and let's prepare to sing the opening hymn," Lizzy said softly.

Several families entered and stopped at the end of the pew where Lizzy and the children sat, then they chose to sit in different pews. Jake sat on the edge of the bench and leaned toward Lizzy, whispering, "Why won't our friends join us? We all took baths last night."

"Quiet," Lizzy placed her finger over her lips, "I don't know for sure, but I'll ask Preacher Booker when church is over. Surely, he'll know."

When the closing prayer was over, Lizzy instructed the children to go to their wagon and wait. She was going to speak to the preacher. Lizzy stood and watched her siblings go out the front doors and down the steps. She sat back down in the pew and waited until Preacher Brooks shook hands with the congregation as they departed.

"Well, Lizzy, it is so good to see you and the children this morning. I have to admit I was a little surprised to see you without your hired hand."

"Mr. Peterson was hurt badly when he arrived at my farm, as you know. He only worked for me to pay me back for taking care of him. He has left and gone home."

"I see. So, the young hired-hand left. Where he is from?"

"He told me that he came from Austin, Texas. His father is a retired judge. Pete runs the farm for his father," Lizzy said. "But, I don't want to talk about him. I want to know why the children and I are being shunned by everyone. What has happened to cause everyone to turn their backs on us?"

"I'm sorry, but I can't control the women folk from wagging their forked tongues. Their husbands can't make them behave when they get a bee in their bonnets. "

"But, what have I done to cause such behavior toward me and the children? Their little friends weren't allowed even to speak to them."

"It all concerns Mr. Peterson staying on your farm without a proper chaperone. They whispered that you were 'living in sin' right in front of the little ones."

"But, Preacher Brooks, for days we weren't sure if he would live or die. He couldn't even get out of bed. After Doctor Hayes arrived and checked him over, he said that Mr. Peterson had to stay in bed another week. The poor fellow had lost a lot of blood."

"Yes, I spoke with the doctor. He also told me he asked you to marry him, but you refused. May I ask why you turned the good doctor down?"

"You're right, he did propose to me. Doctor Hayes is a wonderful man, but he's old enough to be my father. He started doctoring my family when I was a young girl. Doctor Hayes delivered my siblings and doctored Mama until she passed. He's a dear family friend, but I can't marry him just because he needs a nurse to travel with him."

"He didn't say anything about you being his nurse."

"Well, that was in his proposal. He never said he loved me or my brothers and sister. I will only marry for love or not at all."

"I can understand how you feel." He sighed and said, "Bless you, child. I know you're doing a wonderful job in caring for your siblings. Go home and I'll try to stop all this ugly gossip about you."

"Thank you for taking the time to speak to me." Lizzy walked to the front door and noticed all the wagons, single horses, and carriages had left the churchyard. Jake stood holding onto the horse's reins while Joshua and Pearl waited patiently on the top bench.

~

Once home from church, Lizzy put a cold lunch of sandwiches and fresh fruit on the table. She knew she needed to speak with the children about the actions of some of the church members. Once the kids were seated at the table, she said, "People were upset because Pete was living here on our farm with us. Preacher Brooks told me some other things and I will tell you what he said after we have eaten our lunch."

"But, didn't you tell the preacher that Pete has gone away?" Jake questioned.

"Yes, I did, and he said he would spread the word that Mr. Peterson is well and has moved on. He said that should make the womenfolk in town feel better."

"That's not what Mary Lou told me today," Pearl said, shaking her head from side to side.

"When did you get a chance to talk with your friend today?"

"While we were waiting at the wagon. Mary Lou ran over and whispered what the womenfolk want to do to you."

"Well, are you going to tell us what those old bats want to do?" Joshua asked.

"Joshua, what kind of talk is that? What has come over you?" Lizzy raised her voice at the table, which she was taught never to do. She gave the boys a warning look then turned to Pearl.

"Now, tell me what Mary Lou said to you," Lizzy said sweetly, wanting to shake the story out of Pearl.

"She said you're a witch, and I had better hide you. The women want you tied and burned up like a steak." Lizzy's mouth fell open.

"Like a steak? Well done? You mean at the stake? Pearl, you sure you heard her right?" Jake quizzed his sister.

"She said in some places if the womenfolk don't like you, they will tie you to a post, set it on fire, and cook you like a steak."

Lizzy tried to hold her laughter inside, but the last part of Pearl's tale was just too ridiculous. She burst out with laughter until she had to wipe tears from her eyes.

"Lizzy," Pearl reached for her sister's hand. "I ain't never seen you ride a broom. Witches ride brooms and fly around everywhere--." She waved her hands around in the air, "turning people into frogs. We ain't never seen you do that. Besides, you would never turn people into frogs. You're too afraid of those slimy green things."

Pearl's serious statement was too much for Lizzy. She had to leave the table, hardly able to speak from the laughter bubbling up inside her.

Pearl reached to hug Lizzy. "I don't want them to burn you." She wrapped her little arms around Lizzy's neck. "If you're a witch, please get on your broom and fly away to Mr. Pete. He'll keep you safe."

Lizzy rubbed her little sister's back and said that everything would be all right. "We'll have a family discussion in a little while. Finish your lunch while I pour myself another cup of coffee."

Lizzy decided to tell the children why everyone had shunned them today, in simple words that they could understand. She had always tried to be honest with her twin brothers about work and money. Now she would try to make them understand a few facts of life.

Once the children had finished their lunch, Lizzy sat

across the table from them. "First of all, Pearl, I'm not a witch. I can't fly on a broom, and no one will harm a hair on my head. The ladies in town are upset and I want you three to listen to me closely. What the ladies are saying about me is not true. I want you to understand why they aren't pleased with me.

"First, I'm a single girl. I have no man to call my own because I'm not married. The ladies are upset with me because I took in Pete, Mr. Peterson, and allowed him to stay in our house. They believe I should have taken him into town and dropped him off at the doctor's. I knew I couldn't do that. First, he could have died if I didn't stop the bleeding, and Doctor Hayes wasn't at home. He was off on his trip up north.

The ladies don't want to hear our reasons for allowing a strange man to stay in the house without a proper chaperone."

"What's a chap. . er . . one?" Joshua asked.

"A chaperone is another grown person, like a man or woman."

"But who would have come out here?" Jake demanded.

"Right now, that's beside the point. Mr. Peterson was here in the house for nearly a month, along with me and you all. They're saying that I sinned."

"The preacher says people can't know someone has sinned unless you throw rocks at them first," Joshua said.

"You dumb-head, that's not the way that saying goes. Tell him, Lizzy, that he has it all wrong," said Jake, as he walked over to the door and looked out. "I just heard someone riding to the barn."

"Lizzy, that old sheriff rode to the barn. I believe he's coming for a visit."

"Oh, my goodness. Jake, you and Joshua run out, greet him, and offer to take care of his horse. I have to clean off this table. Now, hurry and stall him for a few minutes."

"Can I run and hide, Lizzy? That man doesn't like me, and I'm scared of him," Pearl said as she backed toward the bedroom."

"Yes. Get your dolly and play on the bed quietly. Maybe he'll think you're taking a nap." Lizzy wiped the table and removed her apron. She ran outside onto the front porch and waited for the sheriff and boys to come to the house.

"Good day to you, Miss Lizzy. I was out this way, so I hoped you wouldn't mind a short visit from me." Sheriff Jackson twisted his Stetson round and round.

"Of course, you can always stop at our farm and visit. My brothers will put your horse in the shade, water and give him some oats. Come and sit on the porch, and I'll bring you a tall glass of cold tea." Carrying the tray outside, she said, "I thought you might like a snack while we visit. Have you been busy keeping the peace in our little town?"

"I don't have any trouble caring for Crooksville. The people know I won't put up with foolishness." He drank the tall glass of tea in one big swallow. Lizzy jumped up and retrieved the pitcher of tea from the kitchen. "Let me refill your glass."

"You sure know how to take care of a man," he grinned as he held up his glass, then he leaned forward in the rocking chair as Lizzy sat across from him. "Lizzy, I didn't really drop by here accidentally. I came to speak to you again about marrying me." He held up his hand. "Let me finish. I know you said I was too old for you, but I'm not really. I'm as strong as any young buck in this county. I can work circles around any man I know. I will make you a good husband. It's still possible that you could become a real mama to your own child. I'm not over the hill in that department."

"Sheriff, that's a delicate subject, and I don't appreciate that kind of talk."

"Now, come on, Lizzy."

"Miss Lizzy to you, sir.

"Lizzy, you aren't as innocent as you like people to believe. You had a young man living under your roof for a month of Sundays, and I ain't dumb or blind. I could see how he looked at you in every way."

"I think it is time for you to leave and please do not come to 'visit' me again." Lizzy attempted to stand, but the sheriff put his large hand on her knees.

"You cannot get rid of me so fast, Missy. I have a proposition to put before you."

"And what kind of deal do you want to make with me? Speak your piece and leave."

"I want you to agree to become Mrs. Marvin Jackson in two weeks or . . . ," he lent forward, clapped his fingers together, and grinned. "I'll have you declared unfit to care for your brothers and that little princess. I have a lot of pull and power with the judge in town."

She bolted to her feet. "On what grounds can you prove me to be unfit, as you stated? Everyone in this county knows I'm a good Christian and a loving sister to my siblings."

"No, oh no, they haven't heard the real truth about you and your young man, Pete Peterson. I'll tell them how he has lived with you alone, and he shared your bedroom. He has been seen at the pond swimming naked in broad daylight with your little ones. They watching both of you frolicking together."

"How dare you twist the truth into lies about me?"

"Oh, I have witnesses to call to testify against you. Doctor Hayes and Mrs. Johnson. Both of them will tell what they have witnessed. The judge will be very interested in what they have to say." He watched the color drain from Lizzy's face.

"By the way, once the children are taken from you, they will be taken by train to Waco City to the Orphanage Home, where you'll never be allowed to see them again." He stood, using his elbows to hitch up his pants and stepped off the porch. As he started to walk away, he stopped. "Two weeks, no, Lizzy, one week. I've changed my mind. I'll carry out my plan, if I don't hear from you." Whistling, he strutted to the corral fence and leaped on his horse, like so many young men. He was trying to impress his future bride with his youthfulness. Lizzy fell back in her rocking chair and placed her face in her hands. "Dear heavenly Father, please help me . . ."

"Mama Lizzy, who are you talking to now? That mean old man is gone. I thought I might pee in my pants waiting for him to leave. I've got to go to the outhouse," Pearl declared.

As Lizzy watched Pearl race around the house, the twins crawled out from under the front porch. Lizzy couldn't believe what she was witnessing. "What in the world were you two doing hiding under the porch? Are you both afraid of the sheriff, too?"

"We ain't afraid of him, Lizzy, but we wanted to hear what he talked to you about. We know he has already asked you to marry him, and you told him no." Jake said, wiping the dirt from his overalls.

"We figured he came out here to beg you to change your mind. We heard him say that if you don't marry him, he'll send us to the Orphanage Home. Can he do that?" Joshua asked, as he shook his head to get a spider web out of his hair.

"Boys, I don't like it one bit that you eavesdropped on my conversation with another grown person. That is very impolite." She turned Jake around and wiped dirt off his back. "I wouldn't be surprised if you boys have fleas on your bodies," Lizzy laughed.

"Come on now, Lizzy. Tell us what you're going to do. Are you going to marry the sheriff in a week?"

"I am not going to marry anyone anytime soon. I will only marry a man that I love. So, please don't worry so much. I promised mama I'll always take care of you and will not allow anyone to take you away from me."

"He sure sounded awful mean to me, Lizzy," Jake said, very concerned.

"I'll tell you what let's do. Go get the two tubs off the back porch and fill them with water. It's sweltering this afternoon and a dip in a tub of water should feel mighty good, and if you have fleas, you'll drown them," Lizzy said as she stepped off the porch to walk around to the back of the house.

Chapter 11

Early the next morning, after breakfast and the chores were completed, Lizzy told the children that they were going to town. She had some business to take care of at the tax office and needed to get some supplies at Mayberry's Mercantile.

"Can we get something sweet?" Pearl asked.

Lizzy smiled. "I had planned a surprise for you, but I will tell you now. How about we have a treat at the new bakery? I heard the bakery serves sandwiches, so we can eat lunch there. What do you think?" Their large smiles said it all. "I guess you like the idea, so let's get dressed and have fun today."

~

"What do you mean, Mr. Hardy? I'm here to pay the taxes on the farm. Why can't you take my money?" Lizzy didn't understand why her old friend wouldn't take her money.

"The sheriff was in here a few days ago, and he said I wasn't to send you a notice about your late taxes because you'd be selling your place soon."

"Sheriff Jackson told you this?" Lizzy questioned. He only nodded yes.

"I see. Mr. Hardy, how long have you known me and my family?"

"Golly, Lizzy, I have watched you grow up to become

the pretty lady you are. I was here when your folks bought the farm."

"So, you know that if I was going to sell my parents' farm, I would have come to you and talked to you about it. Wouldn't you agree I would have done that?"

"Certainly. I told the sheriff that I couldn't believe you would sell out unless you married and had to leave the county. He said you would marry soon and be living in town with him." Mr. Hardy shook his head. "I really was surprised, butI didn't want to get on his bad side, so I kept my comments to myself."

"Here's my tax bill and I have the payment in full. Please take my money and apply it to my taxes." Lizzy counted the money and waited for a receipt. "For your information, Mr. Hardy, if I plan to sell my farm, I'll discuss it with you. I have no idea what the place is worth, and I know you would advise me. And I'm not marrying anyone, especially the sheriff. He has asked, but I refused." Lizzy placed her receipt in her bag, smiled, and bade Mr. Hardy good day. The children were waiting in the wagon. "Let's drive to the stable and leave the horse and wagon while we shop and have lunch. We can pick up our supplies on our way home."

As they strolled toward the mercantile, Sheriff Jackson stepped out of his office blocking Lizzy's passage. "What a wonderful surprise, Miss Lizzy." He looked down at the children but didn't speak to them as they hid behind their sister.

"Did you come to give me your answer about our little deal? I'm ready whenever you say the word." Sheriff Jackson smiled broadly.

"My answer is the same as the first time you asked, and I'm not changing my mind. Good day to you." Lizzy reached for Pearl's hand and pulled her from the back of her skirt.

The sheriff refused to move out of their way. Beet red in the face and with neck veins bulging, he snarled. "You're going to be sorry you refused me. The judge will return to town in a few days, so get ready to hear from him."

Lizzy seethed inside at his misuse of his power. "You don't scare me. Now, get out of our way. We have business to take care of." Lizzy pushed the boys ahead and picked up Pearl, who clung to her neck.

Lizzy and the children hurried into the mercantile. The children rushed over to give Mrs. Mayberry a warm hug. "Mercy, how you young'uns have grown," she said as she patted them on their backs. "And, Lizzy, it's so good to see you." Mrs. Mayberry took Lizzy by the arm as the children pressed their noses against the display cases. "What is this I hear? You going to marry the sheriff? Is this true?"

"No, I'm not. The sheriff threatened me if I don't agree to marry him. But I'm not going to marry any man that is as old as Papa or one I don't love."

"What kind of threats has he made to you?" Mr. Mayberry asked when he overheard Lizzy speaking with his wife.

Looking around to make sure the children wouldn't overhear their conversation, she whispered. "The sheriff says he can prove I'm unfit to raise my brothers and sister. He'll have them taken away from me, and I won't ever be able to see them again."

"What does he plan to do with the kids?" Mrs. Mayberry quizzed.

"He said the judge would place them in the Waco Orphanage Home. I can't believe the sheriff would be so cruel just because I don't want to marry him."

"We've heard rumors about you having a young man at your place, but I understand from Preacher Booker that he has left." Mr. Mayberry opened a big jar and gave the children a candy treat.

"That's true. We had a young cowboy at my place for a few weeks, but he was almost dead when he arrived on his horse. He'd had been shot, and the bullet went all the way through his side. He'd lost a lot of blood, but by God's grace, I was able to nurse him back to health. Doctor Hayes came by on two occasions and checked him over."

"So, he's the young man that came to church on Sunday with you?" Mrs. Mayberry asked.

"Yes, he's a good Christian man and after he got better, he helped repair my leaky barn roof, and the fence in the pasture, and he built a new hog pen for our new pig."

"Did he sleep in your house?" Mr. Mayberry's eyes narrowed.

"Yes, at first he did, but I slept with the children in the boys' room. Later we made a room for him in the barn. Doctor Hayes said that we couldn't move him to town for another week. I have no idea what's got all the womenfolk stirred up over this young man being on my farm. For goodness sake, I wasn't ever alone with him with three children living under my roof."

"Have you come to town today to give the sheriff your answer?" Mrs. Mayberry looked out the big display window. The sheriff's on the boardwalk across the street. He's in a conversation with Mr. Hardy and Doctor Hayes."

"I came to town today to buy supplies and pay my overdue bills. First I went to the tax office to settle my back taxes and Mr. Hardy refused to take my money. Sheriff Jackson told him not to take any money from me, because I was going to sell my property after I married him. I couldn't believe he had done that so I insisted that Mr. Hardy take my money, and I told him that I wasn't going to marry anyone."

Mr. Mayberry scoffed. "He must be sure you would agree to wed him."

"Not now, because we ran into him just before we came in here. He asked me if I had come to give him an answer. I told him I had not changed my mind. He got so angry, and he told me I was going to be sorry. He'd talk to the judge when he gets here in a few days, and I should expect to hear from him soon."

"Jim, how can we help Lizzy with this problem?" Mrs. Mayberry glanced at her husband. "Can't you speak with the sheriff?"

"You know he has no use for me. I wanted to elect someone other than him as our town sheriff because I didn't feel he was of good character. When we have a council meeting, he orders me around. He says things like I need to move the apple barrels inside or move our brooms elsewhere. Of course, I don't pay him any mind."

"Don't worry about the sheriff, Mrs. Mayberry. But if he does take me to the judge, will you be there for me? I'm afraid I will need people speaking up for my reputation."

Mr. Mayberry rolled his eyes. "Gracious, you're the most respectable young woman in this town. Of course, we will be there for you." Mr. Mayberry rubbed his chin. "I'll speak with Doctor Hayes about these threats that the sheriff is spouting."

"Lizzy," Jake walked over to her. "Can Joshua and I have a bag of marbles?"

She touched his back. "That would be a good game for you boys. I'll let Pearl choose something, too. Mr. Mayberry, I want to settle my feed bill and order this list of supplies." She handed the list to Mr. Mayberry and led Pearl over to the dolls on display.

Once Pearl had chosen a pretty pink gown for her new dolly, Lizzy told Mr. and Mrs. Mayberry that she would pick up her supplies on the way home, but for now, she was taking the children to lunch at the sweet shop.

Mrs. Mayberry whispered for Lizzy's ears only. "Lizzy, did you inherit some money?"

Laughing, Lizzy shook her head no. "Mr. Peterson paid me for taking care of him before he left. But, please don't say anything."

"We'll have your supplies waiting for you when you're ready to go home. Have fun at the sweet shop."

~

Mr. and Mrs. Mayberry watched the little family walk down the boardwalk.

"I'm very concerned about what lies ahead for Lizzy. I don't trust Sheriff Jackson at all. He's furious and if he wants something, nothing will stand in his way," Mr. Mayberry said as he dropped Lizzy's money in the cash register.

~

After the long day in town, the children were exhausted and didn't put up a fuss about retiring for the night. Lizzy was pleased that the children had a good time shopping and eating lunch in the new bakery. She hadn't had extra money in a long time to spend on the children, and it made her feel good to see the smiles on their little faces. The dark side of the day was how the townspeople all avoided her and the children. She knew they were watching, but her smiles weren't returned. Everyone acted like they were strangers.

Once the children were settled in bed and their prayers heard, Lizzy sat in a rocking chair on the front porch to enjoy the cool breeze. Blue quickly stood and gave a loud bark at something blowing in the wind. "

"Quiet, Blue," Lizzy said as she rubbed the dog's back. "Now, be a good boy while I pray to the Lord for guidance. I have no idea why all this trouble has come down on us."

Chapter 12

As Libby and the children drove into town the next morning, she remembered what the note she had received from Judge Mathis' clerk said. *An Inquiry about the guardianship of the three children, Jake, Joshua, and Pearl Montgomery is in question. Please appear before Judge Mathis Wednesday, August 18th at 10:00 a.m.*

Once Lizzy arrived in town the next morning, Lizzy hoped she'd be able to meet with Judge Mathis alone to plead her case. But, that was not to be. Instead of meeting with the judge in his office, she discovered the meeting was to be held in the church.

When Lizzy and the children arrived at the church, they discovered every pew was as full as it was on Sunday morning. Preacher Booker's wife said she would take the children to the parsonage. "I don't believe this is a meeting at which the children need to be present," she whispered.

"Mrs. Booker, why are all these people here? It looks like the whole town is present. Are there more cases to be heard? I thought mine would be a private affair, with only Sheriff Jackson and the judge."

"No, dear. The sheriff announced that everyone should come and hear what he has to say, so, as you can see, they came out in droves. I'm sorry, but remember God is with you."

After the court was called to order and the clerk read the charges against Lizzy, the proceedings were over in less than fifteen minutes. Without even questioning her or allowing her to defend herself, the judge ruled that Elizabeth Marie Montgomery was an unfit person to be a guardian to her three siblings. She would be escorted to her farm to pack the children's belongings and tell them goodbye. The train would arrive in Crooksville at noon tomorrow to take the children to the orphanage in Waco, Texas.

The judge would not allow anyone to speak in her defense. He wouldn't let Preacher Booker, Doctor Hayes, Mr. Mayberry, or any of her closest friends say a word. The sheriff had done a good job in distorting the truth; she had a strange man in her house, frolicked naked at the lake, and shared her bedroom with him.

The judge banged his gravel, he refused to listen to Lizzy's pleas, and her tears had no effect on him. She had never known such a cold-hearted man. He didn't even ask to see the children or question them about how she cared for them. He never met her eyes.

The sheriff stood at the judge's side and smirked. "I'll take Miss Montgomery to her farm and collect the children's things. She can go to the parsonage and tell them goodbye."

"Fine." The judge banged his gavel again and said, "Court is adjourned."

Everyone stood and filed slowly out of the church. Many of the women hung their heads and whispered to each other. Some of the ladies even had tears in their eyes. Lizzy heard one woman say she was a good person who loved her siblings.

Sheriff Jackson took a strong hold on Lizzy's elbow. She cringed, whipped around, and shook her arm loose. "Don't you dare touch me! If you ever touch me again, or even look at me, I'll claw out your eyes. You will not be going to my farm with me. Mr. Mayberry will retrieve my children's things and bring them to town." Lizzy glared at him. "God will punish you for all the lies you told today, and this is not the last of this so-called trial. I will get my children back."

"But the judge said I would take you to your farm," he

spouted at her.

"Do you want to see daylight tomorrow?" she spewed out. The sheriff didn't know how to respond. She narrowed her eyes. "You come near me or my farm again, and I will shoot you . . . dead." Lizzy took Mr. Mayberry's arm and marched to the parsonage.

Lizzy had no idea how she would tell her beloved siblings they would be leaving their home and going to Waco, Texas, to live at an orphanage. The boys knew what an orphanage was because they'd heard the sheriff say they should have been sent there long ago.

Walking into the parsonage, she asked to speak with the children alone. She gathered them, and they went into Preacher Booker's office. "I have some unsettling news to tell you. Sheriff Jackson took me before a man called a judge. The sheriff was angry because I wouldn't agree to marry him."

"Thank goodness for that," Joshua said.

"Please let me finish before you all speak. I'm having a hard time explaining what has happened." She looked at her beautiful siblings as they stared at her, like expectant baby birds waiting to be fed by their mama. "The sheriff wasn't truthful today, but the judge believed him. The judge wouldn't allow me to speak on my behalf or yours."

Lizzy was struggling to talk, but she had to tell the truth. "Because of what the sheriff said about me, the judge will no longer allow me to be your guardian. You'll have to leave me and go to the Orphanage Home for a little while."

"But, Lizzy, I don't want to go away. You're my mama," Pearl cried.

"How long will we have to be away from you?" Jake asked, wiping away tears.

"I can't tell you that, but I will come for you very soon. I've been thinking about a plan, and if it works, you'll be home soon."

"When do we have to leave?" Joshua asked, rushing into her arms. She patted him on the back. "Tomorrow, I'm afraid. There's a train at noon. I have to say good-bye to you now."

"We can't go home with you today?" Jake asked.

"I'm going home with you now, Mama Lizzy. I don't want to go away. Please tell them we ain't going nowhere." Pearl was crying and holding on to Lizzy for dear life.

"Oh, Pearl, my baby girl. I tried telling the old man I couldn't allow you to leave me, but he wouldn't listen, but I will be very near you every minute of every day. I will be in your heart at all times. You will be in my prayers until I can bring you back home. Please be good and listen to the boys. They will take good care of you, won't you boys?"

"You know we will, Lizzy. We'll watch out for each other and try to be brave." Tears streamed down their scared faces as they wrapped their arms around her neck.

The door opened a crack, and Mrs. Mayberry peeked inside. "It's time to go, Lizzy."

Lizzy stood on shaky legs and patted Pearl on her back one last time. The child had cried until she had the hiccups. The boys clutched onto her skirt until she left for the front door. "I love you so much and I promise I'll see you all very soon," she whispered.

Once she shut the door she could still hear the boys bawling and Pearl began to scream at the top of her lungs. "Ma...ma Lizzy!"

~

Mr. Mayberry hugged Lizzy tight. He knew she was hurting. Over the years, he'd watched this young girl grow into a lovely young woman. Her heart was broken, and he felt like his was too. "Come, let's go to the farm so I can return before dark. I'm not a young man anymore, and I don't like to travel the roads at night."

"Thank you for going with me. I would have died before I let Sheriff Jackson take me anywhere. That man is a disgrace to his badge. Mr. Mayberry, I wish I knew why he wanted to marry me. He certainly doesn't love me because we've only talked a few times. Do you think he might have his eyes on my farm?"

"Now, that's a possibility. You do have some of the richest land in the county, and I heard rumors about the train company wanting to buy more farms," Mr. Mayberry commented.

~

After Lizzy had packed the children's clothes, she scribbled a note for Mr. Mayberry to send in a telegram to Pete Peterson in care of Peterson's Farm in Austin, Texas. She placed a few dollars in his hands. "He told me if I needed him, he would come. I need him, now."

Mr. Mayberry nodded. "I will be happy to send this to him as soon as I get back to town."

"Please don't mention this telegram to anyone. Tell Mr. Smitherman to not tell anyone about this message." She held up her hand to keep Mr. Mayberry from speaking. "I know telegrams are personal, but he does talk. As far away as we are from town, I know everyone's business."

"I will threaten to collect his big bill at my store if he talks," he said, chuckling.

She cupped her hands to her heart to keep from shaking. "Please ask Mrs. Mayberry to help my children onto the train. Tell her to tell them I love them so much."

"She'll see they're taken care of." He turned to climb in his wagon but stopped. "I'm so sorry this has happened. We'll pray for you. Please come and see us soon."

Lizzy watched Mr. Mayberry drive away then she entered the house that seemed bigger and emptier than ever before. She eased over to the boy's room and sat down on Jake's bed. "Oh Mama, I'm so sorry I have lost the children, but I promise you it's only temporarily, and I'll get them back." The room felt too confining so she went onto the front porch. She looked into the dark sky and watched the stars twinkle. Staring at the dark clouds floating above, she prayed, "God, please help me."

Lizzy sat in a rocking chair and listened to the frogs and

crickets settling in for the night. Blue had walked over and settled at her feet. Suddenly he stood with his hair raising up on his back causing Lizzy to jump. He hurried to the edge of the porch and howled at an approaching carriage. Once the carriage grew closer to the house, Lizzy recognized Doctor Hayes.

Lizzy stood and backed toward the front door. She didn't want to see anyone, especially someone who was supposed to be her friend. Good manners dictated that she invite him onto the porch, but she was so hurt and angry, it was hard to even acknowledge his presence. "What are you doing here?" she demanded.

"Miss Lizzy, I'm so sorry for what happened today at the church. I never dreamed that Marvin would go so far as to have the judge take the children from you. Earlier, I heard rumors that he wanted to marry you, so I thought if you married me, you would have never had to worry about the children. He'd gotten drunk and made threats about getting rid of the children after he married and sold your farm. I should have told you, but I thought if we married, well . . . that didn't work."

"No, it didn't, but if you had told me that he had plans to take my children and sell my farm, I could have taken my siblings and gone far away. I never believed that the sheriff would tell those vicious lies about me. The judge didn't even allow anyone to speak for me."

He sighed. "I know. Many of the townsfolks were prepared to speak on your behalf. That's the reason I went to see the judge before I came out here. He's staying at the hotel, and I went to talk to him about you and the children. He was drunk. I mean very drunk. Dollar bills were lying all over the table along with four empty bottles of whiskey. "He asked if I wanted to make a bigger donation to him for another decision about the pretty Miss Montgomery. I didn't realize at first what he meant." The doctor shook his head.

She huffed. "So that's how the justice system works. Come and sit a spell on the porch.

The doctor took a seat next to her. "There was no talking to him. The judge just laughed and picked up the money and let it flow over the table and floor. He said the sheriff is five-thousand-dollars poorer now, but he was pleased with my decision. Now, he's going to get married."

"How can he marry without money," Lizzy asked, peering at the doctor.

"The old fool said the good sheriff is going to sell his bride's farm for a bundle because the train company wants to build a line right dab in the middle of her pastureland. Once he made that statement, he fell onto the bed and passed out. I did check to see if he was still breathing before I left."

She stood and paced back and forth on the porch. "Sheriff Jackson has lost his mind. Doesn't he know that he and Judge Mathis can go to prison for what they've done to me and my children?" She plopped down in the rocker. "Does he think that he can make me marry him, after he's ripped my children from me?"

The doctor huffed, "I personally think he has lost all common sense. If he comes out here, don't allow him in. He's still the sheriff, even if he is a greedy drunk and he can be dangerous. Tomorrow, I'm going to hold a secret council meeting, and hopefully we can get the judge sober enough to retract his decision about you. It's going to be my word against Marvin's, but I have to try. I will keep you informed." He stood to leave.

"Wait, Doctor Hayes. If you want to help me, I need a big favor. I wasn't going to tell anyone, but I find I need help. I'm leaving here tomorrow with the children. No one will know I'm on the train. I need someone to come here every morning and night to care for my animals. Of course, I don't know how long I'll be gone, but would you ask Mr. Peacock, at the stables, if his oldest son would do this for me. I have money to leave with him for feed and other expenses. He can actually stay here at night and go back to town after caring for my animals every morning. Will you ask him for me but please keep my travel plans a secret?"

He smiled at her. "Yes, Miss Lizzy, I will do this for you. If Mr. Peacock's son can't do this, I promise I'll find a dependable person to take care of your place." Doctor Hayes reached to take Lizzy's hand, but she hid her hand under her skirt.

"Miss Lizzy, if and when you have another chance to get the children back, I have made a list of all the things you accomplished over the years. I will demand to speak on your behalf. God bless you on your trip." Doctor Hayes climbed onto his carriages and turned the flame back up on his lanterns and drove down the lane toward town.

~

Lizzy walked back inside the front room. It was so quiet and empty. All she could think about was how that crazy sheriff had bribed the judge. She wondered where he got so much money. She sat down in her rocking chair, placed her face down in her hands and cried until there were no more tears. No, she told herself. Tomorrow was just a few hours away. She was going to get her siblings back, if her plan worked.

Walking into her bedroom, she opened the chest under the window, then she reached into the bottom and pulled out her mama's black widow dress. She stood and placed it up against her body. It would be perfect for her plan. Quickly, she took her largest carpet bag and lifted it on the bed. She filled it with clothes for herself and the children, several of their prize processions, and a few medical supplies.

Sitting down on the bed, she thought about traveling on foot. She would wear her heavy boots and a pair of her father's khaki breeches and shirt under the long black dress. Once, she and the children were on the road, she'd remove the heavy clothing.

Yes, this plan will work. My children will never spend a minute in the orphanage.

~

Early the next morning, Lizzy drove her horse and wagon to Mr. Peacock's stable. Even thought it was early, she was nearly soaked with sweat under the heavy black dress. She stopped the horse inside the stable and jumped down by Mr. Peacock's oldest son, Toby.

"Good morning, Miss Montgomery," Toby said, glancing around to make sure their conversation wasn't overheard. "Doctor Hayes asked if I would help you with your farm animals while you're away. I told him I would."

"I can't thank you enough. Please make yourself at home in my house. There's food in the cellar and in the well house. Take this envelope of money. It should keep you going for a while. Use what you need for yourself. If you need more supplies, Mr. Mayberry will let you put it on my account at his store." Lizzy looked over her shoulder. "Will you do one more big favor for me?" Before he could answer, she requested that he go and purchase her a train ticket to Waco. Please don't let anyone know you're purchasing it for me."

"I'll go now before a crowd gathers." He took the money and raced off.

Lizzy stood in the crowd of passengers, watching her siblings stand in a long line of orphans. The children were all dressed in ragged uniforms of brown shifts for the girls and short pants and shirts for the boys. What had happened to her siblings' clean Sunday clothes?

She teared up as the children were herded like cattle into an empty box car with no windows for air. Her heart sank for the children. She said a silent prayer for all their safety. Once the conductor yelled 'all aboard', Lizzy filed into the passenger car and took a rear seat where she wouldn't be noticed. The porter asked if he could store her carpetbag and basket in the luggage car, but she declined.

Lizzy closed her eyes but all she could see were her babies standing in the long line with the other poor-looking orphans. She wondered where all those children came from. An older couple with dour expressions were in charge of the orphans. Sighing, she could still see her littles ones wearing a long tag around their necks with a big number printed on it.

The twins were holding Pearl's little hands to prevent her from getting out of line. The old woman in charge slapped and screamed at little boys who pushed and shoved each other.

Lizzy wiped her eyes under her black veil. She could still hear the judge announce to a roomful of her friends and neighbors that she was an unfit person to care for the children, therefore they would be placed in the Waco Orphanage Home. She was never to see the children again.

Lizzy wanted nothing more than to make thought to make the sheriff suffer by telling him a lie. She remembered the satisfaction on his face when she told him they could wed, but she needed a week to prepare things. He sauntered away whistling and gloating like a rooster. She was sure he'd tell others that she had agreed to marry him. What a fool he would look like when everyone discovered she had left town.

Several hours later, the train stopped to take on water. The older couple in charge of the orphans had a porter open the boxcar and allowed the children to get down to relieve themselves. The burly man screamed at the boys to turn around and take a leak beside the train. He told the girls to squat and do their business. There was no privacy for the little ones.

Lizzy got down, stretched and pretended to take a walk. She strolled past the line of children. Glancing around to make sure no one was watching, she stopped when she reached her siblings. She touched Jake on the arm and passed him a note that read, "I'm going to pretend to faint. Jump down in the ditch and lean against the wall."

She continued strolling until she neared the woman in charge of the children. Swooning, she pretended to faint. "Oh, my goodness." The older woman screamed for a porter as she bent down to help Lizzy.

The porter bent down next to her, "She's too hot with all those clothes on."

While the couple were busy with Lizzy, Jake, and Joshua, grabbed Pearl. The three of them leaped down in the deep ditch and pressed their small bodies up against the dirt wall.

An older boy standing in the doorway of an empty boxcar watched as three children hid from the other orphans by jumping into a deep ditch. He smiled and thought the three were pretty smart. He leaned forward to glance up the line. He saw the lady who had fainted, stood and began walking toward the back of the train.

The conductor yelled 'all-aboard' and the train began to chug, rattle and blow steam as the children filed back on the train. The widow continued walking toward the back of the train when the big burly man grabbed her arm. "Come on, lady, you're going the wrong way. Let me help you back to the passenger car."

The old woman in charge of the children waved at her husband, the big burly man who was attempting to help Lizzy back on the train.

When the boy realized the lady was struggling to get away from the man, he stood and lassoed the big guy. The rope dropped across his shoulders. The man turned the woman loose and had to jog to keep up with the train, while tugging on the rope. The boy, with help from another stranger in the boxcar, pulled the burly man inside the moving car.

"What's the big idea? You could have killed me," The man bellowed over the noise of the moving train. "I need to be in the other boxcar with those brats. Why did you lasso me?"

"You were hurting that lady," the young boy replied.

"I was only helping her back into the passenger car," he roared to be heard over the noise of the train.

"Really, we heard her screaming for help. You were accosting her. Ain't that right?" The boy looked to the other man who had assisted him. He grinned, showing a big missing tooth and yelled, "Yep."

"That's a lie." The big man removed the rope from his body and stormed to the open door of the boxcar.

"Sorry, it's our word against yours if you want to report us." The boy sat in the doorway of the boxcar, happy that he helped the lady that was dressed in widow weeds.

~

As the train traveled down the track, Lizzy watched until it was out of sight. Hurrying over to the ditch, she breathed a sigh of relief when she saw her three siblings, safe and sound. She couldn't believe her plan had worked so well. Reaching down into the ditch, she lifted Jake and then pulled Joshua and Pearl to safety. In a circle, the four of them hugged and cried for joy.

"Lizzy, we thought we'd never see you again," Pearl said, crying.

"I promised you I'd never allow anyone to take you away from me. I'm sorry that you had to endure the last two days, but I have you back with me again and I'll never let you go. Come, we need to get out of here and find a place to hide. I have a carpetbag of things we'll need and a basket of food."

Chapter 13

Pete's train ride to Austin, Texas was a much shorter trip than riding his horse from Crooksville. The engineer blew the train whistle over and over, announcing their arrival. As soon as the train wheels squealed to a stop, Pete jumped from the passenger car onto the platform.

A porter came running to him. "Do you want me to get your horse out of the cattle car for you?"

"Hello, Jerome, good to see you, old man," Pete yelled over the noisy train. "Yes, I'll help you lead him down the gangplank. I can saddle him once he's settled on the ground."

"Your father arrived from the capital yesterday, and I drove him out to the farm. I bet he'll sure be glad to see you," Jerome said, smiling from ear to ear.

"I'll be happy to see him, too."

Once Pete had saddled his horse, he gathered his carpetbag and headed home. It felt good to be back around familiar places and people. Anxious to get home, he kicked his horse sides and galloped across a field toward his family's home place. Home sounded mighty good to him.

It wasn't long before Pete rode under the large archway that displayed the name, *Hundred Acres Farm and Horse Ranch*. Pete smiled at the pretty grounds that surrounded the front of the house. This was a beautiful place.

A couple of farmhands ran from the back of the house and smiled. One young man young man grabbed his horse while the others pounded him on the back.

At the formal dinner, Pete sat at the right side of his father. All the family members were present, and they had many questions about his journey across the western state. Pete described the small towns he'd traveled through and recounted stories of some of the people he'd met. He saved telling his father about his injury and his stay in Crooksville until after they were settled in his study. He wanted to tell his father about his injury and his stay in Crooksville after they were settled in his study. He wanted to discuss his future plans and he hoped that his father would understand.

Pete didn't know what the future would hold for him, but he had to go back to Lizzy. With the sheriff and doctor, both sniffing after her, she didn't need to be alone with those two men. He was sure that Lizzy didn't want to marry either one of them, and he was afraid for her.

After dinner, Pete and his father settled in front of the fireplace. It was too warm for a fire, but the room was a cozy place where his father enjoyed sitting. Once they were comfortable, his father smiled at Pete and said, "You should know by now, I can almost read your thoughts, my boy. What do you want to discuss with me?"

"I could never hide anything from you," Pete laughed and removed his boots. "You don't mind, do you Father. They're still new, and I haven't broken them in yet."

"Please make yourself comfortable." His father smiled and took out a cigar. He rolled it around and smelled it before he lit it.

"I'll start at the beginning of my trip to Crooksville. A small town about three hours from Waco," Pete said.

"I'm all ears, my dear boy," Father said, as he puffed circles in the air.

"I had stopped in a town, Perryville, and decided to stay over and have a nice dinner and sleep in the hotel. After my meal, I wandered into a saloon and played poker with a couple of cowboys. After winning a lot of their money, I spent the night and got an early start the next morning. I had traveled almost to Crooksville when those two cowboys shot me in the side. Somehow, I got away from them.

After a while, I had lost a lot of blood and I was nearly unconscious, but I managed to hang onto my horse. Later, I woke up in a small farmhouse with a lady and her three siblings. They told me my horse walked into their yard and I was lying over on the saddle. They took me in and nursed me back to health."

"How long were you with them?" Mr. Peterson inquired.

"Almost a month. I can tell you that leaving that little family was the hardest thing I have ever had to do. I'm afraid I lost my heart to my beautiful nurse, Lizzy Montgomery." His father didn't react to his news but continued to puff on his cigar.

"People were beginning to talk about me being alone on the farm with her and the children. After I was well enough to travel, I stayed another week as her hired hand on the place. Lizzy has two twin, seven-year-old brothers and a doll of a five-year-old sister. I helped the boys' repair the fence, a leaky barn roof and we built a new hog pen."

Pete's father laughed. "Don't you mean they helped you? Seven years olds are too young to do those things by themselves."

"Well, they really were a big help. And they were pleased that we accomplished so many tasks that needed to be done."

He took another puff of his cigar. "What's this young lady like who nursed you?".

Pete couldn't help but sigh. "Lizzy is a beautiful, young lady with a loving and kind heart. She became the guardian of her siblings after her mother died, but she's more of a mother to them than a sister. Lizzy works hard on the farm; selling eggs and making butter and cheese to sell." Pete grinned, "She's never idle."

"What are you planning on doing about your new woman?" his father asked, smiling.

"First I wanted to come back and make sure the place was still in good order Samuel is a good foreman and with the help of my two brothers, I needn't have worried, but I do feel responsible for the place when you aren't here."

His father tapped his cigar on the ashtray. "Even though you are my youngest, I have always been able to depend on you more than the other two. They are good workers, but they aren't the leader that you are. Having said that, Pete, you have a life besides this farm. If you must leave to court your new love, then go with my blessing. I hope you'll bring her back here to live."

"Thank you, Father. I have several things I want to do here before I leave again. I'll let you know when I plan to go back to Crooksville."

~

Early the next morning, Pete was out in the barn brushing his horse, when Evelyn came from the house waving a note addressed to him. "Pete, a young boy just delivered this note to you. It must be important."

"Thanks," he said, ripping the folded paper open. *"Pete, I need you. Please come. Miss Montgomery."*

Pete couldn't seem to think straight. He stood staring at the note. *I need you* were the words that jumped off the paper. He remembered telling Lizzy that if she needed him, he would come running. Something bad had happened was his last clear thought before he started running to the house.

Chapter 14

Lizzy and the children watched until the train was out of sight. She was thrilled that her plan had worked, and she had the children back. Glancing around she knew she had to take her siblings away before the man in charge noticed them.

"Jake, can you carry the basket while I carry this carpetbag?" Lizzy scanned the area, focusing on the fenced field.

"Sure, I can do anything now that we're away from the train, and that mean old woman. She was a devil, for sure." Jake commented.

"You'll have to tell me about your experience later. Joshua, take Pearl's hand and stay away from this track. We need to walk in that direction." Lizzy pointed to the west. "We'll find a place to get out of the weather. Those clouds are turning black and roiling in the sky."

Lizzy lifted the barbed-wire fence, and the children crawled under it to reach a smooth path. As the boys held the wire wide for Lizzy to crawl through, her dress got caught in several places, and the sharp barbs stuck into Lizzy's skin. She got untangled and stepped back on the opposite side of the fence. She reached down and pulled the black garment over her head. The boys watched in shock as their sister was stripping off her clothes in front of them.

Once she had removed the heavy, black dress, the boys blew out a breath. "Thank goodness, Lizzy. We didn't know you had on more clothes." The boys rushed closer to the fence. "Where'd you get those breeches?" Joshua asked.

"These pants belonged to your grandfather's. I figured it would be better for me to wear them while we walked in the woods," she said, hugging her brothers.

"Now, let's get moving and find a place to get out of the weather."

After carrying Pearl, who cried herself to sleep, and walking for miles on a path previously made by others, Lizzy saw a cluster of large rocks in the shape of a 'V'. She motioned for the boys to stop and asked them to poke around the ground for critters. Small pellets of rain started falling, so Lizzy quickly reached into her carpetbag and pulled out a light blanket. She lifted Joshua onto the top of the rocks and together, they layered a few heavy stones on the blanket to hold it in place. Lizzy placed the carpetbag, basket, and Pearl under the blanket roof.

She had the children sit and lean against the rocks while she handed each one a sandwich and an apple. The children gobbled the food down and wanted more.

"This is the first thing we've had to eat since last night, and it was only a small bowl of soup." Jake peeked in the basket.

"I'm not sure that was soup," Joshua said. "It smelled awful, so while I was studying it, a bigger boy took mine away."

"I guess you're hungry, but we must save some food for later. We'll find a small town or village tomorrow. With this storm, we'll have to stay here tonight."

"It's all right, Mama Lizzy. It's like a playhouse that you've made for me before. We can bundle together to stay warm." Pearl smiled and appeared happy to be with her Mama Lizzy.

Lizzy reached in the basket and pulled out matches and the children's name and number tags. After stacking a few pieces of wood, she set the papers on fire and pushed them under the wood. The children warmed their hands and soon huddled together and fell fast asleep. Lizzy took out her heavy black dress and bundled it around the children.

As Lizzy walked around the small area, several drops of rain rolled onto her back and dropped down the front of her shirt. The water was so cold. As she prepared to sit down, several more large drops of rain soaked her shirt. She stood watching the rain cascade over the blanket.

Wet and cold, she lay down in front of the children and prayed. She thanked the Lord for being able to rescue the children and prayed that Pete would get her message and come back to Crooksville. It occurred to her he wouldn't find her at home if he did come. How would he know where to look for her? Finding a comfortable spot to sleep was hard because she was chilled to the skin. She scooted her body closer to the children, and soon exhaustion overcame her wet body and she fell into a deep sleep.

~

Dreaming, she heard the children speaking softly. Remembering her babies were safe and sound, she curled into a knot and attempted to get comfortable.

"That's our mama, Lizzy," Pearl's voice sounded very far away. Lizzy couldn't imagine who the child was talking to.

Still exhausted, Lizzy slowly opened one eye and saw two long, tan legs straddling her body." She gashed, fear coursing through her. The legs were large with heavily developed calves. Looking up, she saw a tall, shirtless torso wearing only wore a loincloth that barely covered his lower body. Lizzy shook her head to clear the cobwebs. She hoped that she was dreaming, but when she opened her eyes wide, Jake and Joshua were squatting down beside her.

"Lizzy," Jake whispered, peering up at the big man standing over her. "We're surrounded by Indians, but so far they haven't tried to scalp us."

When the man offered his hand to Lizzy, the boys jumped back. She took his hand and let him pulled her up on her bare feet. Swaying, she nearly fell forward. She wondered why she was barefoot before everything went black.

~

The large brave caught Lizzy before she hit the ground. He stared at the children and asked, "Has she been sick?"

The boys quickly shook their heads. They followed the man as he carried their sister over to a large rock. He took out a large colorful rag and began wiping Lizzy's sweaty face.

~

Mercy, she thought, as her eyes opened. What a handsome man. He had long black hair held back with a bright yellow and green headband, big crystal blue eyes and rosy lips. She had never seen an Indian in real life, and surely not one so handsome.

"Where did you come from?" Lizzy asked, her eyes taking in more Indian braves.

"I could ask you the same," he said, peering down at the young boys. "Our village is less than a mile from here. We were hunting when we saw your fire, but waited for daylight to make sure you were alone with the children. Where is your man?"

"There is no man. We're searching for a small town or an abandoned shack to hide in."."

"Are you running away from a white man or the law?"

"Are you going to scalp us," Joshua asked.

Pearl came running over to Lizzy and grabbed her around the leg. "Maybe they're going to boil us alive and eat us!"

The big brave's mouth twisted into a frown. "What have you taught these little ones about my people?"

Surprised at her children's comments, she didn't respond.

"No little ones," the man said, "we don't scalp people and we don't boil people. We aren't going to hurt your mama or you, unless you misbehave. Come, gather your things and let's go to the village. Food will be ready once we get there. I'm sure you're hungry."

Lizzy held the children tight and asked the handsome

brave. "How is it you speak English?"

"We'll talk later. Your skin is hot. You may be sick. I need to get you to our camp. Later, you can tell me why you're on our reservation. Now, let's move. My friends are ready to get home." He motioned toward the young braves who stood waiting.

The big brave walked ahead of them with the young braves following close.

In one quick motion, a young brave snatched the carpetbag from Joshua and the basket from Jake. Another two braves picked up the boys and tossed them high upon their shoulders. Suddenly Pearl was removed from Lizzy's back by a young brave. He placed her on his shoulders, and she giggled with delight. Relieved, Lizzy rubbed her shoulders as she followed the group.

The big Indian never glanced back as he marched to the village. When they arrived, many young Indian maidens, older men, and children of all ages gathered to greet him and the other braves. One maiden called him the chief's son.

The medicine man, with a painted face wore a colorful headpiece of feathers. He rattled a funny-looking object on a stick as he danced among them. "Go away, old man," the brave said. "You aren't needed here and I don't want you scaring the children."

"Can he perform tricks?" Jake asked, looking around at the other people.

"Woman," the brave asked, "what have you taught these young'uns?" The brave shook his head as a pretty young girl approached and made a hand gesture.

The brave smiled at Lizzy "This young maiden is Morning Glory. She'll take you into her teepee and feed you. Go with her." The brave walked away. Lizzy had no idea if she would ever see him again.

Jake watched the young maiden as she motioned them to follow her. "Is she a dummy?" he asked.

Lizzy was shocked that he would ask such a question. "Where did you hear that word? And before you say another word, no, she doesn't speak English. She's using hand language to communicate with us."

"Tommy says Alex, the boy that cleans the schoolhouse, is a dummy because he can't talk. So, she . . . ." Jake continued.

"Be quiet and don't say another word. If and when we get home, I'll have to teach some serious lessons to you three. Witches, Indians and now dummies. Mercy," Lizzy said as dizziness assailed her.

~

Lizzy took Pearl's hand while the boys followed the pretty young girl into a large teepee. Two older Indian women sat in from of a fire. One was stirring a pot of something that smelled wonderful. Lizzy felt her stomach growl. The other woman was gathering wooden bowls and spoons.

The young maiden motioned for Lizzy and the children to sit. "She doesn't have to tell me twice," Jake said, "I could eat a cow."

"Cow, beef," the young girl said as she passed a bowl to Pearl. "Baby eat first in my teepee. Other teepees, men, eat first." The young maiden smiled and bowed her head.

"Thank you," Lizzy said smiling at the girl. "Pearl is my baby's name."

"Pearl," the girl repeated. "I like." When she passed the boys a bowl, Lizzy gave them a stern look.

"Thank you, Miss," the boys said at the same time.

"Man, this is so good," Joshua said, who happened to be a very picky eater.

"Lizzy, will we sleep here tonight or will they make us leave?" Jake wiped his mouth.

Well, I don't think we're their prisoners," she said groggily. "Maybe that brave will show us which direction we should travel. I didn't know we had walked onto the Indian reservation. As one of the women attempted to pass Lizzy some food, Lizzy coughed and tried to sit up but fell back. "I have heard about this place, but I had no idea we were near it," her voice trailed off.

. She was so hot and could hardly keep her eyes open.

The woman felt Lizzy forehead and declared to the others, "She's sick. Go get Old Woman."

Lizzy's heavy eyes opened just a bit. The young maiden came back into the teepee with an older woman. She motioned for the children to move away from Lizzy. Watching as the young maiden prepared them a bed, the older woman opened Lizzy's shirt and laid her head against her chest.

"I hear a rattle. Woman has trouble breathing." She said something to the young maiden and left.

"Is Lizzy sick?" Pearl asked.

"Yes, Old Woman medical doctor make a poultice for her." She patted her chest, "and some honey to drink for cough." She placed Pearl on the pallet and motioned for her to sleep.

"What does that old medicine man do?" Pearl asked. "Why was he dancing and jumping all around them when we arrived?"

The maiden wrapped a blanket around her. "He can do things but doctoring not one of them. Now sleep. White woman better tomorrow."

~

Later, the old woman returned. The children were resting on the opposite side of the teepee. The young girl named Pearl had gone to sleep, but the twin boys were watching. The old woman placed a thin layer of bear grease on the young woman's chest and laid a hot cloth that contained boiled, wild onions. The white woman groaned but didn't wake. Old Woman shook a jar that contained honey, water, and a few chopped onions. She motioned for the young maiden to help the white woman up so she could spoon the honey mixture into her mouth. The white woman shook her head, but the older woman forced the mixture into her mouth and covered it with her hand making her swallow.

"She will need honey many times during night, and I change the poultice each time. It must be hot to do good." Old Woman nodded at the maiden girl.

The handsome brave entered the teepee. He asked Old Woman about the white woman's health. "She be good in two days. Her fever high but she sweating a lot. That good."

"I appreciate your help with this woman. She's not any danger to our tribe. The woman didn't know she was on the reservation. She is running from someone or something. After she's well, I will convince her to tell me." He walked over to the boys. "Ah, you're still awake. Go to sleep. You need rest. You'll have a big day tomorrow." The brave bent down and covered the twins with a soft blanket of deer hides.

After the brave left the teepee, Joshua whispered. "What did you think he meant about a big day tomorrow?"

"I'm not sure, but they aren't going to harm us. Go to sleep," Jake said, pretty sure they were in a safe place.

Chapter 15

Pete reread the note as he packed for the return trip to Crooksville. Lizzy needed him. He had no idea what could have happened so soon, but it didn't matter. She needed him, and he would be leaving on the afternoon train.

After discussing the problem with his father, he visited his two brothers. He apologized for leaving the farm so soon, but it couldn't be helped. Pete thanked them for understanding and promised to return as quickly as he could.

Months ago, they'd planned to ship two hundred cattle to the fall market, and they'd hired men to help. Pete told his brothers he couldn't stay and head up the big herd, but he was sure they could handle everything. He could see the disappointment in his brothers' faces, but his father understood and that was all that mattered.

His father had said, "Pete, you'll have a lifetime to take care of this farm once you settle your love life. Don't worry about this place. The men can handle anything that comes up. And, I'm not so old that I can't still handle a few problems."

Pete climbed on the train with the peace of mind that the farm was in good hands, but he was worried sick about Lizzy and the children. After what seemed like hours, the train pulled into Crooksville before the town closed down for the night. Pete retrieved his carpetbag and walked to the stable. Mr. Peacock, the owner had retired for the evening, but his son, Toby, was bedding down the boarded horses.

"Good evening, young man. I need a horse. Do you

have one that I can use for a few days?"

"Sure, Mr. Peterson. I told my pa I bet you'd be returning."

"How do you know me? And why were you sure I would be coming back?" Pete had never met this young man before.

"I'm Toby, and I saw you when you came into town with Miss Montgomery, and you went to church with her." Toby walked to the double door and pushed it closed. "You know that she ain't here anymore. She left the same day they took the children. So sad. My momma cried."

He frowned. "Wait, just a minute. Are you telling me that Miss Montgomery isn't here in Crooksville, and her children are gone, too? Where have they gone?"

The boy slapped at a fly on his neck. "Golly, I thought you knew. The judge took her brothers and little sister and shipped them off to that old orphanage home in Waco, and the same day, Miss Montgomery left town. I'm taking care of her farm while she's away."

"You're telling me Lizzy is not at her farm now, right?"

"Yes, sir. I go every night to Miss Montgomery's farm and care for the animals, spend the night at the farm and take care of the animals each morning before I come to work for my pa."

Pete walked around in a circle, stopped, and asked the boy. "Do you know if the judge is still in town?"

"Yep, he lives at the hotel on the third floor. He keeps his horse and carriage here."

"How long has Lizzy and the children been gone?"

"Hmm, about five days. Sheriff Jackson came in here today and boy, he was mad. Miss Montgomery was supposed to marry him, and he discovered she left him high and dry. He was in here yelling at my pa like it was his fault she had left town. Miss Montgomery didn't take her horse and carriage. She left on the train."

"Are you sure she took the train and not the stagecoach?"

"Look, Mr. Peterson," he said, peering at the door. "She asked me to get her a train ticket and I did, but no one else knows this, so please don't tell on me."

Pete frowned. "I won't tell on you. So, as far as you know, she traveled away from here on the same train the children were on when they left to go to Waco?" Pete asked, trying to make things very clear in his mind. It sounded like something Lizzy would do.

Toby nodded. "She was dressed in a long black dress with a black veil covering her face. When I told Mama about seeing her at the station, and how she was dressed, Mama said she was wearing widow-weeds. Mama could understand why she dressed in all black because she knew Miss Montgomery felt like part of herself had died."

"Toby, you have been a big help to me. I'll go to the hotel and get me a room. Tomorrow, I'll begin my search for Miss Montgomery."

The young man smiled. "You might want to talk with Doctor Hayes. My pa said after the judge declared Miss Montgomery unfit, the doctor went to see him later that night."

"My word, I can't believe that she was proven unfit. No one could have cared or loved those children more than she." Pete shook his head. "I'll speak with Doctor Hayes first thing in the morning. You said earlier that Miss Montgomery was going to marry the sheriff?"

"Well, right after the judge sent the children away, the sheriff bragged to the whole town that Miss Montgomery would marry him. My pa said he didn't believe it because the sheriff is the only person that brought evidence against her."

Pete frowned. "I don't know why he would tell everyone she would marry him. She didn't even like the man, and he frightened her, too. But, if she marries anyone, it will be me. I don't know how or when, but I'll bring her brothers and sister back home."

"Can I tell my pa what you just said?" Toby smiled.

"Yes, but let's keep all the other things you told me

quiet," Pete said as he followed Toby as he picked out a horse. Pete paid Toby for the rental of a horse a week in advance and rushed over to the hotel to rent a room for the night. Early the following day, he ate a quick breakfast in the hotel dining room and hurried to purchase a train ticket to Waco. He had his horse boarded in the cattle car so he could ride directly to the orphanage home when he arrived in Waco.

~

Later that day, Pete stood in the orphanage's office. "What do you mean the Montgomery children aren't here?" Pete asked Mr. Cummings, the director of the Waco Orphanage Home.

"We were expecting the three children to arrive with the other fifty or so homeless children, but they never arrived. The attendants who always bring the children to us, said they had escaped and believed they got off at the first watering station."

"Escaped?" Pete repeated. "So, they're treated like little prisoners as they travel?"

"Well, of course not prisoners. They have to keep them close so they'll arrive all together. Somehow, they lost those three."

"I can assure you, Mr. Cummings, if those three children show up here, they won't stay long. They have a sister who loves them very much, and she'll take them home—with me."

"Sometimes, the children are never found. Good luck locating them," he said, returning to shuffling papers on his desk.

Pete stormed from the home and rode his horse back to the train station. His plan was to travel toward Crooksville but get off at the last watering station where Lizzy and the children took their leave from the train.

Chapter 16

Lizzy struggled to open her eyes. She rubbed one eye and, finally both opened to see her twin brothers squatting at her side.

"See, I told you she was trying to wake up," Jake said.

Once Lizzy was completely awake, she got a better view of her brothers. They both were shirtless, wearing headbands with a single colorful feather sticking toward the sky, and their faces and chest were covered with stripes of different color paint. They looked like two Indian braves preparing for a war party.

Joshua hurried outside the teepee to find Pearl, dressed in a light brown Indian shift with long strips of soft leather at the hem, the neck was decorated with beads, and she wore soft leather moccasins. Her lovely blond curls were braided and hung down to her shoulders. "Come Pearl," Joshua said "Lizzy needs to see you. She's better."

Lizzy smiled when she saw her baby sister dressed like a Indian maiden. As she reached to hold Pearl, the Old Woman gave the children orders.

"Move, little braves," Old Woman commanded. Both boys and Pearl leaped up and moved back from Lizzy. Old Woman moved Lizzy's arms and hands. She laid her ear down to listen to her chest. Old woman smiled and patted Lizzy's hand. "You good now." Then she motioned for Morning Flower to come. "Tell woman she must go to the bushes, have a bath, and eat a hardy meal. She better, but still weak. "

"Yes, I'll care for her now. You rest. You haven't slept all night," Morning Flower told Old Woman.

Old Woman moved Lizzy's arms and hands. She laid her ear down to listen to her chest. Old Woman smiled and patted Lizzy's hand. "You good, now."

The older woman motioned for Morning Flower to come. "Tell woman she must to go the bushes, have a bath, and eat a hardy meal. She is well but still weak."

"Yes, I'll care for her now. You rest. You haven't slept all night," Morning Flower told Old Woman.

"Morning Flower, I must get up and have a moment of privacy," Lizzy said.

"I am here to help. Can you sit up?"

"Yes, I think so, with a little help. I'm starving, too," Lizzy commented with a smile. Lizzy noticed her three siblings staring at her, Pearl dressed in an Indian dress, her blond hair braided. "I will be back in a minute, and you must tell me what you have been up to while I was sleeping. The three smiled and stepped back while Lizzy and Morning Flower left the teepee.

After Morning Flower helped Lizzy wash the bear grease off her chest, she scrubbed her with a bar of hard soap. Lizzy's long hair lay plastered to her head and smelled. Fussing, Morning Flower didn't want her to wet her head, but Lizzy won the battle, she had to be clean all over. Old Woman said Lizzy could catch another chill with a wet head, but she quickly dried it by the fire, using a rough drying rag. Once she was clean, Lizzy felt human again.

Morning Flower served her a bowl of venison stew. Lizzy thought it was the best she had ever eaten and wished she could have the recipe.

When it was time to dress, Old Woman brought an Indian shift for Lizzy to wear while her shirt, breeches and undergarments were drying. She dropped a pair of soft moccasins in front of her.

"Your boots are wet but will be dry tomorrow,"

Morning Flower said.

Lizzy remembered her siblings dressed in Indian duds, so she had no choice. Besides, it was for only a day. They would be able to leave the village tomorrow.

While Lizzy was resting on a pallet of soft blankets, the handsome brave entered the teepee. He didn't look like the scantily dressed brave she had first met. His features made up the perfect male specimen. He had a strong jaw, straight nose and high cheekbones. His straight hair was black as a raven, and he had intelligent, dark brown eyes. The man was dressed in long leggings with short leather fringe down each side and a sleeveless soft, deerskin vest with crisscross leather down the front holding it together on his chest. The plain red headband he wore to hold back his long black hair was the only bright color on his bronze body.

"You look well," he said to Lizzy. "Old Woman and Morning Flower have taken good care of you?"

"Yes, they have been so kind to me. I can't thank them enough," Lizzy said as she covered her legs. "I had no idea I was so ill. I'm grateful to you, too, for bringing my siblings and me to your village."

"You're welcome." He glanced around. "Your little ones are enjoying themselves. They have been playing cowboys and Indians."

"May I ask your name? I can't keep referring to you as the big handsome . . . I mean brave." Embarrassed to her toes, Lizzy looked away.

Smiling, he said, "I am called Yuma. It means Son of Chief. My name has great honor among my people."

"May I call you Yuma?"

"Please do. I will call you Lizard?" He frowned at Lizzy.

"No, mercy, my name is Elizabeth, but everyone calls me Lizzy."

"I like that better," he said with a big grin. Lizzy wondered if he was teasing her. "May I ask you how is it you speak perfect English and most of the others only know a few words?"

"After I become almost a man, the Army soldiers drove my people like a herd of cattle to this reservation. I was angry that my people were driven off our land. The government accused my people of burning and raiding white people's farms and killing every white person in their view. All lies, but my father couldn't convince the army we were innocent. So, after a while, the soldiers needed a scout or guide. They chose me and while I lived with them for several years, I listened and learned their language."

"That's a shame the government can get so many things wrong. Believe me, I understand about having lies told and not being able to defend yourself."

Yuma studied Lizzy for a moment. "Is that the reason you're on the run?"

"How did you guess I'm trying to hide from someone?" Lizzy watched as Yuma folded his large body and sat beside her pallet.

"It was easy, woman. You dressed in men's clothes, had very little provisions, protecting three little ones, and with no plan as to where you were headed," Yuma said waiting for her to deny his assumption of her situation.

"That about sums it up," she smiled. "I packed in a hurry, but I had no choice. I'm sure the sheriff and others are looking for me and the children. But I pray they will never find me. I'll never let them take my siblings from me again."

"Your story interests me, so start at the beginning and tell me what made you run." He watched the woman's eyes cloud with tears, but he found himself fascinated with the white woman.

"I don't want to keep you from your tribe. It's obvious your people depend on you." Lizzy knew that this Indian brave was an important man in the tribe.

"Yes, they do, but everyone is busy. The children are playing, and we have time for a long talk, so please begin. I want to help if I can." He wanted to learn more about this strange woman who had bravely adventured away from her home.

Stubbornness was Lizzy's nature when it came to talking to strangers but it would have been childish, especially when she didn't have anything to hide. She was reassured that his people weren't going to harm her and the children. Lizzy sighed and began when Pete first came to her farm. She explained how she nursed him back to health, the sheriff's and doctor's proposals and how angry the Sheriff became after she refused to marry him. She told Yuma how the judge ruled she was an unfit guardian after believing lies spewed by the sheriff and not being able to defend herself. Then she spoked about the children being placed on the Orphanage Train and how she got them off." Lizzy wiped away tears as she said, "You know the rest. Thank the good Lord that you did find us."

In an instant, Yuma frowned. This man, Pete, where's he now?"

"He was well enough to travel, so he went back home to Austin. His father owns a large farm and Pete takes care of it for him while his father works at the capitol building."

"Sounds like this Pete fellow's father is an important man. Maybe he can help you."

"I did send Pete a telegram before I left town and asked him to come to Crooksville. I remembered later that I wouldn't be there even if he did come."

"I want to ask you a personal question. However you want to take it," Yuma said. "I notice whenever you speak about this man, your face lights up."

"Ask away. We don't seem to have any secrets between us now."

"This man Pete. . . he's a friend or lover?"

"Gracious!" Lizzy's face flamed. She looked toward the teepee door and all around the room before answering. "He's just a friend. When he left my farm, he said he'd be back. I hated seeing him go because I was beginning to have feelings for him. He felt the same for me."

"What is it you liked about this man? Can he protect you, provide you a home, plant your fields, teach your boys to grow into strong men, and care for you like a man should?"

Lizzy stared at this handsome Indian who seemed to have changed right before her eyes. He seemed to be a caring man one minute and then like a demanding father who wanted to know answers she couldn't give.

"Pete Peterson is a good man who will care for me and my children. I know he will never harm us."

"If he cares for you, he'll be coming to Crooksville if he isn't already there and if he's any kind of man at all he will be on your trail soon. My men will be watching for him."

She peered at him, amazed at his perceptiveness. "Do you really think he can find us in this wilderness?"

"Yes, he'll come. When a man has a woman in his heart, he'll find her, if he's any kind of man."

Lizzy suddenly got frightened and sat on her knees. "If he can find me, the sheriff and his men might be able to also."

"My people will be on guard. But never fear. The sheriff will not get near you or the children. My braves will see to that." Yuma stood, then walked out into the bright sunshine.

Yuma needed to get away from the white woman. He like everything about her, and if that Peterson man was not to his expectations of a man, she will never leave with him. She will become his woman.

~

After the sun had set, the Indian braves built a big bonfire and all the Indian tribe gathered around. Yuma's father, the Chief, sat with a few other elders while the women sat behind many young braves. A large Indian beat on a deerskin drum. It wasn't long before many of the braves and little boys jumped up and danced around the fire. Many of the boys chanted in a singsong tone. The women hummed words along with them.

Jake and Joshua, along with the younger boys, wearing Indian paints on their bodies, danced around the fire. Pearl sat with Lizzy and clapped her hands. She asked Lizzy if she could dance with the boys, but Lizzy told her this was an Indian ritual only for boys. Pearl twisted her little body and attempted to stand a couple of times. Lizzy held onto her to make her sit quietly like the other little girls.

The drummer stopped and all the Indian braves sat down. Joshua and Jake came and sat down next to Lizzy. Suddenly, Pearl was standing in front of the circle. Lizzy started to pull her back down beside her, but Old Woman shook her head. She made a hand signal that suggested to let her be.

Pearl glanced around at the Chief and all the other Indians. Everyone grew silent as they looked upon the little white girl. Now that she had everyone's attention, Pearl raised her hands in the air and uttered in a loud voice;

> "*Twinkle, twinkle little star, how I wonder what you are,*
> *Up the world so high, like a diamond shining,*
> *When the big sun is gone, when it shines up there,*
> *Then show your little light.*
> *Twinkle, twinkle, little star.*"

When Pearl finished, she smiled at the Chief and took a bow.

Then, the unexpected happened. The Chief waved at Pearl and said, in perfect English, "More, more."

"Say it again, little Pearl," Morning Flower said, as she placed her hand across her shoulders.

Pearl seemed thrilled that the old man liked her poem, so she started singing it Lizzy had taught her.

"*Twinkle, twinkle,*" Pearl was surprised to hear all the women and young Indian maidens sang along with her, repeating "*Twinkle, twinkle, twinkle.*" Excited. Pearl sang louder, waving her hands over her head. All the females copied Pearl. They sang the word *Twinkle* over and over and waved their hands, too.

Lizzy, Jake and Joshua sat together and watched Pearl

sing the song. She had forgotten many words, but she still entertained the tribe. Pearl had taught the Indians a new English word they enjoyed singing.

Chapter 17

"Listen to me, old man. I tell you now, that gal won't escape me!" Sheriff Jackson stomped circles in his office. "She's going to be sorry when I catch her, too," he slurred as he watched Judge Mathis' face turn white.

"Now, look here, Marvin. I'm not going to be a part of any violence. You can't harm Miss Montgomery physically. I won't be a part of that," Judge Mathis declared as he pulled on his starched white collar. "You'd best calm yourself before you make any rash decisions."

"You old drunk. Do you think I'd harm her where it might show? But right now, I'm going to the tax office to have old Hardy place a For Sale sign on her farm. She won't have a place to return if she ever shows her face around here again. Then I'll collect the money from her farm. I'd planned to marry her and sell the place right away. Now that she has abandoned her farm, I'm claiming it."

"I'm sure you don't have the right to do that. Besides, Mr. Hardy won't sell her farm without her permission." The judge walked toward the door. He needed to escape from the sheriff because he would get them all in big-time trouble.

"You just run and hide away in your hotel room and drink yourself into a stupor. I'll take care of old man Hardy. He'll do what I tell him, or else." Sheriff Jackson used his elbows to pull up his pants as he ran his hand through his hair. He needed a bath and shave, but he didn't care about his appearance when he had other important matters on his mind.

Sheriff Jackson entered the tax office and pushed Mr. Hardy into the backroom. Then he grabbed Mr. Hardy by the throat, nearly lifting him off the floor. He shook the little man several times and said, "You'll prepare a paper that says Lizzy instructed you to sell her farm and give the money to me. Do you understand what I'm telling you to do? If you don't, your little girl will come up missing, never to be found again. She'll bring a lot of money at the border of Mexico. "

Mr. Hardy cringed. "No, please, please, don't harm my family. Yes, I know what you want from me. I'll prepare the paper, whatever you say, and I'll have my wife sign Lizzy's name. Please, I'll need a few hours, and I'll go and put up the For Sale sign." The sheriff turned him loose and grinned. "Now that's more like it."

Walking Mr. Hardy back into the front of the tax office, he hesitated momentarily as he held the door open. "If you need to tell anyone about our little talk today, think about your little girl. I know Bonnie very well."

"No, I won't tell a soul." Mr. Hardy sat down in a chair and watched the sheriff stroll away. "Oh, Lord," he prayed, holding his head in his hands, "please help me."

~

Pete was disappointed that he didn't find the children at the Waco Orphanage Home. And looking around Waco, he didn't find any information that Lizzy had been there. He left the Waco home and purchased a ticket for the train back to Crooksville. Once there, he'd go to the farm and hope to find a clue where Lizzy might be headed. He planned to get on another train, get off at the first water station, and start his search. It was hard to believe Lizzy would get off the train in an isolated area with the children, especially in an area surrounded by wilderness.

Pete arrived in Crooksville and got a hotel room to have a hot bath and a good meal. He went to the stable and spoke with Toby, the young boy who worked at his father's livery stable.

"Hello, Mr. Peterson," Toby addressed him. "Did you see the kids in Waco?"

"Afraid not. I was told that Lizzy and the children got off the train before it reached the city. I'm going to ride out to her farm and see if I can find any clues about where she might have planned to go. Have you heard any news about them?"

The boy shrugged. "Well, only from my Pa. He said that Miss Montgomery's farm was up for sale. My pa is very confused about it because he couldn't believe she told Mr. Hardy at the tax office to sell it for her."

"I can't believe that either. If Lizzy had him sell her farm, he'd have to know where to send her the money; therefore, he would know where she would be."

"No, that's not what Pa said. He said the sheriff would get her money." Toby glanced over his shoulder and said softly, "He said the sheriff bragged that Miss Montgomery said he could collect the money for himself."

"What?" Pete nearly yelled.

"Please, Mr. Peterson. I shouldn't have repeated this to you, but I know you care about Miss Montgomery. My Pa and some of the other council members are silently looking into the sale of her farm. So many people knew that Miss Montgomery was afraid of the sheriff, and she never planned to marry him, even though he said that she was going to."

Pete scratched the back of his head. "It looks like he is trying to sell her farm and take the money since she has left town. Maybe he and the judge are in this deal together."

"Please don't say I told you any of this. Pa will skin me alive if I cause trouble with my big mouth." Toby said as he walked into the stall to retrieve Pete's horse.

"I won't say a word, but I will keep my eyes and ears open now that you have informed me what's happening. I'll be back later, but tomorrow I'm going to track Lizzy after she gets off the train. You can tell your Pa. I know he cares about Lizzy."

~

Early the following day, Pete arrived at Lizzy's farm. As he rode his mount over to the water trough, Toby came out of the barn. "Morning, Mr. Peterson. You said you would come out here, but I wasn't expecting to see you so early."

"Morning Toby. I couldn't sleep and I wanted to catch the afternoon train and begin my search for Lizzy." Pete walked over to the For Sign nailed on the fence post.

"Has your Pa said how much they are selling this place for?"

"I heard this place was worth about six hundred dollars or a little less. The sheriff said he wanted a thousand dollars because some railroad Tycoons were buying up farms and land near here."

Pete frowned. "What does the sheriff plan to do with all these animals?" Pete pointed at the two mules and the dozen head of cattle in the pasture.

The boy shrugged. "I believe he is trying to sell everything that isn't nailed down. Pa is so angry that he's stealing Miss Montgomery blind." Toby tossed a saddle on his horse, preparing to go to town.

"I'm going over to see Mr. Johnson and talk to him about Lizzy's animals. I want to see if I can make a deal with him. Don't mention this to anyone," Pete said as he waved goodbye to the young man.

Pete was pleased to see Lizzy's farm had been well taken care of since she had been gone. Toby had been keeping the place clean and the animals well-fed. No way would the sheriff take the farm away from Lizzy. Nor was Pete going to allow him to sell the animals Lizzy and the children loved.

The boys had practically raised all the chickens even though they had to run from the old rooster many times. Now, if Lizzy and the kids were home, they'd be preparing to take care of a new bunch of little piglets in a few weeks. When the cows dropped their calves, then they had helped clean them up and sometimes even bottle-feed a few. There was no way the children would come home and find all their animals sold.

Pete rode into Mr. Johnson's front yard and was welcomed by Mrs. Johnson. "Well, young man. We thought we'd never see you again." Her voice had an angry tone.

"Now, Gertie," Mr. Johnson said as he walked from the barn. "That's no way to welcome our guest." Irritated at his wife, he motioned for her to return to the house. "Get down, young man, and tell me why you've come," Mr. Johnson said.

"Thank you, Mr. Johnson. I'm sorry you've formed a bad opinion of me, but believe me, I hope to change your mind." Pete slowly slid off his horse and waited for Mr. Johnson to speak.

"Come, let's walk to my barn, and you can tell me why you have come to see me."

"Thank you, Mr. Johnson. I've come back to Crooksville because Miss Montgomery sent for my help. Now she and the children are gone, but I'll find them. But, I am concerned the sheriff has placed her farm up for sale. He's also planning to keep the money for the sale for himself. Have you heard anything about this?"

He scratched his head. "Afraid so. There aren't many secrets in Crooksville."

"I was told that he's planning to sell Miss Montgomery farm animals--the cattle, pig, two mules and chickens. I cannot let her come home and find all the animals gone. The children will be devastated."

He shook his head. "Someone has got to stop that man, but I'm afraid I can't do much."

"Maybe you can. If I purchased all the animals, would you board them here? I will pay you monthly for your time and all the extra feed. I can't allow that man to sell her livestock."

"Do you know how long you'd want to board the animals with me? I have plenty of my own livestock to care for."

"I could hire a youngster to come out every afternoon to help you with them. Once I settle Miss Montgomery's legal problem, she'll be back home with the children."

"You know, Mr. Peterson, I have watched that young lady grow into a lovely woman and one her mama surely would be proud. She has taken those children to her bosom just like they were hers. Yes, I'll be happy to help you with the animals. The sheriff will not get his hands on her animals if I have them mix in with mine."

"He's not going to get the farm either. I will buy it and have the money placed in her bank account, and I'll bring in a lawyer to ensure Sheriff Jackson cannot steal her money, because I believe he has Judge Mathis in his pocket."

"You know, son, I have often wondered if that old man is really a judge. You might want to check into his past."

"Thanks, Mr. Johnson. I'll do that after I get the farm and animals out of the sheriff's greedy hands, then I'll have Toby get some help to herd the cattle and other animals over here. Do you need to have something built for the chickens?"

"Oh, no. I have a large chicken house and the pig can go back in with the others she came from."

"Toby will bring you anything you need for the animals. Would you like to get your own cattle and chicken feed or do you want Toby to haul it out to you tomorrow?" Pete asked as he watched his horse drink water.

"Toby can bring the feed in their livery wagon. He'll know how many bags I'll need for a few weeks."

Pete pulled his wallet from his vest pocket and handed Mr. Johnson several significant bills. "Will this be enough to board the animals for a few weeks? I'm sure I'll be back soon, and if not, I'll instruct the banker to pay you more money."

"Son, I hate to take this money, but times are hard, and this extra money will come in handy. I won't say anything to my wife about you purchasing the animals or the farm. If I leave her guessing, she can't spread any gossip." Mr. Johnson shook his head. "Sometimes I would love to give her a good shake, but I don't approve of abusing womenfolk."

"I understand, but if she doesn't know anything, she can't cause a problem." Both men smiled as Pete rode toward town. He was anxious to get back to town, purchase Lizzy's farm, and buy a ticket for the afternoon train.

Chapter 18

Pete rode into the livery stable where Mr. Peacock and his son, Toby were working. "Hello, young man," Mr. Peacock said as Pete tossed the reins to Toby.

"Howdy," Pete replied. "I just returned from Miss Montgomery's farm, and Toby has done a good job caring for her animals. Mr. Johnson will board all her animals at his place. I will pay him, of course. He will need feed and hay for the cattle, mules, and chickens. I want to pay you for whatever you think he will need for several weeks. I hope you won't mind delivering the feed to his farm. If he needs more supplies before I return, please allow him to have an account with you. I'll pay the bill when I return."

"Sure, I'll happily let him have whatever he needs for the animals. I trust you to return," Mr. Peacock grinned.

"Does that mean I won't have to spend the night at her farm anymore?"

Pete looked around the stable to make sure their conversation wasn't overheard. "Yes, Toby, I'm heading over to the clerk in the tax office to purchase Libby's farm. I don't want the sheriff to know anything about the sale until I am out of town, which will be this afternoon."

"Wait a minute, Mr. Peterson. Old Hardy, responsible for placing the For Sale on Lizzy's property, has left town. He packed up his family, and they went on a short trip. I asked him how long he'd be gone, but he only shrugged. I questioned him about the tax office but he only said people will have to see Mr. Grimes at the bank if they had any business."

"Did he get scared and leave town or was this trip already planned?" Pete wondered out loud.

"He wasn't talkative when he came in for his carriage. I questioned him about his sudden trip, but he told me to mind my business. That's when I knew something was wrong. In all the years I have known Hardy, he has never gone on a trip with his wife."

"I'm going to start over at the bank. I'm sure Mr. Grimes can help," Pete said. "I don't want the sheriff to know what I'm up to."

Pete strolled down the old gray boardwalk and pretended to be window shopping until he got to the bank. He entered the busy bank and asked the clerk at the first window if he could speak with Mr. Grimes.

"Yes, sir. The sheriff is with him now, but I believe he's about to complete his business with Mr. Grimes." The clerk looked over his shoulder toward Mr. Grime's office door where the sheriff was shouting at his boss.

Pete walked around the bank and pretended to read notices on a bulletin board that hung on the wall. In a few minutes, the sheriff stormed out of the banker's office madder than a wet hen. The sheriff slammed his Stetson on his messy hair, never glancing at the other customers.

"You can go in now, Mr. Peterson," the clerk said.

"You know me?" Pete quizzed the clerk.

"Well, I saw you in town with Miss Montgomery once."

Pete lifted his chin and smiled. "Everyone soon learns everyone's name in a small town."

Mr. Grimes stood in his doorway and offered his hand to Pete. "How can I help you today, Mr. Peterson?"

"I hope you can help me, sir. I'm here to make an offer on Miss Montgomery's farm. I understand that Mr. Hardy has left town, and I was instructed to come and see you."

"It seems there's a lot of interest in Miss Montgomery's place. The sheriff was in here, but he left angry. I hope I can help you," he said, frowning.

"Do you mind if I ask you a personal question?" Pete waited for the banker to respond.

"Ask away. If I can answer, I will."

"Is the sheriff interested in purchasing Lizzy's property?"

"No, but he seems to think he can collect the money once the property is sold. But that won't happen as long as I'm President of this bank. I have never given money to a person . . . oh well, I probably already said too much."

Mr. Grimes motioned toward a chair for Pete to have a seat while he sat down behind his oak desk. "Now, let's get down to your business."

"I want to buy Lizzy's farm to keep it out of Sheriff Jackson's greedy hands. I will keep it in my name until she returns home with the children."

"I can take your money and give you a Bill of Sale, but it won't be recorded until Mr. Hardy returns. If he doesn't return in a few weeks, the city council will post his job. In that way, the sale of the property will be legal, and I'll hold the proceeds of the sale in her account. I can assure you, the money will be Miss Montgomery's. I am shocked the sheriff would even think that he could collect her money. He said she would marry him, making him practically next of kin." The banker shook his head. "I told him that if they had married, I would give him the money, but she left him at the altar," he said, grinning.

"I can tell you that Lizzy would have never married the sheriff. She and the children were afraid of him, and the last time she saw him, she told him to never speak to her again."

"I can understand that. The sheriff can be hard to deal with, but he has met his match with me. He can't intimidate me. Now, Mr. Peterson, how do you plan to pay for the farm?"

"Cash money if that is suitable?"

"Cash is always good. Are you planning on making an offer or paying the posted price?" Mr. Grimes watched as

Pete counted out the purchase price.

"I'll pay the asking price. It's worth the amount. I'll not be buying her animals. Mr. Johnson will board them until she returns, but I want all her furnishes and personal items to remain in the house."

"You'll need to place new locks on her doors," Mr. Grimes suggested.

"Mr. Peacock and his son Toby said they'll keep an eye on the place, along with Mr. Johnson, while I'm searching for Lizzy and the children."

"Good luck in finding her. The sheriff said that he's forming a posse to search for her as well."

"Why does he need a bunch of men searching for her? Can't he look for her by himself?"

"I know he could, but I suggested he get a group of men to accompany him. I believe if Miss Montgomery is found, she'll be a lot safer with others presence. I don't trust Sheriff Jackson. If he's alone, he might do her harm."

His brow furrowed. "Yes, I see what you mean. The sheriff will regret the day he lays one hand on her." Pete hurried out the door and walked to the train depot. After purchasing his ticket, he returned to his hotel room and repacked his carpetbag. He still had an hour before the train departed, so he entered the hotel dining room.

Before being led to a table, Sheriff Jackson stepped into his path. "So, I hear you are going on a search for my fiancée," he said as he picked his teeth with a toothpick.

"I'm afraid you're mistaken. I'm going to look for Miss Montgomery."

"That's who I am speaking about. She will marry me just as soon as I find her."

Pete noticed that everyone in the dining room was watching and listening. He didn't care for an audience. "Good luck in finding her and your marriage.".

Pete stood in the doorway of the Pacific railroad train as it traveled toward Waco City, Texas. He was anxious for the train to stop at the watering station where he would begin his search for Lizzy. The train rocked, rattled, and exhausted large amount of steam from under the wheels. Pete watched as the conductor and several porters leaped from the train before he stepped down onto the wooden depot where many buckets were lined up to be filled.

He walked back to one of the cattle cars and shoved open the large door. The stink almost took his breath away. Tying a handkerchief over his nose and mouth, he climbed inside and lowered two heavy, wooden planks to the ground. His horse raised his head, excited to see his master. Pete untied the rope that had secured his horse to a rail and walked him over to the opening. He made sure the walkway to the ground was sturdy before he began to lead his horse off the train.

A porter raced to Pete's side and asked if he could help with the animal. "Thanks, but I got him. You can replace the boards back inside the car, if you really want to help."

"Happy to oblige, sir." The porter lifted the boards and shoveled them back inside the train. Meanwhile, Pete checked over his bay horse. Once Pete had secured his saddlebags, bedroll and rifle, he climbed on his prize animal. He quickly turned to the porter and tossed him a silver dollar as he slowly walked away from the tracks toward the open wilderness.

Chapter 19

Pete rode along the stretch of the barbed-wire fence when he noticed something black on the barbwire waving in the breeze. He leaped down and examined the bit of material and the ground surrounding the area. Almost in a trance, he examined the area beyond the fence. Next to the side of it, a well-worn path veered away and went deep into the forest. Pete felt a pounding in his chest. He was almost positive he had found Lizzy's trail.

Pete took a pair of work gloves and wire cutters from his saddlebag. He had learned from working on the range at home, a cowboy was always prepared. He opened the barbed-wire fence to let his horse cross on the opposite side. Pete attempted to repair the fence as best as he could, so other animals would not mosey onto the railroad tracks.

He decided to walk the path instead of riding. His horse followed but occasionally stopped to take a bite of tall grass. Pete laughed and rubbed his animal's nose. "I'm getting hungry too, old boy."

A few minutes later, Pete tied his mount to a tree and scanned the area for a clearing to make camp for the night. He had a coffee pot, coffee grinds, and the making for a sandwich or two. He had tied a bag of oats on his saddlebags for his horse. After filling the coffee pot with water from his canteen, he made a small fire and placed the pot over it. After feeding his horse, he settled back on a large rock to rest. He was so tired, he was asleep in minutes.

Early the next morning, a light dizzy of rain threatened to fall. The air felt cooler which was a nice change. Pete decided to check the area before he built a fire to cook breakfast. As he walked for a mile or so on the smooth path made by others, he didn't noticed any signs of Lizzy or the children. He climbed on his horse's back and headed deeper into the wilderness. He came upon a narrow, well-worn path made by many footsteps.

Pete jumped down from his horse and listened. He was sure he heard voices from a language he didn't recognize. Whoever it was must surely have moved further down the path. Pete moved cautiously and listened. Suddenly, he ducked deep into the bushes, and he could almost smell the man or men. His intuition told him that he was in great danger.

. At that precise moment, his ears detected muffled voices. It sounded like the men were angry as one of them raised his voice. Pete was sure he must be near the Indian reservation he had heard about in this part of the country. He prayed the Indians were peaceful. Every move he made must be calculated carefully or he could end up in their hands. Sitting on his knees until they were cramping, he knew he must stand. With cautious steps he began to penetrate the forest undergrowth toward a ridge of rocks.

Beech and chestnuts trees were so thick they towered over him making it hard to move. Large clumps of briers and clinging vines grabbed his legs and stuck into his clothes, some punctuating his skin.

Once Pete got closer to a creek bed, he noticed a small cave. He surveyed the area and lit a bundle of small dry tree limbs to view the inside of the cave. He wasn't surprised the cave had been used by others. After he went back outside of the cave, the sky opened up and the rain came pouring down. He grabbed his horse and pulled him inside the dark cave. Once he settled his horse, Pete build a large fire, spread his clean bedroll on the ground and rested. He was hungry, but he was also exhausted. He would rest and then prepare something to eat later. He tossed and turned, attempting to get comfortable on the hard ground because he'd hardly slept at all since he'd learned of Lizzy's disappearance.

As he drifted off into an uncomfortable sleep, he heard his horse whinny and moved around. As he sat up, someone hit him over the head and black spots flashed before his eyes as he slid into oblivion.

~

Several Indian braves stood over him while one untied his horse and leaped on his back, calming him down. The Indians tied Pete's hands and feet to a long stick and lifted the pole onto their shoulders. They strung him up like a roast pig over a barbecue pit. The Indians marched like soldiers with Pete's head dangling backward to the Indian village with their big prize.

The sunrise cast a shadow over the campsite as the braves carried their prey into the front of Yuma's teepee. Many of the Indian women laughed and poked sticks at the white man's body.

Yuma came out of his teepee and peered at the white man as he slept like a babe. He looked at the brave still perched on the big Bay horse.

"Where did you find this man and this animal you've seemed to be laying claim to?" Yuma asked a tall brave.

"The animal belongs to that man, but I can only control him if I'm on his back. He's a wild horse."

Pearl came out of the Old Woman's teepee to relieve herself in the bushes when she passed another teepee. Why were so many people milling around so early? She noticed a man tied on a large pole strung between two trees. His head was dangling backward. She wanted a closer look so she peeked around a big, heavy-set woman. Pearl couldn't believe what she saw. She screamed as she raced over to the man, "Pete, oh Pete, what have they done to you?" She rushed to Pete's head, lifted it and held him close to her little chest. Blood dripped from his scalp onto her body.

A young brave rushed to Pearl to get her away from their prisoner. Pearl turned and kicked the brave in the shin. He hopped on his hurt leg as Pearl began screaming, "Mama Lizzy, Mama Lizzy!"

~

Once the child screamed the name, Pete, Yuma realized who this man on the pole was. "Untie him and get Old Woman to examine to his head wound." He lifted a screaming, wild child away from the hurt man strung up on the pole.

"Shush, child. We will care for your Mama's friend." Yuma held Pearl in his arms. Once she was sure the Indian braves wouldn't harm Pete, she calmed down and pressed her head on Yuma's shoulder.

The Indian braves cut Pete down and carried him into Yuma's teepee and dropped him on a pile of deerskins blankets. Pete moaned but continued to sleep. Yuma hoped that his braves hadn't done too much damage to this young man, whom he remembered the woman said was her friend.

Lizzy heard Pearl screaming. It took her a moment to realize that she wasn't dreaming. She noticed that Pearl wasn't in the teepee so she bolted up, slipped on her moccasins and went outside, where many Indian women and men formed a circle around the fire. She noticed the sun rising over the treetops and wondered what had caused so many villagers to be up so early.

"Mama Lizzy, Pete's here. They tied him up like a pig to be cooked, but they took him in there." She pointed to Yuma's teepee.

Pearl practically leaped out of Yuma's arms as she screamed at Lizzy about Pete. Lizzy walked to Yuma and took Pearl from him. "Tell me what's going on, please," she asked the chief's son.

"Your friend has come as I said he would. I'm afraid my braves found him and hit him over the head while he slept. He has yet to come to. I have Old Woman looking after him in my teepee. You can go in to see him once she comes out."

Pearls' face was full of anger. "Mama Lizzy, they tied him to a pole like he was a witch. Remember what I said the women wanted to do to you. They were going to burn him up!" Pearl crossed her arms, being so dramatic.

Yuma glared at Lizzy. "Where does she get such wild ideals?" he asked.

"It's a long story, but she tends to confuse things. Please don't ask me to explain this wild tale." Lizzy said as she tried to peer in the doorway of Yuma's teepee.

The Old Woman soaked Pete's hair with warm water to see to the bloody wound. The gash on his head wasn't deep. The Old Woman wasn't concerned about the bloody area because she had learned that head wounds bled easily. However, she'd hoped he would wake while she doctored him, but he remained unconscious. She didn't want to leave this man alone because she worried he might not wake.

Old Woman walked to the teepee flap and motioned for white woman and Morning Flower to enter. "This man not opened his eyes," she said to the young maiden. "Tell White Lady to try to talk to him."

Lizzy bent down on her knees next to Pete's pallet. She looked at Morning Flower and Old Woman. She felt uncomfortable speaking to him in front of others, but if talking to Pete would help him wake, she would try.

"Pete, this is Lizzy. Please try to open your eyes and let me know you'll be all right." She lifted his right hand and placed it next to her cheek, then she kissed the palm of his hand.

Lizzy continued to speak softly to Pete as she pushed wet hair off his forehead. In a quiet moment, his eyes slowly opened.

Pete seemed to be in a trance as he raised his blue eyes to Lizzy. They were dark with worry. His gaze had a strange mixture of familiarity that had always drawn Lizzy to him. As their eyes met, a sense of harmony existed between them.

They were able to communicate in a manner that was more profound than spoken words. Not even the few weeks of absence had changed the intense feelings that existed between them.

Lizzy was still shocked by his presence in the village, but she didn't want to show how thrilled she was. The couple looked at each other. Pete seemed to be waiting for Lizzy to make the first move.

After a good moment of silence, he let out a faint sigh and reached for her hand. Apparently, he didn't care what the women surrounding them thought. "Oh my Lizzy, I'm thankful you're safe."

He said *my Lizzy*. His startling words surprised her momentarily, but then she realized what he meant. She wanted to jump into his arms, but four eyes watched them. Ropes were tied around Pete's wrists. He wouldn't be able to hold her. Lizzy went to the door of the teepee and called Yuma to come inside. "Yuma, please untie Pete's wrists and ankles."

"Of course, I thought the young braves had already done that," he said. "I'll tell the women to bring your breakfast, and something for him. The boys and Pearl can eat with the other children."

Lizzy shook her head. "My boys are going to want to see Pete. They are very fond of him and I'm sure they're worried."

"I'll go get them now. Then, they can eat with you before they go fishing. and prepare to go fishing. Some of the older braves are taking the younger children to the river. They'll catch our evening meal." With a frown at Pete, he left the teepee.

"Lizzy, who's that Indian?" Pete said as he watched the tall, man leave.

"His name is Yuma. He's the chief's son. Fortunately, he found the children and me in the woods the morning after a bad rainstorm. He brought us to his village and Old Woman saved my life. I had a high fever and a terrible cough.

Yuma and the village people have been good to us. I told him about you and Sheriff Jackson. He told me his braves wouldn't allow anyone to take us away from here if I didn't want to go with them. I do feel safe here."

"I'm glad you found a safe haven for yourself and the children but I also know the son of the chief has deep feelings for you. Of course, I can't blame him because I lost my heart to you soon after meeting you."

"Oh, Pete, I feel the same toward you, too." Lizzy immediately sat down beside him and took his hand in hers. She rubbed his wrists where he had rope burns from being tied to the pole.

"Pete, Yuma's a nice man. You're wrong about him having feelings for me. He's just the one who rescued me and the children, and he has been kind in every way. He has made sure the children are well-cared for, too.

"Lizzy, a man knows when another man cares for his woman. You are my woman, I hope, and I believe Yuma would love to see me ride off into the sunset alone." He smiled and pulled her closer.

"Let's not speak any more about him. Do you hurt anywhere besides your head? Did they hurt your side where you'd been shot?"

"No, only my head, but it isn't pounding like it was before. I hope we'll be able to travel tomorrow."

She frowned. "But Pete, I can't take the children back to my farm. Sheriff Jackson will come for them and try to take them from me again."

"Not if we get married once we arrive in Crooksville. He smiled weakly up at her. "Will you marry me, Elizabeth Marie Montgomery?"

She posted her hands on her hips. "I'm surprised you remember my name."

"I remember everything about you; your beautiful face, your kind heart, and you have so much love to give."

She bent over him to give him a gentle hug. "Oh, darling, there's so many special things about you. You're kind, loving, and too generous with your money. You left me way too much money for what I did for you. As you told me to spend it wisely, I paid the back taxes on the farm and caught up all my other bills in town."

"Pete, Pete!" the boys, along with Pearl, came shouting inside the teepee. Lizzy had to stop them from leaping on Pete's stomach as he lay on the pallet.

Down on their knees in front of Pete, they hugged him as he hugged them back. Pete rubbed their hair and told them how pleased he was to see them. "We're happy to see you, too. We didn't think we'd ever see you or Lizzy again when we left the church," Jake said, as he tried to fight back tears.

~

Yuma stood watching the scene between the stranger and Lizzy's children. An angry streak went through his body. He didn't want to witness the children sharing the same feelings for this man as the white woman did.

"Come boys, the young braves are waiting for you to eat your breakfast and go fishing. So hurry along now. Pearl, you go with the braves today and they'll teach you and a few of the other girls how to fish, too."

Once the children were gone, Yuma sat down in front of Pete and Lizzy. "I have sent the children away today, because my braves spied some white men traveling close to the reservation. It may be that lawman who is looking for you, Miss Lizzy. If they come near, we will hide you both. I will not let him take you away." Yuma stood, and without any further instructions, left the teepee.

Pete attempted to sit up but he still felt dizzy. "Lizzy, I want to hold you if only for a moment, but I smell worse than a grizzly bear. I need a bath. Maybe I can go to the creek and get clean."

"I don't care how you smell. I want you to hold me." Lizzy slipped down onto the pallet and placed her arms around his shoulders. "Now, is that better?"

"Yes, so much better." Being so close together, they opened their hearts which added so much to what they were feeling. They held each other in comfortable tenderness for minutes. Lizzy waited for her cowboy to confess his love for her, but the words never came. They continued to sit content, and secure in their newfound relationship until Old Woman appeared in the doorway of the teepee along with Morning Flower

"Old Woman said that she came with Morning Flower to check on her patient.

"Do you think that I could go to the creek and take a dip? I smell to high-heavens." Pete asked Morning Flower so she will translate his request.

"Let me get two braves to help you walk. You must not get your head wet." Morning Flower repeated the Old Woman's instructions. In a few minutes, Pete and two big braves walked to the creek. After Pete was clean and prepared to leave, the braves saw strangers riding toward the village.

The sound of horse hooves in the distant made Yuma enter the large teepee. "Where is your man, Pete?" Lizzy had heard the horses too. She leaped off the pallet and rushed to Yuma. "Two braves helped him walk to the creek to bathe. Is it Sheriff Jackson and his men?" Lizzy asked.

"Afraid so. Stay very quiet," he said as he stared out into the darkness. Morning Flower appeared with a cardboard sign that read, "Stay out, Measles" written in Sioux. Yuma tacked the sign over the flap of the teepee door.

The braves pushed Pete over to a large tree. One of the men motioned for him to climb the tree and stay quiet. Another brave gave Pete a hand-up and lifted him to the first branch. He motioned for Pete to climb higher.

Chapter 20

Yuma and his father, Chief Viho, stood at the edge of the village. Many armed brave, with bows and arrows, formed lines behind them. Several braves rode beside and behind Sheriff Jackson and his posse, chanting challenging phrases.

As he stood his ground, Yuma signaled his braves to take their leave from around the men. Sheriff Jackson stopped at the edge of the Indian's village. One of his posse eased his horse close to the sheriff and said in a low, nervous voice. "I don't like this. There are many Indians ready to kill us if we make a wrong move, so watch what comes out of your big mouth."

"Shut your trap. I know how to handle these heathens," he replied.

~

"Why are you here?" Yuma asked the Sheriff in perfect English. Yuma noticed how pale the big man turned once he realized he understood what he had called the Indians.

"We, my men and I, are searching for a white woman. She was on the train that passed a few miles from here. Once the train stopped, she got off and wasn't seen getting back on."

"So, you think us *heathens* might have captured her?"

Sheriff Jackson blushed. "Maybe not captured, but possibly given her shelter. She's wanted by the law, and if you have her hidden, you're harboring a criminal. I can have my men destroy this place in a blink of an eye," Sheriff Jackson said.

Some of his braves moved forward. Morning Flower was quietly repeating the English words for the Sioux braves.

Yuma didn't react. "I wouldn't try something like that if you want to take another breath. My men are ready for war. If you don't believe me, just look around."

The Sheriff rose from his saddle and glanced around at his surroundings. There had to be at least a hundred or more Indians circling him. Some of the braves were hanging out of trees with their bows loaded with arrows pointing down at his men.

"We aren't here to cause a war. I only want the white woman called Lizzy Montgomery. If she's here, you must turn her over to me. She's wanted by the law, but she promised to be my wife. I am deeply hurt that she left town without informing me."

"You lie," he said, stepping closer to the sheriff. "Why would you want a woman that is wanted by the law?"

"I'm not lying. Lizzy ran away when the judge said she couldn't care for her siblings, but I love her and want to marry her."

Yuma stared at the fat man who was sweating like a pig. "What about her siblings, as you called them?" Before the sheriff could answer, Yuma said, "Who is caring for this woman's siblings now if she can't?"

"Oh, the children have been placed in a nice Waco home. She doesn't have to be concerned about them any longer." The sheriff smirked at the Indian. "I want to search your village. I believe the woman is here." Sheriff Jackson got off his horse, but the other men remained in their saddles. They wanted to leave with their scalps and hoped the big-mouth sheriff didn't make the Indians mad.

"Come, I'll walk with you while you search the teepees." Yuma signaled his braves to back away and allow the man to follow him closely.

As they neared each teepee, Yuma called out, and the women came out of their teepee and stood quietly by the flap.

The Sheriff peeked inside each teepee until he went to a larger one with a cardboard sign nailed to the door.

"What does that sign say?" The sheriff could speak a few words of the Sioux but had yet to read any.

Yuma frowned. "Measles."

"I've had measles when I was a young boy. Move out of my way so I can search this teepee." The Sheriff started to enter the teepee, but Yuma stepped before him."

"Enter if you wish, but your white doctor who came earlier said they may have smallpox. My people are very sick."

The sheriff stopped in his tracks. "Smallpox is a deadly disease. It could wipe out this whole village."

Yuma looked into the distance and replied sadly, "We've lost two people already, but enter the teepee if you dare."

The sheriff backed away from the front entrance. "We'll go now but if I find out you are hiding the white woman from me, I'll come down hard on you and your braves."

Yuma and the braves watched as the angry man got on his horse and signaled for his men to follow. He turned to see his father standing beside his teepee.

"I am proud of you, my son. You didn't show any fear of the white lawman." The old chief sat down in front of his teepee with some of the other older tribesmen. Yuma watched his father pass a large pipe to the older men. Each man took a puff, passed it to another, and smiled. The older men liked to pull the wool over any white man's eyes who came to their village. It was their revenge for being stripped of their land and placed on a reservation.

Yuma and his braves watched as the sheriff and his men left the reservation. All the braves and Pete relaxed and walked back to their teepees with a sigh of relief that there wasn't any gunplay. Yuma went into the teepee and told Lizzy that the men had left and he hoped they wouldn't come back with the threat of smallpox in the village.

~

Lizzy was so frightened she felt her stomach churning. She raced outside and went deep into the bushes to relieve her upset belly. After heaving her guts out, she sat on a log to pull herself together.

Suddenly, the world went dark when a cloth bag pulled down over her head. She struggled to lift the bag off, but whoever had done this to her tied a rope around her neck to hold it in place. She screamed, but the hot air from her breath only made breathing more difficult.

A large person grabbed Lizzy and threw her body across his shoulders. The bumping up and down on the big man's shoulders made her even more nauseous, but finally he stopped and tossed her body across a horse. She felt one of her soft shoes slip off, and a saddle horn poked her stomach as she tried to move her body further back onto the saddle. The horse swayed sideways when her captor leaped upon the horse. His hand pressed her down onto the neck of the animal as he trotted off.

Listening to the heavy breathing of the man who had kidnapped her, Lizzy was sure it was Sheriff Jackson. He would be the only person who would do something like this. Yuma had said the sheriff and his posse had left the reservation, but the sheriff must have turned around and hid in the woods.

Lizzy attempted to slip off the animal, but the big man held her tight. He hit her hard on the back of the neck, and everything went totally black.

~

The sheriff gave Lizzy a little shake, but she didn't even flinch an eyelid. *Oh well*, he thought, *she'll be easier to handle unconscious.* Marvin couldn't keep a smile off his face as he rode toward town. He outsmarted the chief's son and the whole Indian tribe. He had sent his posse back to town while he slipped behind the village teepees watching and waiting for Lizzy to appear.

The sheriff had a gut feeling the Indian's chief son was lying. He could almost feel Lizzy's presence in the village. He would take her back to his place and make her marry him. He wanted her farm, and he was going to have it. The Pacific Train representative had told him that Lizzy's farmhouse and land would be theirs by eminent domain. They had to have it. The survey showed her farm directly in the path of the new railroad lines.

After hours of traveling to his little house, he was sweating like a hog. As he lifted his prize off the horse, her head fell backward. He quickly untightened the rope that held the bag over her head. Her face was red, and her lovely curls were soaking wet. Marvin used his hand to fan her awake, but that didn't work. Judging from the red bruise on the back of her neck, he figured she'd have a walloping headache for a few days. He hadn't intended to harm her, but what was done was done.

He carried her into his house and laid her on the dirty bed. Exhausted, he plopped down in a chair and stared at Lizzy as if he hadn't seen a woman before. Sadly, it had been a long time since he'd entertained a decent woman in his little home.

Sheriff Jackson moved to the bed and patted her cheek to coax her to awake, but she slept on. He prayed he had not killed her. No, he hadn't hit her hard enough to kill her. *She was breathing evenly,* he thought.

"Come on, Lizzy, girl. Open your eyes." He patted her face a little more forceful, but she made no response. Marvin removed her shoes. Maybe that would wake her up. Once he lifted the hem of her deerskin dress, he noticed she was wearing only one moccasin. The one missing would be a clue to anyone tracking her. *Too bad. Everyone would know soon enough.*

Sheriff Jackson looked down at Lizzy and gritted his teeth. He did wish he hadn't struck her so hard. Maybe he should loosen her clothes. He knew she wasn't wearing the typical ladies' undergarments as he handled her. The deerskin shift was soft against her slim, lifeless body.

~

Lizzy opened her eyes in vengeance. Anger catapulted her into a sitting position before she leaped off the bed to face her surprised captor.

Sheriff Jackson opened his mouth to say something as he jumped back from the angry woman.

"If you touch me again, I'll claw your eyes out!" Lizzy screamed with her hands curled out in front of her.

The sheriff laughed. "I believe you said that to me before." Grinning, he stepped toward Lizzy.

"Stay away from me," Lizzy said as she glanced around the room where he had taken her. "Where is this place?"

"I have brought you to your future home. Once we're married and you sell your farm to the railroad, you and the children will live here with me. I know it isn't huge, but we'll add extra rooms as needed." A grin spread across his face, "If the children want to live here."

They will not live here, and neither will I. When are you going to understand that I'll never marry you?" Lizzy grabbed the back of her neck and rubbed it. The pain was excruciating. When she glanced up, the insufferable man had moved close.

Lizzy darted to the right to evade his arms, but Sheriff Jackson grabbed her around the waist and forced her to face him.

"Never say never, sweetheart. You'll marry me if you want to ever see your siblings again. The Headmaster of the orphanage is a friend of mine and will do whatever I instruct him to do."

Lizzy suddenly realized the sheriff had not seen the children at the village, so he thought they were still in the home. *Good, let him think they're still there, and they'll remain safe out of his reach.* Pete, Yuma, or Morning Flower would take good care of them.

Chapter 21

Yuma turned to Morning Flower as the sheriff and his men left the village. "You and the women did well." Just then, Lizzy turned and raced into the woods.

Morning Flower said, "She'll be fine soon. Nerves has given her an upset stomach."

After a few minutes, Pete walked to the edge of the woods and called to Lizzy. When she didn't answer, Yuma joined him. "I can wait for her if you want to see to your braves." Pete started walking toward the woods, but Yuma stayed right beside him.

"I want to make sure she's all right," Yuma said, giving Pete a no-nonsense look.

"Lizzy," Pete called. When she didn't answer, both men hurried in the direction they believed she went. "Lizzy!" Pete called her name again. Still no answer.

Then they saw it. A little distance from a fallen log lay a moccasin. Yuma searched the earth and saw a horse track. "Someone has taken her away."

"It couldn't have been anyone but that crazy Sheriff Jackson. He must have slipped back and waited for Lizzy to come outside alone. There's no one else who would have kidnapped her. I need to leave for Crooksville now," Pete declared.

"I'm going with you," Yuma stood his ground and announced. "I care deeply for her and want to ensure she's safe. Her brothers and sister can stay here where they'll be well-looked after. Once we know she's safe, I'll come back for the children and bring them to her."

"You don't need to come with me. Lizzy will marry me as soon as I can arrange it after I find her. She'll be safe as my wife." Pete pushed Yuma out of his way.

"Or she could marry me. I greatly regard the white woman and she'll be good for me and my people. I think she likes me, too."

"I know she loves me," Pete said as he hurried into the large teepee to talk to the children.

"Has she ever said those words?" Yuma asked.

"What words?"

"That she loves you?"

"Well, in not so many words, but she said she cares for me like I care for her. That's the same as love," Pete declared, as he entered the teepee. The children's eyes darted from one man to the other.

"No, it's not. We'll see who Lizzy loves and wants to spend her life with after we have her safe," Yuma said. "I need to find Morning Flower to tell her our plans." He disappeared out the tent.

"Pete, what happened to Lizzy?" Jake stood on his pallet while Joshua knelt, waiting for Pete to answer.

Pete kneeled down in front of the little boys. "Sheriff Jackson came to the village and took Lizzy by force back to Crooksville. Yuma and I are leaving in a few minutes to go and rescue her. I know the sheriff will not harm her, but he has no right to take her away from here."

"We know that he wants to marry her . . . but she said she'd die first," Joshua said. "She's scared of him."

"I was going to take us back to Crooksville today, but now, I want you to stay here with Morning Flower. Please help take care of Pearl." Pete smiled and hugged each boy. "We'll all be together soon."

~

Both men chose two good horses and packed their saddlebags with grub to camp overnight on the trip to

Crooksville. Pete felt uncomfortable in the presence of Yuma, but they both had one common goal-- to get Lizzy away from the sheriff.

Once the two men arrived in Crooksville, Pete suggested that they go directly to Lizzy's farm, which belonged to him. The front door and all the windows were boarded up. It looked as if something was going on at the farm. He wondered if the railroad representative had made a deal with someone, not realizing Pete owned the farm. He was surprised that Mr. Hardy had not informed whoever that he had purchased Lizzy's farm a couple weeks ago.

Pete pointed to the door. "Tear those boards off the door while I rip the ones off the front windows. Let's get fresh air in the house." Pete never dreamed he would find his house all boarded up. What was going on with Lizzy's house?

After building a fire in the stone fireplace, he went to the kitchen stove and made a fresh pot of coffee. Yuma walked from one room to the other. "Nice little house," he said.

"At least whoever boarded the place didn't take any of Lizzy's furniture and personal items. She would have been heartbroken if they had taken her mama's things."

"Where do you think the sheriff has taken Lizzy?" Yuma asked.

"He has a small house in town, right off Main Street. I think we should sneak into town before sunrise in the morning. He'll never expect us to storm his home so early. After we rescue her, I'll send a telegram to my father. He's a retired judge, but can still serve over cases if called upon. I want him to give Lizzy another opportunity to clear her name so she can raise her siblings. Judge Mathis took the children away from her. He only listened to the sheriff's testimony and wouldn't allow other witnesses to speak for her. The sheriff has him in his pocket, but that will end soon after my father arrives.

"Lizzy is a brave woman. That's what I want in a wife. She will be good for my people," Yuma said, spreading his bedroll in front of the fireplace. Pete listened to that comment but made no reply. Lizzy belonged to him, not to the Indian.

"There're two beds in that room and a bed in the other bedroom. You don't have to sleep on the hard floor," Pete said as he watched Yuma prepare for sleep.

A loud noise came from the front porch. Someone or something was stomping around outside. Pete grabbed his pistol and opened the front door. Laying curled up by the swing was an old man who smelled like an outhouse. Pete noticed the old man's body shook as he tried to get comfortable. He took his foot and nudged the old man.

"Leave me be. Go pick on someone else. This is my place," the old man responded.

Pete bent down and made the old drunk sit up. "Hey, fellow, who are you?"

"Where's Marie? Tell her to come and take care of me."

"Who's Marie?" Pete wondered as he asked the old drunk.

"My . . .w. . .wife," he stutters. "Where's my Lizzy? She'll take care of me."

Pete realized that this old drunk was Lizzy's father, who had left the family years ago. Even being in a drunken state, he could find his way home. Pete couldn't imagine how Lizzy would feel once she learned that her pa had returned after all these years.

"Yuma," Pete called. "Give me a hand with this old man. This is Lizzy's pa, who deserted his family years ago. He's drunk and smells awful. We can put him in the boys' room for tonight."

"Man stinks. He needs a good dunking before Lizzy sees him," Yuma said.

"Yep. I guess we should clean the old guy," Pete said. "I'll heat some water. Bring in the tub off the back porch. We'll give him a good dunking and put some clean clothes on him. Then we'll add his rags to the fire."

After the tub was full of hot water, Yuma picked up the

old man, sat him naked in the warm water and poured buckets of water over his head. He spit, sputtered and flailed his arms. "You trying to drown me?"

Pete entered Lizzy's bedroom and opened the big chest in the corner of the room. He dug to the bottom and found some of the old man's clothes. He found a red union suit, overalls, and a plaid shirt. There were several pairs of thick socks. Pete bundled everything in his arms and closed the lid. He went to the boys' room and found Yuma drying off the man. "I found some of his clothes in Lizzy's room. She saved his things. Lord, that's one skinny old man." Pete said, looking the man's body over as Yuma helped him dress.

"Good gracious, look at all the dark bruises and whip marks all over his poor body. He has been mistreated by someone," Yuma said.

"I need a drink," the man demanded. Through blurry eyes, he frowned at the two strangers.

"You need food and sleep, but for now, sleep is what you're getting." Yuma practically carried the old man to the nice clean bed. He pulled back a quilt and pointed to the bed. "Get in and sleep off that liquor. Lizzy will be home in the morning, and she needs to see her pa sober," Yuma said.

The old man fell into the bed. His head hit the pillow, and in just a minute, he was snoring.

Pete stood looking down upon the man. "Wonder where he has been for the last few years? Lizzy told me he left them high and dry right after Pearl was born. Her mama died a year later. She's surely going to be surprised. I hope she'll be pleased to see him. Let's leave for the sheriff's house before dawn."~

The two men saddled their horses, Yuma's stallion and Pete's bay. They had chosen the two fastest horses on the reservation. Both men hoped they could get to Sheriff Jackson's house on Main Street without being seen. They rode hard into the morning darkness, praying their rescue of Lizzy would go well, and not have to hurt anyone.

Sheriff Jackson couldn't sleep. Something didn't feel

right. He pulled on his pants and peeked in on Lizzy, who was sleeping. He walked onto the porch and looked up and down the street. Everything seemed quiet, so he returned inside and crawled back into his bed. He was exhausted. It wasn't but a few minutes before he was snoring and fell into a deep sleep.

~

Pete and Yuma tied their horses a short distance behind the Sheriff's small shack. They crept to the back wall and peeked in a window. Lizzy was lying on a bed asleep. Yuma went to the next window and listened. He could hear the Sheriff snoring. He hurried back to Pete and watched as he raised the window. Yuma cupped his hand so Pete could be lifted inside the house.

Once he reached Lizzy, he placed his hand over her mouth, causing her to sit straight up. Pete put his finger over his mouth, motioning her to remain silent. She immediately grabbed the back of her neck and mouthed "*all right.*" Pete picked her up off the bed and carried her to the window. He helped her sit on the windowsill, waiting for Yuma to lift her down. After she was settled in Yuma's arms, Pete climbed through the window to the ground.

After slipping on his boots, Pete caught up with the other two as they raced across the small yard to their horses. The two men climbed on their mounts with Lizzy settled in front of Pete, which brought a frown from Yuma. He wanted to carry her but this wasn't the time to make a scene. Lizzy's safety was the most important thing now.

After another tense thirty minutes of concentrating on keeping Lizzy safe in front of him, they finally arrived at the farmhouse. Pete silently thanked the good Lord, they had made it back, safe and sound. He whispered in her ear, "You're home and safe now. I'll never let that man harm you again even if it means I have to hurt him."

Lizzy leaned back trembling against Pete's chest. Pete led his horse to the front porch allowing Yuma to lift her down. The brave held Lizzy in his arms and waited for Pete to get down from his horse to open the front door. After Yuma positioned her on the floor, her legs were wobbly, but Pete grabbed her around the waist and guided her to a rocking chair. Yuma sighed as he watched Pete's hands circled Lizzy, so he immediately built a fire to warm the room.

"I'll take care of the horses this time, but next time you'll do it. Don't touch her while I'm in the barn," Yuma said.

Pete grinned and watched as the big Indian went out the door. Snoring came from the boy's bedroom. Lizzy attempted to get up, but Pete touched her shoulder to keep her still.

"Lizzy, be prepared for a surprise," Pete said as he stood before her.

"A surprise? Who's in that room?" Lizzy sat on the edge of the rocker.

I"It's your pa, Herman Montgomery? He showed up early tonight. Your pa was in pretty bad shape, but he's sleeping now. He asked for 'Marie.' Is that your mother's name?"

Lizzy nodded as she sat frozen in the rocker.

Pete told her about her pa rolling around on the front porch, and that they hadn't questioned him. She would have to do that in the morning.

"Come on now, Lizzy. You've had a hard night. Why don't you rest for a while, and later, you can be reunited with your pa." Pete took her hand and led her to her bedroom, giving her a reassuring smile as he closed the door.

Lizzy moved slowly toward the bed and sat down. She lowered her head into her hands as many questions came to her. The back of her neck ached, giving her a bad headache, but she couldn't stop thinking about her Pa. He'd returned after nearly five years. Would the twins remember him? Pearl was less than a year old, so of course, she wouldn't have any remembrance of him. She wanted to hear why he just up and left her, Mama, and the children. Mama had been sick and she needed him. In the morning, she'd demand answers. He better have a good excuse if he thinks she'll allow him to stay here. She was the head of her household now.

Chapter 22

Yuma was up and walking barefoot in Lizzy's front room. He went into the kitchen and picked up the coffee pot. It had been a long time since he had to make coffee over a campfire, much less over a stove. He lifted the lid off the pot and tried to remember what went into it to make coffee.

Lizzy's voice made Yuma spin toward the doorway where she stood as he held the pot in one hand and the lid in the other.

"Good morning, Yuma. Are you going to make coffee this morning?"

"Well, I have made it before, but it has been a long time. Since my scout days," he said, grinning. "I can't remember how much water and coffee I'm supposed to put in. Our old cook placed eggshells in the bottom but . . ." He looked so pitifully at Lizzy.

"I'm happy you weren't able to make it. Old eggshells? Mercy, I can't imagine what the coffee would taste like," she said, laughing. "Here, give me the pot. I'll make it." Looking in the cupboard, she sighed, "I was going to cook breakfast, but the cupboard's bare. I'll need to go into town and get some supplies before I bring the children home."

"Pete has already gone to town. He's planning on picking up supplies and will send a telegram for his father to come here." Yuma walked over to his pallet and slipped on his moccasins. "I better go check on the horses."

~

Lizzy hurried back into her bedroom and tidied her hair. She looked in the closet and was pleased to find her day dresses were still there. Selecting one, she removed the Indian shift Morning Flower had loaned her to wear. Feeling like her old self, she walked back into the front room and discovered her Pa standing in the doorway of the boys' room.

Both of them stood staring at each other. Lizzy felt tears welting behind her eyelids. As much as she wanted to hate this man standing before her--wrinkled, old, pitiful-looking, she couldn't. Taking several giant steps, she was standing directly in front of him. "Oh, Pa," she cried. "I can't believe you're home." She threw her arms around his shoulders and sobbed.

When he trembled, she pushed back and looked him in the eyes. He was so sad. Standing before her wasn't the giant of a man she remembered. He was much shorter, and his overalls practically hung loose on his thin frame. It had been five years since she had seen him, and how he'd aged.

"Come, Pa and sit with me in front of the fire. Yuma is outside carrying for the horses, but I made coffee. We have a lot to talk about."

"Lizzy, I don't see my little ones. Where are they?" Pa asked, glancing around the room.

"That's one of the things we need to discuss, but Pa, believe me, they're fine. You'll be so surprised how big the twins are and little Pearl is a smart, beautiful little girl. I am so proud of them."

"Oh, I'm so pleased to learn this. I hope the children will be happy to see me."

Tears sprang in Lizzy's eyes again. Her Pa reached over and slid a single fingertip down her cheek. "My daughter, you have the softest heart of anyone I've ever met. I had no idea how you were going to accept me after I so many years have passed."

"I'm sure you'll tell me where you have been." Lizzy used the hem of her dress and wiped her eyes. She gave her pa a sweet smile. "Pa, you have to know the children won't remember you. I'm sorry to say I haven't spoken about you to them, and they haven't asked. They don't remember Mama either. Remember, they were very young when you left us."

"I remember now. You'll never know how sorry I have been I couldn't get back home before now. I tried to get away but was always caught." He looked down at his bare feet.

Lizzy didn't know what to think. It sounded like her pa might have been in prison, but she wanted to wait for him to tell her in his own way.

"Here's a hot cup of coffee. Pete Peterson will return soon with some food, and I'll cook a nice breakfast."

"Who are these two men? Is one of them your husband?" Pa asked.

"No. I'm not married."

"But, daughter, you're so lovely and certainly of marriage age. I can't imagine why you haven't been snapped up by some young man. You looked so much like your Mama. She was as pretty as a princess. Her hair was soft and light as a star's twinkle. Your mother turned a blind eye to my hidden liquor still because it did help put food on the table. She never scolded me for drinking too much of my own liquor. No man could have had a better woman as a wife." The old man wiped his eyes.

Oh, Pa. Mama loved you so much. She grieved herself sick after you left. She never believed you just ran off, but we didn't have any other reason why you left us." Lizzy sipped her hot coffee.

"Pa, I have had marriage offers, but I will only marry for love. I don't need a man to take care of me. Over the years, I've learned to stand on my own two feet and care for my siblings."

"Of course. I wouldn't want you to marry a man just for security or to avoid becoming an old maid," he muttered as he jiggled his coffee cup.

She chuckled. "I guess people say *I'm on the shelf* at twenty, but I don't care how much they gossip about me. I can guess what they're saying with Sheriff Jackson chasing after me."

"What'd you mean? Is that old man still around. And did you say he's the law?"

"Yes. He's the sheriff of Crooksville." Lizzy's head snapped up and she said, "Now, I remember. He came here. I was only sixteen when he asked if he could court me. This was before he was the sheriff. He had just arrived in town and met me on the boardwalk." Lizzy smiled at her Pa. "He came out here, but you took the shotgun off the mantel and chased him away. You told him he was old enough to be my pa and he'd better not set foot on our farm again."

The grizzle man set his cup on the side table and held his hands before him. "I'm afraid that was my downfall. A few days after I chased him off the place, two rough men came riding out to the pasture where I was working. They got down off their horses, pointed their pistols at me and said I was going with them. I fought them off, but one of them hit me over my head and when I woke up, I was at the border of Mexico. Money exchanged hands for me and I was carried to a Mexican farm where my legs were chained to the other men. I became a field hand and a prisoner for years. I tried to escape once, but got beaten up so badly for the effort, I prayed to die." Pa wiped the sweat off his forehead and sighed. "During the years, I heard Marvin Jackson's name mentioned several times."

"Oh, I'm so sorry. We thought you had just gotten tired of Mama being sick and all the babies. Mama cried and said she knew something bad had happened to you, but we had no idea where to look."

"Can't believe that man is still around. I better stay out of his sight. There's no telling what he might do to me if he discovers I escaped and made it home."

"So, you are telling me Sheriff Jackson was in a kidnapping scheme to sell American men to the Mexicans?" Lizzy stood as she heard Pete driving the wagon to the front porch.

"Later, I want you to tell Pete and Yuma all about the

sheriff. These are good men who have helped me. I will introduce you to them when they get settled inside."

"I met them last night. They tried to drown me," he said as he opened the front door for Pete to come inside with a large bag of white flour over his shoulder.

Lizzy wasn't sure what her Pa meant, but she walked out on the front porch to gather a few small bags from Yuma.

After Pete and Yuma left all the supplies in the kitchen, Pete approached her father and asked how he was feeling after a good night's rest. "Fine." He replied. "You can call me Herman." Staring at Pete, he said, "I'm starving. Lizzy is going to cook a big breakfast since you brought some supplies."

"I hope you told Lizzy where you've been for years. She must have forgiven you since you're still here."

"Yes, I have a wonderful, forgiving daughter. I hope to make it up to her and the children once I regain my strength," Herman said.

"We'll have a discussion after breakfast," Pete said,

"What's my daughter to you?" Pa asked, wondering about Pete's attitude toward Lizzy.

"I'm the man that will marry her very soon." He said as he poured himself a cup of coffee.

Lizzy overheard Pete tell his Pa he was going to marry her. He had not even said he loved her or even proposed. Her heart fluttered. Pete had her heart, but confusion flowed through her. She couldn't believe he was telling her Pa he would marry her when she was proven to be an unfit guardian. She'd never consider marriage until her brothers and sister were back home.

Lizzy prepared bacon, scrambled eggs and flapjacks for breakfast. The men hurried to the table and waited for Lizzy to take her seat. She motioned for them to sit while she poured them a fresh cup of coffee. Pete said a quick grace, served the platters around the table and watched Lizzy as she stood in a corner of the kitchen.

"Come, Lizzy. I know you have to be hungry. It's been a while since we have eaten anything," Pete said.

Lizzy moved slowly to the table and took a seat next to Yuma. He smiled at her and offered her a platter of bacon and eggs. "Are you all right," Yuma asked.

"I have a lot on my mind. I miss the children, even though I know they're fine with Morning Flower and Old Woman."

"Yes, they're in good hands," Yuma said. "After we eat, can we talk alone?"

Pete heard Yuma's request. "Why do you need to talk with her alone? What do you need to discuss with her that I can't hear?"

"I'll be happy to talk with you . . . alone, Yuma." Lizzy glared at Pete, daring him to say anything else.

Pa's eyes darted from one man to the other. Something was going on between these two men and whatever it was, Lizzy wasn't happy. He was going to let his daughter take care of the problem.

Yuma and Lizzy walked outside to the corral fence. Both stood staring at the two horses as they jumped around. The weather was cool, which made the animals frisky.

"What do you want to talk to me about Yuma?" Lizzy smiled sweetly at the handsome Indian.

Yuma shifted his feet until he stood in front of Lizzy. He had finally gotten the nerve to speak with her, so now was his opportunity.

"Lizzy, will you do me the honor of becoming my wife under the Indian stars, my gods and man? I want you to be my woman," he said matter-of-factly. "You are special and with your knowledge and other ways, you'll be good for my people. And, we could have many papooses that would grow to be brave and knowledgeable in the white man's world."

"My goodness, Yuma. I never dreamed you thought of me in that way. I'm surprised and I guess a little honored. You're a nice man. A girl would be lucky to have you as her protector and father of her children. But, Yuma, you and I live in different worlds. You live in the wilderness and provide for your family by hunting and living off the land. I'm a city girl who lives on a farm and can go into town and purchase whatever my family needs. My brothers and sister love playing with the little braves, but they'd already asked me to take them home."

"My heart has never felt this way about another woman. I can make you happy," Yuma said, his eyes hardening.

"Yuma, Morning Flower has been in your life for years. I suspect you aren't even aware of how she feels for you."

"Morning Flower? Good gracious woman. She's a child I have watched grow. "

"Yes, she'd grown into a young woman. She has feelings for you. Her lovely brown eyes follow your every move. I can't believe you haven't noticed."

"But, Lizzy, I feel my heart belongs to you. I will protect you with my life. I will teach your brothers to be strong men and great warriors. You'll never have to fear any man again."

She rested her hand against his cheek. "No, Yuma, your heart belongs to Morning Flower. When you return to the village, you'll see the love in her eyes for you. I know she's heartbroken that you left the reservation to accompany Pete and me." Lizzy took his face and turned it to look into her eyes. "I am a practical woman, not a silly romantic girl in love with you. Morning Flower is beautiful, young, and has romance in her heart. Give her a chance and you'll find romance: a young lady in love with the handsome chief's son."

Just then, the door swung open, and Pete exploded from the front porch and pushed between Yuma and Lizzy. "Now look here, my friend. Lizzy is my woman. She will never be yours, understand?" Yuma was speechless. He didn't know how to respond to Pete.

Lizzy's face flamed red and she couldn't hold back her temper. "Listen to me, Pete. I care for you but you aren't my boss. I can make my own decisions. *I am not your woman.*

You've never proposed or confessed your love to me. No man will tell me what I can or can't do. So, please go back in the house. Yuma and I haven't finished with our conversation."

"But Lizzy, I wanted him to know that. . . I'm sorry. Please forgive my intrusion. I didn't mean to sound like a bully." He hurried into the house and flopped down in a rocker next to Herman.

"I can't believe my sweet daughter raised her voice to you," Herman said.

Pete gave Lizzy's Pa a hard stare. "I can hear sounds almost from town sitting in this here rocker next to the open door. Lizzy wasn't talking softly."

"Well, you and I know she's a sweet woman, and I guess I deserved her angry words. I've got a lot to think about," Pete said, looking down at the floor. He couldn't ever remember Lizzy raising her voice in anger at him or the children, but she certainly attacked him with her temper. He learned this morning that the gal he loved could certainly stand on her own two feet.

Chapter 23

In a moment of peace and contentment, Yuma and Lizzy stood close together at the corral. The two horses settled down and hung their heads over the corral fence, waiting to be rubbed. Lizzy reached for Pete's large bay and patted his nose.

"Yuma, you're really a wonderful man. I wish I hadn't already given my heart to another man. But I'm afraid, our worlds are so different. You'll be a happy Indian once you arrive home. A beautiful young maiden will greet you." Lizzy reached for his hand as they walked back to the porch.

"I'm going back to feed the horses some oats Pete brought back from town. Don't be too hard on him." Yuma nodded toward Pete. "We're both happy to have you safely home."

Lizzy stood on the porch step and watched the tall, muscular Indian walk to the barn. She glanced at the open front door and sighed. She needed to go inside to apologize to Pete for her outburst. Lizzy entered the house and froze when Pete jumped as if he had been shot from a cannon. Herman hurried out the front door leaving Lizzy and Pete alone. "I'm sorry," she murmured.

"You don't sound sincere, and you won't even look me in the eye. Are you still angry? Aren't I even worthy of a glance?"

Flushing with guilt, Lizzy licked her lips. Maybe she had made too much out of his action in front of Yuma. "I realize

I need more self-control, where you and I are concerned." Strolling into the center of the room, she said, "I'm eager to have things settled between us."

Pete seated himself on the settee. "I also realize if I'd practiced more self-control, you wouldn't have lost your temper. I deserved everything you said."

Lizzy hung her head. "Pete, I can't make plans for the future with the sheriff's influence in town. I'm still judged to be an unfit guardian for my siblings. Before anything else, I must clear my name and have a safe home for them."

Pete patted the settee for Lizzy to take a seat beside him. "Listen, I sent a telegram to my father this morning. I asked the boy who works at the telegraph office to bring his reply out here. Maybe we will hear from him today."

Lizzy cocked her head to the side. "I don't understand."

"My father is a retired judge. I mentioned that before. He's an important man and I'll ask him to have another public hearing to clear your name and have the children returned to us legally."

Lizzy sat quietly and listened. Pete said the word "us." She smiled for the first time.

"Yes, my love. I want more than anything to marry you." Pete slid off the settee down on one knee. "Lizzy Marie Montgomery, I love you with all my heart. Will you consent to be my wedded wife?"

"Oh, Pete," Lizzy sighed.

"I've prayed about all of this, and I don't want to wait any longer. I want to take care of you and the children forever."

Lizzy slid down on the floor in front of the man she loved with all her heart. Gently, lovingly, they met the passion of the other, sharing sweet kisses until too much heat flared between them.

Pete pulled back from Lizzy and said, "You haven't given me an answer."

Lizzy pressed herself more tightly against his chest. "Yes," she said, giggling.

Pete gave her a warm gaze and Lizzy felt a fluttery tenderness as she said for the first time, "I love you."

The couple hugged each other tight, sharing more kisses, until they heard a slight cough coming from the doorway. They jumped apart and laughed. Pete helped Lizzy stand as Yuma and her pa stood looking down at them.

Lizzy's warm smile sent tingles down Pete's spine as she led him to stand next to her pa. "May I have your permission to marry your wonderful daughter?" He lifted Lizzy's hand and kissed her fingertips.

"My daughter has taken care of herself for years. If she wants to marry you, I'll not stand in her way. I want her to be happy. If she's happy, then I give you both my blessings."

"Thank you, Pa," Lizzy hugged him and said, "I do love him."

"I promise to make her, the twins, and Pearl as happy as I can for the rest of my life." Pete pulled Lizzy into his side.

A warm rush tingled from her lips to her toes as Pete kissed her. Lizzy rested in the circle of his arms, feeling more cherished than she'd have ever thought possible.

~

Dusk was creeping over the farm. Yuma sat on a giant hay bale, staring over the pastures near the barn. One knee rested under his chin. He heard a flutter of noise but ignored it. Suddenly, a gunshot whizzed past his head and hit the barn door. Hesitating only a flash, he dove to the ground.

Yuma frowned, anxious and confused. He lay still and glanced out the door. Pete rushed out onto the porch with a rifle in hand.

"Yuma, are you ok?" Pete shouted.

"Yes, but someone might still be out there. The shot came from the front of the house." Yuma crawled on his belly until he reached the front porch steps.

"You think the shot came from Sheriff Jackson?"

"He's the only one with any reason to shoot at us."

"I think the same, but what will we do about it? Should

we saddle the horses and go after him?" Yuma said.

"No, since it appears he's gone, maybe it was a warning."

"Listen," Pete said, "a rider is approaching the house. Take cover beside the porch until we see who it is," Pete commanded Yuma.

"Mr. Peterson," a young voice called. The young telegraph boy leaped down from his horse and began walking to the porch.

"My goodness, Mr. Peterson, you nearly scared me to death. I didn't see you." The boy held the telegram in his hand as he looked at the tall Indian.

"Sorry, son. Is the telegram from my father in Austin?"

"Yes, Sir. I'm sorry it's late, but it wasn't dark when I left town."

"Thank you for bringing it. Can you wait for me to read it? I'll probably have a reply." Pete opened the telegram and grinned. His father would catch the train tomorrow and arrive in the late afternoon.

"I would like to send a note to him. Let me go inside and write it out for your father." In just a few minutes, Pete came out with a written note and a couple of dollars for the young man. "I appreciate your assistance with this note. Would you like to water your horse and refresh yourself before heading back to town?"

"Thanks for the money. I'd better get back to town. Ma will be holding supper for me." He waved the new note, tucked it in his shirt, and rode away.

"Good news, Yuma. My father will arrive tomorrow, and we can get Lizzy's name cleared. As a judge, he will listen to people that know Lizzy well and confirm her abilities. He won't put up with the Sheriff and his shenanigans."

"Lizzy will be so happy to hear this. Once her name is cleared, I'll return to the reservation and bring the children home."

"I'll go with you," Pete said.

"No, you need to stay with Lizzy. The sheriff may try

something else. If he comes out here, I'm afraid her Pa won't be able to handle him alone."

"I'm sure you're right about that," Pete commented. "Let's all go into town tomorrow and meet the train. We need to go early. I want you to drive a wagon back to your reservation which I intend to fill it with supplies for your people. Winter is coming and I noticed thread-bare blankets in the teepees. This will be our way of saying thank you to your people for helping care for us."

Yuma laughed. "If Pearl hadn't recognized you, it's no telling what my young braves would have done to you."

"Thank goodness nothing serious happened, so I feel fortunate. I want to get some coffee pots for your women. Coffee made in a tin can is pretty bad," Pete said, shaking his head.

"Man, you act like an old woman," he grinned and walked inside the house.

The next morning, Pete saddled his horse and hitched Yuma's mount to the flatbed wagon. Yuma, Lizzy and Herman rode in the wagon as Pete led them to the Johnson's farm. He went inside and asked the couple if they would please come into town at about four and attend the court proceeding. "My father will preside over Lizzy's new inquest concerning the children."

"We'll be happy to be there. The Sheriff wouldn't allow us to speak the last time," Mr. Johnson said as he looked at Yuma and Herman.

Pete rushed back to his horse, and they all continued toward town. After Pete at the parsonage, and spoke with Rev. Brooker about Lizzy's new inquest, Yuma continued to the Mayberry Mercantile to get the needed supplies. Pete joined Yuma and recruited Mr. and Mrs. Mayberry to attend the inquest, which they were pleased to do. Afterward, Pete handed Mr. Mayberry a long list of supplies to fill, then he led Lizzy, Herman, and Yuma to the hotel restaurant for a nice lunch while waiting for the train.

Lizzy had little time to take in the makeshift courtroom. It looked a lot different from the make-shift courtroom in the church.

A bustling stir came from the large room. The front door swept open. Reverend and Mrs. Brooker hurried inside and sat in the second row.

Sheriff Jackson entered the room, wearing his gun belt low on his hips and a smug grin on his red, sunburned cheeks. He strolled over and stood in front of Lizzy.

Beside him, Judge Mathis stood, with his head hanging low, not meeting Lizzy's eyes. He side-stepped Sheriff Jackson to take his seat behind the big oak desk.

Pete's large hand gripped the Judges' shoulder and led him to another chair. "Sorry, Judge Mathis," Pete said, "Since you haven't passed the bar exam in this state, we have a real Judge presiding over this case. Judge Peterson, a retired Judge from Austin, will be conducting this meeting."

"What?" Stuttering, he understood and smiled. "Good, I'll just watch and learn." Pleased that he didn't have to hurt the lovely young lady anymore, he sat with a sigh. Sheriff Jackson glared at him, but he didn't even acknowledge the angry faced man.

All those that were asked to attend, along with many curious townsfolk about the prominent judge who'd shown up, came into the courtroom and took their seats. Pete took Lizzy's arm and sat her down directly beside the judge's desk.

A short stocky man wearing a black robe entered the room. He smiled and bowed in front of Lizzy. "You must be Elizabeth Montgomery. My name is James P. Peterson. I'll be calling witnesses to testify about you being judged as an unfit guardian for your siblings. We will begin as soon as I call the first witness."

Everyone stood as the Judge stood behind the desk. "You may be seated. I always open my cases with a prayer. If the gentlemen will remove hats and gun belts, I'll pray. He closed his eyes.

"Father, our hearts are full that we have the freedom to serve you. Please give me the wisdom to render a fair verdict after listening to your servants. I pray I will make a fair decision, and it will be accepted by all. Amen"

"Today, we will hear witnesses for Elizabeth Montgomery. In the former hearing, no one was allowed to speak for her reputation, good or bad. I'm opening the case because in these kind of cases people are allowed to offer their judgement of a person. So, I will be calling on Rev. Brooker first to say whatever he wishes to express about Miss Montgomery's role as guardian to her young siblings."

After thirty minutes, all the witnesses had expressed their beliefs that Lizzy was more than a wonderful guardian to the children, she was like a mother. Everyone who testified said she was a Christian girl who had taken care of the children since their mama had passed. No one mentioned that Pete Peterson had lived under her roof for a month while he was healing from being wounded.

Sheriff Jackson stood and raised his voice, demanding to tell how Lizzy allowed a man to stay with her, but he was quickly placed in contempt of court.

The man didn't sit down, but whipped around, slapped his Stetson on his head, grabbed his gun belt and stormed out of the room.

"After listening to all these wonderful praises about you, Miss Montgomery, from these prominent citizens, I declare you to be a fit guardian for your siblings. This case is closed."

Pete and Lizzy hugged each other. Everyone was thrilled for her little family and came up to say so.

"His father took him by the arm. "Pete, I recognized that man who claims to be the Sheriff. I want to talk to you about him when we get to the hotel. I never forget a face and I'm sure I've seen him before."

"Father, we don't want you to stay at the hotel. We have room for you at the farm."

That's just fine, son. I'll like that. Who is that man?"

Pete's father asked as he looked at Herman holding onto Lizzy's arm.

"Father, I would like for you to meet Lizzy's father, Herman Montgomery."

"I'm proud to meet you, sir. I hope we'll be good friends," the judge said, holding out his hand to Herman.

"I've never been called sir, before. I kinda like it," Herman said, smiling. He took Lizzy's arm and walked out of the courtroom.

"Let's get to the store and pack the supplies for my trip to the reservation. I know you're anxious to have the children home." Yuma said as he leaped on the wagon.

"Yes, I am. I want to go with you to get them." Lizzy said, holding Yuma's arm.

He pulled her arm away. "No, you must stay here. Pete will need help transferring all your animals back to the farm, and besides, your pa still needs care. I'll be setting a good pace going and coming."

She smiled at the tall man. "I know you're right, but I can't hardly wait to see them. I've never been away from them this long. I know they're safe, but I want them home with me."

Chapter 24

Pete decided Yuma should take the train to the first water station from Crooksville. Once the train stopped, the porters would help Yuma pull the wagon and horse from the train.

In the dusky afternoon, Yuma drove the wagon onto the reservation. Soon a crowd of children and young braves surrounded him. They chanted and raced alongside him as he walked toward his teepee.

"Welcome home, my son," said Viho.

"Happy to be back, Father. I come for White Woman's children. I must return them to their sister."

"Yuma, Yuma," Pearl raced to him. Stopping and looking around, she screamed, "Where's Mama Lizzy?"

Yuma bent down on one knee and gave her a big hug. "I've come to take you home. Where are your brothers?"

"Here we are!" Jake said, circling Yuma.

"First light, I'll take you home. Your sister can legally care for you again, and the sheriff will not bother her anymore."

"That's good news. I like it here, but I want to go home," Joshua said.

"Believe me, I do know. I'm ready to settle down with my village people, too."

Standing up, Yuma looked over the children's heads and saw Morning Flower. She was staring at him as if it was the first time she had ever laid eyes upon him. Yuma gently pushed the children to the side and approached Morning Flower. He gazed into her big, brown eyes and saw more than friendship. Before he knew what overcame him, he pulled her into his arms. Her slim body melted into his chest as he lifted her face only inches from his. "I missed you," he said softly.

"I'm happy to hear that. I've missed you, too." Morning Flower was almost lost for words. Her heart was hammering in her chest. She was thrilled the man she loved for years finally said he had missed her.

"I have food prepared in your teepee."

Giggles resounded from Indian maidens watching the romantic action between them. Morning Flower felt herself blushing, so she grabbed Yuma's hand and pulled him into his father's teepee away from spying eyes. She closed the flap, leaped into Yuma's arms, and kissed him. "It's about time you noticed me."

"Well, a certain white woman told me I should open my eyes to my surroundings. I'm pleased that she did."

"Oh, I see. White Woman told you I have eyes on you, no?" Morning Flower's tone could have been sweeter.

"Now, don't be angry. Sometimes, men are blind. I'm very pleased to finally notice a beautiful, Indian maiden who has been in front of me for a long time. I have always cared for you, and now I know it's more than caring. I love you, Morning Flower."

Just as he was going to steal another kiss, Old Woman entered the teepee. Yuma's ears were redder than ripe tomatoes.

"Let's feed this Indian," Old Woman chuckled.

~

Once the Judge was settled at the farm, Pete and Herman rode over to Mr. Johnson's place to retrieve most of the animals. Mr. Johnson opened the back of his flatbed wagon, placed crates of chickens in it and tied the two milk cows to the back. Pete and Herman herded the horses and the cattle down the road.

"It sure feels good to be useful again," Herman said.

Pete smiled and told him the boys were good farmhands who took good care of the animals, but they could use help for a while."

Herman looked at Pete and pondered what he meant by 'for a while.'

Pete noticed the questionable glance of Herman's face. "I'm afraid Lizzy will to have to sell the farm. The railroad company is buying all the property in the path of the new railroad line. The rails are being laid and coming straight through her farm. I'm sure they'll offer her a good price, but she has no choice."

"Does she know this?" Herman asked, feeling his heart breaking. "I just only arrived home, and I don't want to leave yet."

"I understand how you feel. Lizzy doesn't know yet. But, Lizzy, the children, and even you, won't be homeless. I intend to marry her and we'll move to Austin. I have land and a big house for all of us to live in."

"How does Lizzy feel about moving away from here? She's never lived anywhere but Crooksville."

"I haven't had the opportunity to discuss this with her, so please don't say anything. I'll talk to her tonight after supper."

The chickens were soon turned loose into the chicken yard and the horses and cattle roamed into the corral and pasture. Mr. Johnson waved goodbye, and Pete and Herman entered the house.

Lizzy had the Judge helping her make a couple of pies. He wore a big white apron and flour dusted his face. Pete's father seemed to be enjoying himself in the kitchen.

"Howdy, gentlemen," the judge said. "Come into my kitchen and have a fresh cup of coffee while my helper here—" he grinned at Lizzy, "puts our pies in the oven. She's made a hearty pot of stew and cornbread for us to share as soon as she sets the table," he said, removing the apron.

While Lizzy set the table, she asked Pete, "When do

you think Yuma will bring the children?"

"If he leaves in the morning, he will have to spend one night under the stars, but, he should arrive home the next afternoon. The children will enjoy camping out for one night with Yuma. I'm sure he has many stories to share with them."

She rubbed her arms. "I'm just so anxious to see them."

Pete grabbed her hand. "After we clean the kitchen and put things way, we need to have a discussion. We're going to have to make plans for our future."

"Sounds like a life change for all of us," Lizzy said.

How about we go sit on the front porch? We need to make plans for our wedding, and I need to tell you about some things that happened while you were at the reservation."

"Let me get my shawl. The evenings have turned cool, but we'll have privacy outside."

Pete held the front door open, and they settled themselves in the swing at the end of the porch. "Let me tell you what I did about your farm before we discuss our wedding." Pete reached for Lizzy's hand.

"While you were away, Sheriff Jackson made Mr. Hardy at the tax office place your farm up for sale. He demanded Mr. Hardy give him the money once your farm sold. Mr. Hardy refused at first, but after the sheriff became overly persuasive, he finally agreed." Pete tried to find the right words, as he pushed the swing.

Lizzy gasped and covered her mouth. "I can't believe it."

When I first came to check on the farm, I saw the For Sale sign. I went to see Mr. Hardy, but he had taken his family and disappeared. So, I went to see Mr. McCombie, the banker. He told me that he could sell me your farm. According to the banker, Mr. Hardy knew he could be arrested for doing what the sheriff demanded so he closed the tax office and left town."

Lizzy's face had lost all of its color, and she was shaking. Pete pulled her close.

"I would never allow the sheriff to get his greedy hands on this farm. So, I bought your place. Your money is in the bank." He sighed and took a deep breath. "Now, Lizzy, I never intended to keep your farm from you, but there is a problem. Mr. Leonard, the railroad representative, is purchasing everyone's farmhouses and land. The railroad is coming across your property, and you don't have a choice whether to sell or not. The government will take you to court and demand that you sell. It's called eminent domain. They will offer you a reasonable price—lot more than I paid for it."

"Mercy, a lot did happen in just a few days. It looks like we'll have to move, but where will I go and start over with my siblings and Pa?"

Pete turned to face his love. "Listen, after we marry, we'll move to Austin. We can live with my father in his mansion, or we can stay there until I can build a bigger house. I have many acres and we can have horses, cattle, pigs, chickens, and any other animal the kids would like to have. You can design our house into the home of your dreams."

"This is so much to take in," Lizzy said. "I've never lived anywhere else, but it seems I don't have any choice. What will your other brothers and their wives think about you moving a ready-made family into your father's home?"

"My father has already willed his house and many acres to me. My brothers have their own homes and properties, even though we all work together to maintain everything. They'll accept you as my wife and love the children. Besides, my brothers have small children already so the kids will have playmates. The boys will love Blue."

Lizzy sat quiet for a while, and he let her. She had a lot to consider. "Let's keep my farm in your name, so you can deal with the railroad company. You have a business head so I know you'll not allow them to take advantage of me."

"I appreciate your confidence in me. You're right. I'll not allow them to take your farm for pennies. If they want your house and land, they'll have to pay. The law says they must pay a reasonable price. The children can take Blue and any other animal they want to my farm. We will ship them on the train. The others can be sold to Mr. Johnson or other neighbors."

"Speaking of the children, moving will be hard for them. They'll be sad to leave their friends."

He shrugged. "They can invite their close friends to visit after we get settled. I'll send them a round-trip ticket to Austin, and they can stay a couple of weeks in the summer."

"The boys will love that, but Pete, you'll already have so much expense. At least I can add my money to yours to help build our new house." Lizzy smiled and leaned back into the swing.

"No, I want you place most of your money into a trust for your three siblings. If you save it now, while they're young, they'll have a nest egg when they get older. They can all continue their education. If the boys decide to farm, they'll have money to purchase a home, and get married. Pearl will have a dowry for when she gets married."

She leaned her head against his arm. "You are the most loving man I know. You're always thinking about the future. But, if you don't take my money, I won't have a dowry to bring to you after we marry."

He chuckled. "You already paid me when you saved my life. I couldn't ask anything more from you. Besides, I don't need your money. I've worked and saved for many years, and my mother left my brothers and me a lot. My grandparents were rich. So, you see, we're set for life if we take care."

She sat up. "Good gracious, Pete. Please don't let the boys, and especially Pearl, know this. I don't want them to become spoiled, and I certainly don't want Pearl telling all our friends I'm marrying a rich man." Pete promised and both of them laughed.

Chapter 25

After a lengthy discussion, Pete and Lizzy came inside the house to tell her pa and the judge goodnight. The judge stood, thanked Lizzy for her hospitality and went out the door to the outhouse.

After patting Blue on the head, he began whistling. As he opened the outhouse door, gunshots exploded and hit him in the lower back and leg. He grabbed at the handle and fell onto the ground. He lay perfectly still so the shooter would think he had killed his target.

~

Pete and Herman raced onto the porch. They listened and watched Blue run down the middle of the road after someone. They hurried to the back of the house.

"Herman, hurry! Pa's been shot. He's still alive but he's hurt bad," Pete said as he held the judge's head in his lap.

"Pa, can you hear me?"

"Yep, but I got shot in the back and the leg. My legs don't want to move. Help me," he cried.

"Let me go and get several blankets so we can carry him inside." Herman rushed inside the house.

~

Herman rushed inside the house. "Lizzy, Pete's father has been shot. He's hurt bad . . . listen, someone else is in the yard. Grab that shotgun off the mantel and stand behind the door." Herman bolted onto the porch and saw a flat-bed wagon speeding up to the front porch.

"Help, Yuma been shot. The sheriff shot him." Joshua screamed as he attempted to hold the reins and keep the horse still."

Lizzy hurried out of the house and helped Herman lift Yuma out of the wagon onto the porch. Her pa gently laid the big Indian man onto the porch. "Yuma, are your hurt badly?"

"My shoulder. I was hit in my shoulder, but I'll live."

Herman pushed to his feet. "Great. Can you lie still while I help Pete with his pa? He's been shot, too, but he was hit in the back and can't walk. Pete and I will be bringing him in the house."

"Go get the judge. I'll take care of Yuma." Lizzy took Yuma's head and placed it on her lap."

~

"Mama Lizzy," Pearl sprinted up the steps and hugged her sister so tight she thought Pearl was going to choke her.

"Oh, honey, it's so good to have you home. Where is Jake? I see Joshua."

"He's climbing down from the wagon now. Oh, Mama, the boys saved my life. That mean sheriff would have shot us if he knew we were in the wagon. The boys covered me with their bodies, and we all lay still. "Poor Yuma, I'm so sorry that mean man hurt you," Pearl said as she rubbed her tiny hand across his cheeks.

"Thanks, sweet girl. I'm going to be all right as soon as I get inside. Don't get in Pete or your Pa's way now," Yuma said, his voice weak.

"Pa? Who has a Pa?" Pearl cocked her eyes at her sister.

"Pearl, I don't have time to tell you and the boys about our Pa. You'll meet him in a little while, but for now he's helping Pete with his father. The sheriff shot him too."

"Can I do anything to help? I'm a big girl now. I learned a lot at the Indian village."

"Please scramble inside and get a pillow and blanket for Yuma. We need to make him comfortable while Pete and Pa are taking care of the judge."

Her brothers stood at the bottom of the steps watching Lizzy and Pearl place a blanket over Yuma. Lizzy turned to them. "Jake, come give me a hug. I'm so happy to have you all home."

"Lizzy, we need to move the wagon and unhitch Yuma's horse. We'll be back as soon as we take care of this chore." Jake said, as he and Joshua prevailed into action. Joshua leaped onto the wagon and took up the reins while Jake took the horses' bridle and began leading him to the barn.

Lizzy smiled as she watched her two brothers act like grown men. She was so proud of them. "Yuma, my boys are turning into young men right before my eyes. I do wish they could stay young a little longer."

"They're good boys. You've done a good job, but I believe living among my younger braves have taught them to take on responsibilities," he said, slurring his words. He closed his eyes.

"You're in pain, aren't you?" she gently touched his forehead.

~

Mr. Johnson was entering his house when he heard gunshots. Suddenly, he heard another gunshot, and he was sure it came from the Montgomery's place. He hurried to the barn and quickly threw a blanket over his horse's back and rode as fast as he could toward Lizzy's farm.

Pete had just finished getting Yuma on the porch when Mr. Johnson rode into the front yard. He leaped off his horse and rushed to Pete. "What's happening over here? I heard gunshots!"

"Thank goodness you're here. Please ride into town and bring the doctor back. The sheriff shot my father and Yuma, my Indian friend. My Pa is hurt bad, but Yuma will be all right. He was shot in the shoulder."

"Do you think your father will live?"

"Yes, but he was shot in the back and he says he can't move his legs. Please hurry. We need help."

"I'll ride as fast as I can. I hope he's not on a call," Mr. Johnson said, as he leaped on his horse's back.

~

Pete called the two boys to the edge of the porch. "I need you, Herman, and Lizzy to help me carry my father into the house. It will take all of us to pick him up off the ground. There's a wide board standing by the barn doorway. We'll roll him onto it and I believe we can carry him into Lizzy's bedroom. Mr. Johnson has gone into town to get the doctor."

"I'll get the board," Joshua said, and Jake raced inside to get a couple of blankets. Lizzy and Pete lifted Yuma off the porch and walked him into the boys' room. Lizzy made sure he was comfortable while they rushed outside to bring in the judge.

Lizzy propped open the front door and rushed to pull back the covers on her double bed. Pete and Herman carefully rolled the judge onto the big wide board. With the boy's help, they each picked up a corner of the board and carried it inside. Once they reached the room, they placed it on the edge of the bed and slid him off the board onto the bed. He moaned, which to Pete's ears sounded good. At least his father had some feeling in his body.

After Pete undressed his father, Lizzy washed his face, chest and hands. The judge gave her a smile and asked if he could have some coffee.

"Yes, I'll happily make you a fresh cup. Would you like something to eat?"

"No, child, I'm still full from supper. I'm just thirsty. Coffee sounds good to me."

~

Lizzy hurried to the boy's room to check on Yuma. He lay still as death. "Yuma, are you hurting bad?"

"Indians never complain," he said, but continued to lay perfectly still.

"I'm going to give you a small doze of laudanum to relieve the pain until the doctor gets here." When he didn't respond, she hurried to the kitchen and put a fresh pot of coffee on the stove and took down the medicine. She carried the medicine and a spoon into Yuma's room. "Open your mouth, Yuma, and swallow this liquid. I have some water for you to drink afterwards. This will help with the pain."

Yuma lifted his head, swallowed the teaspoon of dark liquid, shaking his head in disgust. He grabbed the glass of water and drank it all. He shuttered and lay back down, never saying a word.

Both men were laying content when Dr. Hayes arrived. Lizzy led him to look at Yuma first. He had lost a lot of blood, and he couldn't stay awake, even after she was sure the Laudanum should have worn off.

Doctor Hayes turned to Lizzy. "Give the young man more Laudanum for the pain, bring plenty of hot water and lots of clean white rags. I'm going to remove the bullet from his shoulder."

Doctor Hayes and Pete turned his father onto his stomach so he could examine his back. A bullet was lodged at the waistline. "It seemed to have hit his spinal cord but it had not bled a lot. The other bullet lodged in the back of the upper right thigh, which would have caused great pain if the judge had feeling in the lower part of his body.

"Judge, I'm going to see if I can do surgery on your back, but first I'm going to remove the bullet in your leg. Lizzy is going to give you some pain medicine, therefore, you'll not feel anything. Continue to relax and try to go to sleep while I take care of the other man. He has a bullet in his shoulder, and it won't take me very long to remove it. Now, take the medicine and try to sleep."

Several hours later, both of Doctor Hayes patients were sound asleep. The bullet had been removed from Yuma's arm and it would be in a sling for a while. The judge would have to lie on his stomach or side for a couple weeks. The bullet was removed from the judge's leg, but the doctor couldn't remove the other bullet lodged in his back. Doctor Hayes said that the judge needed to go to a big city hospital for further treatment.

Doctor Hayes left and said he would return tomorrow. Lizzy put the children to bed in the room with Yuma while she slept on the sofa in the living area. Pete and Herman stretched out on a bedroll in front of the fireplace.

~

Pete saddled his horse and tied a bedroll on the back. Lizzy stood watching the man she loved prepare to leave. "Please be careful," Lizzy said as she patted Pete's thigh.

"I will. I may be gone for a few days. Once the deputy forms a posse, we'll be headed for the Texas border. Hopefully, the Mexican border patrol will allow us to cross over into Mexico and find the sheriff. If not, we won't have any chance of catching him."

"I hope we'll never see him again. Don't worry about your father. We'll take good care of him."

Pete leaned down and kissed Lizzy lightly on her lips and gave her a small salute. She watched until he was out of sight before she went back inside to check on the children and her two patients.

Chapter 26

As the children sat at the kitchen table, they stared at the old man who Lizzy called Pa. Earlier, she'd told the boys that their pa had left the farm a few months after Pearl was born. They were nearly three and Pearl was just a small infant, therefore, they didn't know this man who sat sipping his coffee and staring at them.

Lizzy had checked on Yuma and the judge and found they were sleeping. So, she poured herself a cup of coffee and took a chair at the table.

"Pa, I want to introduce you to your sons, Jake and Joshua. They will be eight years old in several months and this beautiful little girl, is your daughter Pearl. She turned five last month." Herman smiled and gazed into the eyes of the three children who looked at him like he wasn't real.

"How do we know he's our Pa?"

"Jake! I can't believe you asked that. I was sixteen when Pa left home. Of course, I know our Papa."

Her father chuckled. "Lizzy, I think they're old enough to hear the whole story about why I was forced to leave them, their mama and you. You can tell them or I can," Herman said.

"I'll tell them what you told me," Lizzy said, taking a sip of her coffee before she began. Lizzy told them Sheriff Jackson had men kidnap Pa out of the fields and forced him to work in a labor camp in Mexico. The children seemed to understand since they believed the sheriff could have done something like that to coerce Lizzy to marry him.

"The sheriff figured if I was out of the way, he could marry your sister, and take over this farm. From what I've heard, it seems he has had his eye on this place for years," Herman commented softly.

"Oh Pa, I'm so glad you got to come home. I have always wanted a papa." Pearl slid out of her chair and climbed into her long-lost papa's lap. Tears clouded Herman's eyes and he kissed the top of Pearls' blonde curls.

"That's right. The mean sheriff has always wanted to put us in a home for children who didn't have folks to care for them, but we've always had Lizzy," Jake said.

"Jake's right about that. Lizzy has always been more of a mama than a sister to us. She has taken right good care of us," Joshua said with conviction.

"I want you children to know I never wanted to leave you. I loved your mama, and I knew she was sickly. Those men nearly killed me before they got me to Mexico because I fought, pleaded and begged them to let me go. About two weeks ago, a young girl, who was a captive, knew I had been mistreated and was having a hard time working in the fields. She helped feed prisoners so she slipped me a knife so I could free myself after the men drank themselves to sleep. After cutting my ropes, I was able to sneak out of the campsite. I swam the river to the U.S. border. I hid during the day and traveled at night. I finally arrived here a few days ago. Yuma and Pete took care of me."

Herman watched the twins take in everything he said. Finally, Jake walked over to him. He looked into his papa's eyes and said, "I'm sorry you had a bad time and I'm sorry Lizzy had to care for us by herself, but you're home now." He stood in front of his pa while Lizzy took Pearl off his lap and laid her on a pallet. She had fallen asleep in her papa's arms.

Herman reached for Jake while Joshua rushed out of his chair and both boys hugged their papa for the first time. Lizzy wiped tears from her eyes, and she watched the reunion of an old man and two young boys. Her chest swelled with the love for her two brothers as they welcomed their pa home.

After breakfast the next day, Lizzy asked her pa if he would care for the two patients while she took the children into town. She wanted to tell the Mayberry's she would be bringing in fresh eggs and butter, like before, as long as they are still living on the farm.

"Oh, Lizzy, it is so wonderful to see the children. They look like they have grown a foot." Mrs. Mayberry said as she gave each one of the children a peppermint stick.

"I'm thrilled we are back together and now with Pa home, things are wonderful. Pa is filling out and his health is getting better. He was treated badly in that prison camp, but he's resting, eating good and getting a lot of fresh air."

Mr. Mayberry smiled. "I hope he'll come in to town and see us soon. I know you probably don't remember, but sometime, we would sit on the boardwalk and play checkers together. We solved the world's problem."

"I'm sure he'll come into see you before we have to move to Austin."

"Wait, a minute, I knew I had something important to tell you," Mr. Mayberry said as he led Lizzy to the end of the counter.

"You won't have to sale your farm. The railroad is not going to lay tracks on your land or any farm around here. After construction started, the engineers discovered that the dirt about four feet down was mostly limestone. The weight of the train on those geological conditions can cause voids underneath the foundations, which could cause the tracks to cave in."

"That's wonderful! I mean I'm sorry for the people who wanted the train to come through, but I am so happy that I won't have to move away. I love it here but . . . I have already sold my farm to Pete." Lizzy was so confused she felt dizzy. Mrs. Odem said you probably would marry Mr. Peterson. Is she right?" Mrs. Mayberry asked.

"Yes, we were planning on moving to Austin, Texas where his family lives, but I only agreed to move away because I was being forced out by the railroad. Now, we'll have to reevaluate our options when Pete returns. He's riding with the deputy and posse to the Mexican border. They hope to bring Sheriff Jackson to justice."

"I have never trusted that man. He'd come in here and grab an apple or orange. He dared me to say anything to him." Mrs. Mayberry said as she watched the boys move the checkers around on the checkerboard sitting by the window.

"Oh, Mr. Mayberry, are you sure about the train?"

He gave Lizzy a big smile and nodded.

"I'm so happy I could scream. We won't have to pull up roots and move away," Lizzy sighed and smiled. "I didn't want to leave our little place, sell our animals, and leave Mama . . . well, our little graveyard."

Mr. Mayberry smiled, "Many people don't know I have ten acres of land the railroad wanted to purchase. That's the reason the train representative came and told me about all their trouble. He said they were moving all their equipment ten miles east of here."

"I don't know what Pete is going to think when he finds out I've changed my mind about moving. I have lived here all my life, and I really didn't want to agree to move, but I had no choice. Pete seemed pleased he had a lovely home that he could take me and the kids to live in. He was also very welcoming to my pa." Lizzy walked around in the store talking softly to Mrs. Mayberry.

Mrs. Mayberry picked up a stack of material and gave Lizzy a hard look. "Oh honey, that man loves you and I know he'll understand that you want to remain here. You have a nice farm and all it needs is another room or two added. But I feel he can afford to build onto your farmhouse."

"He may be upset with me, but he has a lot to do when he returns. Dr. Hayes cannot operate on the judge. He said he must be taken to a large hospital. I believe Austin, Pete's hometown, has many doctors who will be able to care for him."

Mrs. Mayberry raised her eyebrows and commented. "That will be perfect for Mr. Peterson. He'll be able to stay at his home while his father has the surgery and recuperates."

"Yes, that will be a good thing. He'll be able to visit with his brothers and other family members. When he arrived at my place, he was on his way home. He had taken a trip to the western part of the state because he wanted to see it, but he never planned to be away from home long."

"Whenever he was around us at the store and in church, he never seemed unhappy until the sheriff lost his senses." Mrs. Mayberry shook her head in disgust. "I'm happy your Indian friend was able to come to Crooksville with you and Pete. That's one handsome Indian," Mrs. Mayberry said, looking over her shoulder for Mr. Mayberry.

Lizzy giggled. "He sure is. While I was at the reservation, it was hard keeping my eyes off him. He is not just good looking, he's polite and nice. He made sure his women took good care of me and the children." Lizzy glanced over her shoulder to make sure she wasn't overheard. "You know, Mrs. Mayberry, Yuma proposed to me. I was in a state of shock because I had no idea he cared for me enough to want to marry me. But I told him that he really loved another. He just didn't know it."

Lizzy walked over to the children and let out a long sigh. "Just listen to me. I'm talking like a blabbing old woman."

"Are you blabbering, Lizzy? You tell me to keep quiet all the time," Pearl said tugging on Lizzy's skirt.

"Now Pearl, I have a surprise for you and your brothers. I want all of you to choose something you'd like to take home. Now, hurry to the back of the store and pick out a toy or a treat to eat. Hurry because we have to get back home and check on Yuma and the judge."

WHERE LOVE HAPPENS

Chapter 27

Once Lizzy arrived home and found both of her patients asleep, she decided to take a few minutes for herself, so she went for a short walk. The sun shot light beams down through the trees. The scent of pine filled the air. Beneath her feet, the pine needles crunched, and twigs snapped. Occasionally Lizzy picked up a pinecone to use later in her fireplace as a fire starter.

As she walked, she kept the farmhouse in sight. She couldn't be gone long. She crossed the path where she had walked with Pete. Her heart swelled. Pete wanted to marry her, but he also wanted to live in Austin. *"Please God. Let him understand I love him but I want to stay on my own land."*

Lizzy sighed and began walking back to the house. Suddenly, she saw a handsome man ambling slowly toward her. "Oh Pete, what a wonderful surprise!"

"Hi honey. I hoped you'd be happy to see me. I left the posse in town and came straight here. How's my father and Yuma?"

"Both were asleep when I decided to take a short walk. Your father still can't move his legs but Yuma is ready to go back to the reservation."

Pete wrapped his arms around Lizzy's shoulders and pulled her into his chest. He gave her a small peck on the lips and then turned her toward the farmhouse.

"I'm sorry to say we didn't catch the Sheriff. The Mexican border patrol wouldn't allow us to cross the Rio

Grande and enter Mexico. The border commander demanded money. The deputy talked a blue streak but the old Mexican in charge wouldn't change his mind. When the deputy mentioned the sheriff's name, it was obvious he recognized it."

"That's awful that they'll protect bad men." Lizzy said. "You look like you've been in the saddle for days. I'll fix you a nice hot bath."

"Some decent grub would be good first. I'm ready for some of your home cooking." Lizzy took his hand and pulled him up the steps into the house.

"Look who is home," Lizzy said, as the children raced to Pete. He stooped down and hugged all three of them at once.

"Jake and Joshua, please go to the well and pull up several buckets of fresh water. I'll heat it so Pete can have a nice hot bath. While you're busy, I'll prepare dinner and Pete can visit with his pa."

"All right sis. We'll get the water." Jake motioned for Joshua to follow him.

Lizzy turned to her little sister. "Pearl, wash your hands and set the table."

"Gosh, I'm going to wash the skin right off my hands. They're never dirty, but I still have to wash them." Pearl drug her feet over to the dry sink.

~

Pete went into the front bedroom where his father opened his eyes. "How are you feeling?" Pete asked as he took his pa's right hand.

"I'm not in any pain, if you want to know. Lizzy makes sure I'm comfortable. She's a great nurse."

"I'm pleased to hear that. What does the doctor say about the bullet in your back?"

"He can't operate. I'm going to have to go to a big hospital, like the one in Austin. I'd like to go there so we can be near home."

"When does the doctor think you can travel?"

"He says I can travel anytime if I get a private car on the train." The judge tried to pull himself up to sit a little straighter in bed.

"Let me talk to Lizzy about getting married before we all leave for Austin."

Pete stood, smiled and released his father's hand. "We have a lot to plan, but I want to settle things here, so we concentrate on getting you well."

The judge squeezed Pete's hand but didn't say anything.

"Come Pete. I have your bath ready in the boys' room. Afterward, we'll have supper." Lizzy peeked her head in and motioned for him to follow her.

In less than thirty minutes, Pete, Herman, and the children were all sitting at the dining room table. Lizzy filled their plates with chicken and dumplings while Jake passed the biscuits.

"Hmmm, this looked delicious," Pete said as he passed a plate to Herman.

"Marie, the children's mama, taught Lizzy to make dumplings. Gosh, she couldn't have been a dozen years old," Herman smiled at Lizzy.

"You're right Pa. Mama taught me to cook at a very early age. I'm thankful she did. We had a lot of fun cooking together."

Pete ate two big helpings of everything. He patted his stomach and said he could hardly move. "Lizzy, after we get the kitchen cleaned, we need to talk and make plans. I'll help with the dishes." Pete stood and began removing plates from the table.

Herman stood and took the plates from Pete. "The children and I'll clean the kitchen. You two go somewhere and talk privately. Come on young'uns, let's get at it." Herman tossed the boys an apron and smiled at Pearl. "Come little lady. You can wipe down the table and sweep the floor.

~

As Lizzy and Pete walked to the corral fence, Lizzy turned and said, "I know you're exhausted and probably don't want to talk about Sheriff Jackson, but I have to know what you're thinking with him still on the run?"

"I'm not sure what he'll do in the future, but with us all gone from Crooksville, I don't think he'll travel to Austin with intent on harming us." He scanned the pasture and smiled when he saw the horses nipping each other.

"I know you helped me by purchasing my farm so the sheriff couldn't get his hands on my money, and I love you for doing that. But you have to know that I have never wanted to sell and leave my home. I've never lived anywhere else. Before, I had no choice but to agree to move when the train was to come through my land, but the railroad has changed their route."

Pete stretched his back and placed his hands at his waist. If this puzzling woman he loved was speaking the truth, their future was in jeopardy. Could he change her mind about her home, but a dozen questions were floating around in his mind.

Her big brown eyes intrigued him. They were clear, intelligent eyes--not like a silly schoolgirl. Even at the young age of twenty-one, she was a strong-willed young lady. It wouldn't be easy to convince her to marry him and move to his home in Austin. A safe haven for sure—a lot safer than remaining here with the sheriff out there somewhere.

"Pete, do you understand why I just can't leave my farm. Pa has finally come home, and mama is buried in our small graveyard. This is to be the resting place for both of them. Besides, I love it here and I know you can, if you are willing, to make this place a very profitable farm. You have already made many repairs." With apologetic eyes, Lizzy stood in front of Pete as she explained her reasons for remaining on her farm.

She tried to read his thoughts, but his facial expression never changed. He stared stone faced, not even blinking an eye. Suddenly, Pete leaned forward and placed a gentle kiss on her lips. He couldn't remain quiet. Quirking a brow to the woman he loved, he said, "You know I want more than anything to marry you, but for now, I can't agree to live here for the rest of my life. I do have an inheritance of a beautiful farmhouse and many acres. Now, like you, I have the responsibility of caring for my father. I have to take him to the hospital in Austin. Hopefully, by going there, he'll be able to walk again."

"I understand, and I want to marry you, too. And I will always be willing to help care for the judge. The children and I already love him."

"I'm not sure what the future holds for him. I thought I had our future all planned out, but now everything is up in the air. You want one thing and I'm torn between my responsibilities back home and my responsibility to you. I hate to say this, but I guess we need to wait to get married."

~

Lizzy sighed, not knowing what to say to the kind-hearted cowboy that came into her life. He made her feel special and loved. She really wanted to marry this handsome young man and spend the rest of her life with him, but he wanted to move her away from the only home she knew. It was a lot to ask now, when she didn't have sell her home and move. Her heart felt like it had fallen to her toes.

Pete stepped closer and pulled Lizzy into his arms. He kissed her eyes, as if doing so, she would know how much he loved her.

Softly moaning, she turned her head from side to side. "I wish I could agree to go with you to Austin, but I have Pa and the children to think about, too. I know the boys want to stay here and I hate to insist that Pa move away from his farm.

As one would force a small child who refused to take medicine, Pete cuddled Lizzy into his strong arms. "It's going to be all right, Sweetheart. Things between us will work out, and in good time, we'll settle on where we'll live."

For a long time, Pete held Lizzy, feeling her breath on his chest as he held her. "Let's go inside so I can check on

Father before I go to bed. I'm exhausted after staying in the saddle for two days." He took Lizzy's arm and led her back to the house.

Chapter 28

After a long rest, Pete joined the family for a hearty breakfast. Lizzy said her pa was helping the judge with his coffee. "The two men are chatting like long-lost friends."

Pete ate and then hurried into the bedroom to visit with his father. "Good morning, Father," Pete said as he walked to the bed. "Good morning to you, too, Herman. Thanks so much for helping my father with his breakfast."

Herman shrugged. "Shoot, he don't need much help. I like sharing my morning coffee with him while the others eat." Herman stood and gave the judge a salute. "See you later, old boy."

"Hey, who's calling me old boy?" Both men smiled at each other as Herman went back into the kitchen.

"Father, I'm going into town and take care of business. I need to see the banker and have the deed to this farm transferred back into Lizzy's name. You knew I'd purchased the farm to prevent the Sheriff from getting it. It's complicated to explain, but I'll straighten it out." He walked over and sat down in a chair by the bed. "I'm going to stop at the doctor's office and pick up your patient file so we can carry it to the hospital in Austin. I'll also purchase tickets for us to travel. When do you think you'll feel like going?"

"I'm ready to go whenever you are. I'm going to miss this little family. Are you planning on marrying Lizzy and living here on her farm?"

He sighed. "We haven't decided on our plans for the

future. We're going to take it one step at a time. The first step is getting you better. How would you feel about moving her and leaving your other sons and their families?" Pete questioned his father.

"How would you like to move here and leave your other sons and their families?" Looking severe, Pete questioned his father.

"Like you said. Let's take one step at a time. We'll have time to consider the future when I'm better."

Why was his father turning the tables on him? Once Pete saddled his horse and bade everyone a good day, he rode into Crooksville. He went straight to the train depot. "I'd like two tickets to Austin and with a private car for my father. He can't sit up very long and will need a bed to rest along the way. Would you know of anyone having a chair with wheels that I could purchase or rent?"

"I don't," the ticket master replied, "but I bet if anyone knows who might have one, it would be Mr. Mayberry at the mercantile."

"Thanks. I'll ask about the chair when I pick up a few supplies later."

"Here's your two tickets and you know, reserving a private car is mighty costly. I guess you have the money to pay for it?"

"Yes. Just give me the total and I can pay now." Pete noticed several people listening to his conversation with the ticket master.

"The train will leave at three p.m. tomorrow. This will give you time to get your father settled on the train. Oh, will you be taking your horse this time?"

"No, I won't need it once we arrive in Austin, but thanks for asking. See you tomorrow." Pete gave the older man a salute and walked around the people who had stood close behind.

~

A stranger was peeking around the building, watching Pete's every move. He scribbled a note and gave it to a young man with a scruffy face on a horse. "Take this to the border. He'll know who to give it to from there." Money changed hands, and the rider took off as fast as his horse would move.

~

A shiny black carriage drove up in front of the house-- Lizzy's first warning that it was time for Pete and his father to leave. Lizzy opened the door and walked out on the porch, grabbing her shawl off the coat rack. A bustling stir bypassed Lizzy as three children rushed ahead of her to greet Pete.

"Mr. Pete, are you coming back?" Jake jumped on the running board of the carriage.

"My plans are to return, but I can't say when. You all know I must take my father to Austin." His gaze swept over the children's heads as he rested his hands on the reins of the two black horses.

Lizzy nodded to Pete, a generous smile spreading across her face. She knew that very little would escape his lips. They had said all that could be said last night.

Beside Pete sat the judge with pillows tucked behind his back and his legs extended. His friendly dark brown eyes beamed at Lizzy and the children.

"When you say your prayers, remember me. I hope to be walking when we return." The judge tugged on Pete's arm and motioned for him to drive forward.

Nodding to Lizzy and the children, Pete gave them all a big smile and said, "I love you all. Boys, take care of your sister and Pa." Pete didn't wait to hear their response as he clicked his tongue to signal the animals into motion.

~

"Lizzy, why can't we go into town and watch Pete and his father get on the train. I know Pearl wants to wave goodbye to them, and we want to see them off," Joshua said.

Lizzy was standing straight as an arrow, wiping tears that were brimming. "All right, let's hurry and get ready. Jake, go to the barn and tell Pa we are all going into town."

After less than an hour, Lizzy, Herman, and the

children drove toward town to surprise Pete and the judge. The closer Herman went to town, Lizzy wasn't sure that gathering at the train station to see the men off was a good idea. She didn't want Pete to feel uncomfortable.

To her surprise, Pete was delighted they came into town. The judge was already made comfortable in his private car and he could see them from his window. He waved enthusiastically. Pete leaped down from the platform and gave Lizzy a strong hug and a kiss. "I'm glad you all came to see us off. Father and I both were feeling pretty low on the drive to town."

"I wanted to see you again, too. Pearl wants to wave goodbye to you and the boys said we couldn't disappoint her. Pearl loves you."

"I hope she isn't the only one," Pete said again as he reached to pick Pearl up.

The train whistle blew, announcing it was time for Pete to get back on the train. As the train pulled from the station, the children waved to Pete and the judge as they traveled down the track.

Lizzy patted Pearl on the back as she rubbed her tear-stained face into her sister's long, pretty skirt. "Come, Pearl, boys, and Pa. We need to stop at the seamstress shop. Afterward, we'll go to the mercantile and buy a treat before heading home.

"Why do we have to go to the seamstress shop? It's so boring waiting for you to get pinned up," Jake said as they approached the shop.

"I'm only going to drop off some material to make a few dresses for Pearl. She is growing like a weed. Now, I won't be but a minute." Lizzy opened the door to the seamstress shop with a bell announcing their arrival. "Come in! I'll be right there." A voice from the back yelled.

Lizzy herded the children to a small sofa and pointed toward a straight-back chair for her Pa. "All of you be very quiet while I talk to Miss Balding, Lizzy said while pointing her finger at the children.

"Lizzy, it's so good to see you. It's been a while." Miss Balding entered the front room. She hugged Lizzy and looked at the children. "Mercy, your brothers and sister have grown a foot since you've been here." She turned to face Herman and asked, "Now, who's this handsome man?"

"Miss Balding, this is my father, Herman. He has been away, but he's home for good now. Papa, this is my dear friend, Miss Ida Balding."

Herman leaped from the chair, removed his hat, and practically gave the seamstress a bow. He blushed fiery red. "It's nice to meet you, madam."

"Miss Balding, I have several pieces of material to make Pearl a couple of new dresses. I have let out all the deep hems you placed in her older dresses. She's growing tall."

"Well, Missy, come with me and allow me to measure you so I can get busy and make you some new dresses." Miss Balding and Pearl left the front room and went behind a curtain.

Herman didn't return to his chair but circled the room several times. "Who is this woman, Lizzy? I don't remember her being in town before I left."

"She had only been in town a couple of years. Mama probably wouldn't have used her anyway because she made all my clothes and hers, too. I can sew a little, but Miss Balding is affordable and I let her help me with Pearl's clothes."

"Is she married?" Herman asked before he knew what he was saying.

"Wow, Pa, I think you like Miss Balding," Jake said, punching Joshua in the ribs. Both boys giggled.

"Hush," Lizzy said to her young brothers as she noticed how embarrassed her Pa was.

"Here she is," Miss Balding said as she led Pearl back to the front room. "I will have her dresses ready in a week from today."

"That's great," Lizzy said, motioning the children out the front door. Herman gave her a shy smile, said goodbye while placing his hat on his head and rushed out the door following the children.

"Lizzy, your Pa is a handsome man. Does he have eyes on a lady in town?"

"No, he doesn't. When he returned, he was very sick and weak, but he's better now." Lizzy was surprised at this unexpected turn of events.

~

"Hey, Mr. Mayberry, Pa got a girlfriend," a smiling Pearl told the store owner after racing inside the dry-goods store.

"Pearl, you best keep a civil tongue in your head. Now, you know Pa just met Miss Balding." Lizzy gave Pearl's shoulder a shake and walked away to talk to Mrs. Mayberry.

"Pearl, you go stand by the door and not say another word about me or Miss Balding." Herman used a stern but quiet voice reprimanding his little daughter for the first time.

"Mercy, Lizzy, whatever gave Pearl an idea like that," Mrs. Mayberry laughed. "I didn't know that your Pa knew the Widow Balding."

"He just met her a few minutes ago. I don't know where Pearl gets her ideas. Pa 's sure embarrassed," Lizzy said as she watched him head to the back of the store. "I brought the kids over to get a treat before we head home. They're sad because we saw Pete and his father off on the train. I hope the doctors in Austin will be able to remove the bullet and he will be able to walk again." Lizzy watched her brothers choose a small bag of marbles and lollipops. She glanced over their head to see what Pearl had chosen, but Pearl wasn't in sight. Lizzy called, but after searching the store, Pearl wasn't inside.

"Jake, look on the boardwalk for your sister. She knows not to get too far away from me."

"She could have gone outside after Pa scolded her," Joshua commented.

Jake came in. "Lizzy, I looked up and down the street, and didn't see her. You don't think a bad man may have grabbed her?" he said, chuckling.

"If he did, he'll return the brat back quickly enough," both boys laughed.

"All right now. Hush that talk, and help me find her. Pa, Pearl went outside, and we can't find her. Come help us look for her."

Everyone walked outside and looked in all directions. "We need to spread out. I'll go this way, up alongside the hotel," Lizzy gestured with her right hand. "Pa, you go a couple doors down and then cut back between the buildings there. There'll be trees and underbrush for a ways. Boys, you go by the residences off to your right and ask everyone you see if they have seen her. She can't be very far." Lizzy was near frantic with worry, but she tried to appear calm.

~

Mr. and Mrs. Mayberry were closing the store when the deputy of Crooksville walked by. "Jeremy. Pearl, Lizzy Montgomery's little sister, is missing. We need everyone to look for her. She walked out of the store about thirty minutes ago and hasn't been seen since."

"I'll gather some men and we'll help look for her. Do you know if anyone went down by the train tracks?"

"No, I don't know, but when I see Lizzy, I'll ask." Mr. Mayberry went in the opposite direction with his wife clutching his arm. "Let's head behind the store," Mr. Mayberry said.

After searching the ground and underbrush, the pair started back to the store when they heard the girl's voice.

"Come to me, sweet thing. I'll take you home."

Mr. Mayberry placed two fingers over his lips for his wife to be quiet. Twenty feet ahead, they walked toward the sound, making their way through the underbrush. They bumped and scraped against the rough brush until they saw Pearl squatting in front of a brown wild rabbit. She held a handful of green leaves in her hands, trying her best to coax the animal to come to her.

Trying not to scare the child, Mrs. Mayberry called to

Pearl softly. Pearl jumped, and the little rabbit hopped out of sight.

"Oh, darn, Mrs. Mayberry, you scared my new little friend. Now, I won't be able to catch it."

"I'm sorry, dearie, but Lizzy and many others have been looking all over town for you. You may have more to worry about than that little creature. Your Pa is very upset that you left the store."

"Well, mercy me. I can't say or do anything right anymore. Shoot fire. I guess I better go with you and show Lizzy I'm all right."

"Would you like for me to carry you, little one?" Mr. Mayberry asked.

"Nah, I can walk," Pearl said as she raced ahead of the couple.

Chapter 29

After supper that evening, Lizzy was still fretting and fussing about how dangerous it was for Pearl to have left the store. Both she and her pa had given Pearl a good scolding.

Lizzy didn't realize how much danger Pearl could have been in until she remembered crazy Sheriff Jackson was still at large and might have taken the opportunity to abduct Pearl. Pete had told her that Sheriff Jackson was hiding somewhere in Mexico and hopefully wouldn't dare come back across the border anytime soon. She prayed he had given up the idea of getting his hands on her farm.

Herman tried to downplay the danger aspect but did counsel Pearl about being alone in town. "A lot of things could happen to a child left unattended. There's gunplay, runaway horses, and drunken men on the streets." Pearl listened and was sure thankful that she hadn't received a spanking for leaving the store.

Lizzy cleaned the scratches on Pearl's face, legs and arms that she received from running through the underbrush as she tried to catch the little rabbit. Thankfully, she didn't need any stitches. Once Lizzy put Pearl down for the night, she spoke softly about the dangers of slipping away from the family while in town. "Promise me you won't do that again," Lizzy said.

"Oh, Lizzy, I'm sorry I went outside the store. Pa was mad, so I sat on the bench by the front door. While looking around, I saw a little rabbit under the boardwalk and wanted to catch it." Pearl yawned big. "Can I get a rabbit to have as a pet?"

"I think that could be possible in the future, but for now, you'll have to show Pa and me that you can be responsible." Lizzy listened to Pearl's prayers, tucked the covers under her chin, and left the room. Lizzy placed the tea kettle on the stove to make herself and her pa a cup of hot tea before retiring.

Her pa studied her. "Lizzy, you need to tell me what Sheriff Jackson has been doing to you since I've been gone. Whenever his name is mentioned, you tense, and tears almost spill over."

Lizzy poured tea for both of them and sat across the table from her Pa. "Oh, Pa, the sheriff has been after me to marry him for years. After he asked you if he could court me and you chased him away, he kept coming around. For several years, he only stopped by but never mentioned marriage again until Pete showed up here. Then things went wild. Doctor Hayes proposed marriage and then the sheriff. I thought they both had lost their minds."

"What about Yuma, the Indian? How did he come to be here?"

"The sheriff was so angry he threatened me that if I didn't agree to marry him, I would be sorry. I did refuse him, so he had a judge-- a friend of his-- declare me unfit to care for the children. The judge ordered them to be placed in an orphanage in Waco, Texas.

"That weasel little varmint. I'd like to –"

But, dressed as a widow, I got on the same train the twins and Pearl were put on, and snuck them off the first chance I could before they ever made it to the orphanage. Luckily, we were near an Indian reservation, and Yuma and his braves found us and carried us to their home. We stayed hidden there for a while. The sheriff and his posse looked everywhere for us. While I was gone, the sheriff had Mr. Hardy, the tax man, place my farm up for sale and demanded that he receive the money." Lizzy shook her head. "I still can't figure out how he thought he could get his hands on my money."

"Gracious, you have had to put up with a lot. Thank goodness you have great friends like Pete and Yuma. I'm so sorry I wasn't here."

"You're right, if you'd been here, these things wouldn't have happened." Lizzy stood and stretched. "I'm so tired, need to go to bed." Lizzy took their cups to the dry sink. "You know what Pa? I'd like for us to start adding to the house. You need a room. Let's draw up a plan for how we want it to look tomorrow. I have extra money to purchase lumber, windows, and a door."

He made her face him. "Daughter, are you sure you want to build onto this house? Maybe you'll change your mind and move to Austin with Pete." Herman moved forward to take Lizzy's shoulders.

"I'll still need to figure out our future. I love Pete, Pa, but I won't give up our home. He can move in with us, or he won't." Lizzy hung her head and walked to her room.

~

The train pulled into Austin, Texas and was met by Pete's two brothers, Will and Jeff. Pete waved to them and hurried to his father's private car where the judge was sitting in the new chair with wheels, waiting for Pete to come.

"We've arrived, and Will and Jeff are here to meet us," Pete said as he reached for their carpetbags. A porter stood behind the judge, ready to push him down a ramp to the train platform. Pete tipped the man and took over pushing his father to meet his other two sons.

"Father, you look wonderful. We were afraid you would be lying on a stretcher." Will shouted.

"Son, I have been shot in the back, but I'm not deaf," the judge winked at Jeff, his younger son.

Will stooped down in front of his father and took his hand. "Father, the hospital is waiting for you to arrive. We thought you should go there and let them get to your surgery as soon as possible. A carriage is waiting. You can lie down in it as we travel to the hospital."

The judge smiled and thanked Will. With my three sons, I don't have to decide anything."

Pete shook his brothers' hands and thank them for making all the carriage and hospital arrangements. "Let's get father to the carriage and be on our way. It's tough to sleep on the train. I know he's ready for a long nap. We did eat well, but the train is so loud it's hard to rest."

The carriage arrived at Austin's hospital and the orderlies and nurses escorted the judge to a nice clean private room. After getting him ready for bed, the surgeon entered the room.

"Mr. Peterson, I'll want to examine you first thing in the morning. I can't guarantee you'll be able to walk again after the operation. If I can remove the bullet, I will do the best I can to repair the lower part of your spine. We're hoping we can do your surgery tomorrow afternoon."

"I'm ready, doc." The judge smiled and adjusted his pillow. "I'm anxious to get this over."

~

Pete rode with his two brothers to the farm, about five miles from the hospital. He was hoping to see his two sisters-in-laws and their children because he hadn't seen his two nephews and niece in months. "How are Evelyn and Marilyn doing?" Pete asked his brothers.

"They're fine, just busy with the community," Jeff answered.

"I was hoping to bring my new bride-to-be home with me along with her three siblings and her pa, but after Father got hurt, we put our marriage off for a while."

"Why did you do that? Did your fiancé refuse to take care of Father?"

"Of course not. Lizzy and the children gave him great care."

"Well, I pray his surgery is successful and he can walk. Marilyn has refused to take care of an invalid. She said that if I bring him home for her to nurse him, she'll pack up the boys and leave me," Will said, shaking his head.

Pete couldn't believe his ears. "Surely, she jests. Father is not a demanding man. Besides, he has enough money to hire a live-in nurse. He'll not be any trouble."

"Listen," Will said. "I discussed this with Evelyn and Jeff, but Evelyn said she's not willing to look after him either. Jeff tried to change her mind, but both girls refuse to help with Father."

"I'm sorry to hear your wives feel this way toward Father. After all he has given us, I would have thought they loved him and would be more than willing to care for him. Your wives sound very ungrateful, which is surprising to me."

"Well, while discussing Father and the things he has given us, both girls feel that Father cheated Jeff and me. He willed this house and the surrounding land to you while we had to build our houses and only received forty acres."

His jaw dropped open. "I never told Father to give me this house after he dies or anything, as far as that goes. I'm surprised your wives wanted this house. Do they want you two to live here together?"

"They'd like having all the servants that live here. We only have one maid that comes each day."

"Those servants are like family. After Mother passed, Father never wanted to let any of them go. Most of them depend on their jobs to feed their own families."

Once they arrived, they headed into the parlor, where Jeff slumped into a wingback chair. "When our wives get a bee in their bonnets, we can't do anything to change their minds."

"If it's servants they want, why don't you hire them some?" Pete asked.

"We don't have room for them to live in and that's what Marilyn wants. She likes to sleep in, and have a live-in maid to feed the boys and get them off to school. She's not a morning person." Will wiped his face with his hand and looked away from Pete.

"For gosh sake, build another room onto your house.

Figure out how to make them happy. You aren't poor." Pete was disgusted listening to the complaints that his sisters-in-law's had.

"No, Pete, that's not the answer. They both want us to lease some of our land to other farmers and they want to move into this house to entertain and have large parties. Marilyn wants me to run for governor of Texas, and I'll need a mansion to look the part."

"Governor? I had no idea you were into politics."

"Well, I'm not, but Marilyn is, and she says she would help me with my campaign and later if elected, she'll be my right hand woman."

"Lord have mercy." Pete ran his hand through his hair. "I need to go to bed. Is my room still at the top of the stairs?" Pete wondered if the wives had already made changes in the house.

"Yes, the servants put clean sheets on your bed and aired out the room. It's all ready for you. I can assure you nothing has changed." Will walked Pete to the bottom of the staircase.

"I'm glad to hear that," Pete picked up his carpetbag and hurried up the staircase. "Good night. I'll have an early breakfast. I want to be at the hospital when the surgeon examines Father."

Chapter 30

Old Mexico

"Hey gal, get your rump over here. Don't make me come and get you," bellowed Sheriff Jackson. "Bring me another shot of tequila and be quick about it," he yelled at the bartender.

Michele Perez looked uncomfortable under the extreme degree of Marvin's gaze. She shuddered at the big man's advances because her man, Antonio, was wildly jealous. "Now, Marvin, you know I can't consort with you. Antonio said he'd kill you if you keep messing with me," she said, turning her back to him.

"I may have to kill your jealous lover if you don't get over here. Do you think that my friends in this 'wonderful establishment' would let your man harm me?"

Many of the young Mexicans cheered and raised their mugs of beer. The sheriff marched across the room and grabbed the beautiful senorita's arm. He pulled her down onto his lap. The young girl struggled and cursed, attempting to escape.

Suddenly, the men backed away from the bar. Many of them hovered close to the wall. The room took on a dim glow as a sizable, handsome man stood in the tavern's doorway. He was dressed in black from head to toe. A giant over six feet tall, wearing two shiny six-guns strapped on his hips, took in the room with one glance.

Marvin chuckled. "Michele, look who's arrived. I hope he has brought the money he owes me, but if not, you'll belong to me." Michele twisted and clawed to get loose, but Marvin held her tight.

Antonio Santana approached the bar and turned to face the sheriff and his woman. He placed both elbows on the bar and relaxed. "Jackson, I won't give you more money. You didn't complete your job. Men crossed the border and are still looking for me."

"I killed the men following you. If more are coming, then you'll have to pay more," Sheriff Jackson sneered.

"Turn my woman loose before I blow your brains all over this room," Antonio said without smiling. The thought of that old man putting his hands on his woman made his skin crawl.

"In a minute, she'll be mine," laughed the sheriff. Suddenly, the sheriff stopped laughing, pushed Michele off his lap, and stood with his legs parted and his right hand close to his pistol on his hip.

Marvin noticed the men in the room waited for one of them to make a move. The last thing he saw was Antonio pushing away from the bar. The last thing he felt was a plug between his eyes.

The room was silent for a second and then exploded with cheers. Several men picked up the sheriff's dead body and hauled it out the back door of the tavern.

"Well, he won't be bothering you anymore," he murmured as Michele leaped in his arms.

"*Sí*, I'm glad." Michele looked at her lover. "Now, he won't bother the young girl across the border. Whenever he was drunk, he bragged he would take her from her family and make her his bride."

"The old fool won't be bothering anybody anymore," Antonio said, with a grin.

~

<u>Austin, Texas</u>

Pete paced up and down the waiting room as he waited for the surgeon to complete his father's examination. His brother, Jeff had fallen asleep and was snoring loudly in one of the overstuffed chairs. Before long, voices came down the hallway into the waiting room.

The surgeon spoke with a nurse before he shifted his attention to the two men waiting for him. Pete took his boot and bumped Jess's leg to wake him up.

"Mr. Peterson, I've examined your father and am happy to report that I'll be able to operate. I'm sure I can remove the bullet, but it will be weeks before we'll know if he can walk again. He'll need a lot of care and attention to help him exercise his legs daily. The bullet is located on the right side of the spine, not in the center, which is good. I would like for him to spend the night in the hospital. My partner and I will do the operation early in the morning."

"Thank you so much, doctor. My brothers and I will be here early in the morning, but I'll stay with him today," Pete said.

"Mrs. Evans, my head nurse, will give you some instructions. I'll see you first thing in the morning." The doctor shook Pete's and Jeff's hands and hurried down the corridor.

~

I'm telling you now Will, I won't take care of your old man. You'd better hire a butler to take care of him before he comes home." Marilyn was almost screeching.

Pete stood at the entrance to the sitting room and listened to his sister-in-law. Marilyn was laying down the law to his brother. He already knew how she felt about caring for his father from Will. Jeff's wife, Evelyn, felt the same way. He never dreamed they were so selfish in all the years he had known his sisters-in-law's. Pete would ensure they never had to take care of his father, even though he was Will and Jeff's responsibility, too.

Marilyn's angry words drained him. It was time to tell Marilyn and Jeff's wife, Evelyn, how it would be after

Father's surgery. "Excuse me," Pete said as he entered the room. "I couldn't help but overhear you talking about Father. I want you to know that Father will be coming here to recuperate after his surgery, but never fear; no one will have to take care of him as long as I'm here."

"So, you sound like you'll be leaving. Are you going back to Crooksville? I understand you have a woman with a bunch of young'uns. You should plan to live there because I can tell you now she'll not like living here."

"First of all, dear sister-in-law, my woman is the guardian of her two brothers and little sister. Her father also lives with her. My woman has never been married, but I'm sure she would love this big house if she decides to marry me."

"Is it possible that she may not marry you?" Marilyn asked with a smirk on her face.

"Even though it's none of your business she doesn't want to move from her own farm. She has never lived anywhere else, and she doesn't want to uproot her siblings or her father."

"Thank goodness for that," Marilyn laughed softly.

"Why do you say that? I believe she would love this house."

Oh, that's right. This will be your house when your father dies, but for now, Evelyn and I are staying here with our children. We certainly don't need another big family moving in."

Pete stood straight and lifted his chin. "Now, you'd better listen to me, Marilyn. If Lizzy decides to marry me and is willing to move to Austin, this will be her home. You and Evelyn will have to move back into your own nice homes."

Marilyn looked at Evelyn. "I can tell you now, brother dear, your 'Lizzy' will not enjoy living on this big farm, so far away from town, with no one to talk or visit with."

Pete shook his head and glared at his sister-in-law. "So, that's the way it will be, is it? You and Evelyn will not accept her into our family." He looked at Marilyn and his brother

Will. "You both make me sick. You haven't asked about Father or how his surgery went." Pete whirled around and left them staring at each other.

Chapter 31

"Lizzy, do you know when Pete will return to the farm? Have you heard from him, a letter or telegram?" Herman asked.

"No, I haven't, but Pa, I know he has been busy with the farm and taking care of his father. The doctor will have to decide if there's anything that can be do to help Mr. Peterson."

"I guess you're right. The kids and I miss him, and we hope he'll return soon and marry you."

"I hope the same thing, but I'm proud he's that kind of man who takes care of his family. After his father is in good hands, I pray Pete will return to me." Lizzy turned and returned to the stove to stir the stew she was preparing for dinner.

"Mama Lizzy, I don't feel so good. I need something cold to drink," Pearl hung onto Lizzy's skirt nearly making her fall.

"Gracious, baby girl, be careful pulling on me while I'm cooking. Here, I'll give you a dipper of cool water." Lizzy dipped fresh water and gave it to Pearl. As she watched her drink, she felt Pearl's forehead.

Lizzy moved the stew off the burner and stooped down to eye level with her sister. "Mercy, child, you're burning up."

"Ain't nobody tied me to a post and set it afire," Pearl commented.

Lizzy smiled, picked up Pearl, and walked into the front

bedroom. Let me look at you." She undressed Pearl and sighed. "I was afraid that's what it was. Mrs. Mayberry said the Wilson boys had a case of measles, and they were at church Sunday."

"I don't want anything those mean boys have. They can just keep their old measles." Pearl reached for her dress.

"I'm afraid the measles are not something you can give back, sweetheart. These red spots on your stomach and back tell me you already have caught a good case." Lizzy instructed Pearl to lie on the bed while she got a pan of cool water and made a paste of baking soda and water. She learned about the paste from her mama when the boys came down with measles when they were three. It helped prevent itching.

When Lizzy returned to the bedroom, Pearl had already fallen asleep. Lizzy spread the paste over the red spots and covered her with a soft blanket. Rest was good for Pearl, so she encouraged her brothers and Pa to be as quiet as possible.

Lizzy walked back to the stove and finished preparing the stew. She mixed a pan of cornmeal and placed it in the oven. "Pa, do you remember ever having the red measles?"

"Afraid so. I got a bad case when I was about ten. I had those red spots in my ears, hair, and even between my toes. I was very sick for about a week, but my brothers had a mild case. They had to stay inside. To past time, they tormented me to death."

"Why did your mama let them do that to you?"

"Oh, she didn't know, and I told them I would get them back once I got rid of those nasty red spots . . . and I did." Herman chuckled, remembering some of the things he did to his brothers.

"When I take your eggs and cheese into town this afternoon, I'll ask Doctor Hayes to drop by and look at Pearl."

"I'm not sure he can do anything for her, but seeing him will be nice. Since Pete arrived and had to remain with us, he hasn't dropped by like he used to. The kids and I enjoyed his visits.

Late into the evening, Doctor Hayes arrived to look at Pearl. The little girl was thrilled to see him. He smiled at her and laid a peppermint stick of candy on the nightstand. "You can have the candy after I examine you."

"I'm sorry you can't marry Lizzy. You know she liked you a lot, but since I'm not old enough to marry Pete, she'll marry him. He's nice but he doesn't bring me candy like you do."

Doctor Hayes sat next to Pearl and listened to her chatter. He smiled as he looked at her back and legs. He hoped she didn't get too many red spots on her face because if the spots were bad, they would scar her lovely face.

"Now, Pearl, Lizzy will cover your red spot with a paste to help with the itching. Please try not to scratch and get the spots infected. I want you to stay in bed and get a lot of rest. You can go sit on the porch, but no running and getting hot. Since your brothers have had measles, they can play with you."

"How long will I have to wear this white paste on my body? I look like a polka-dotted Indian wearing war paint." Pearl pouted.

Doctor Hayes couldn't hold his laughter at Pearl's comical remark. "It will depend on how well you follow my instructions. Probably no more than a week. You should be over the fever and the spots will not itch, but if you're not well in a week, I'll be back out to see you."

Pearl reached for her peppermint stick and laid her head on the pillow. She sighed, she hoping time didn't drag like when that old mama cow was giving birth to her baby.

Doctor Hayes snapped his black bag closed and shook his head as he walked out of the bedroom door. Lizzy stood near the door to hear the doctor and his patient.

~

"Lizzy, I believe Pearl will be just fine. She already has a good case of measles. It will be hard to keep her still for a few days. That youngster is a character," he said, chuckling, "and much too old for her age."

Lizzy agreed and invited Doctor Hayes to have coffee and cake before he had to leave.

"I would enjoy some coffee, and I do have something to tell you," He commented, pushing a strand of her blond hair behind her ear.

"Please," Lizzy quickly pulled back from the doctor. He made her feel uncomfortable. Please sit while I get you some coffee," Lizzy said as she gathered two cups of coffee and nervously cut a large slice of pound cake. With the sheriff and Pete gone, she hoped Dr. Hayes wouldn't start up again.

Doctor Hayes stirred his coffee. "Lizzy, the deputy in town, told me that he got word from a young boy that lives across the border that sheriff Jackson got shot, and he's dead."

"What? How did that happen?" Lizzy's wanted to shout with glee, but she knew in her heart that wouldn't be very Christian. She should have compassion and not be happy that someone had died.

"The young boy said the sheriff was messing with a known bandit's woman in a tavern. The sheriff had been working for this man and earlier admitted to killing several men following Santana across the border. Santana, the bandit, told the sheriff that he might have other men wanting him dead. The sheriff said he would have to pay him more if he did that job. Santana also demanded the sheriff leave his woman alone. Words were exchanged. That's when Santana shot the sheriff right between the eyes."

Lizzy began to tremble as she listened to the horrible events that took place at the border. "Oh, my word. I didn't realize the sheriff was so vicious. I never dreamed he would kill men for money.

"We should all give you a great big thanks for not marrying him. He wanted your farm so he could sell it to the railroad company. I'm surprised that he didn't kill Pete and your Indian friend, Yuma." The doctor drank his coffee and took a small bite of cake. "He died at the hands of a bad man, but he was consorting with criminals. At least you and the children will no longer have to worry about him." The doctor stood and reached for Lizzy's arm, but she stepped back.

"Thank you for sharing the information about Sheriff Jackson. I'll tell Pa so he won't be looking over his shoulder every time he's working outside. I'm relieved that he won't be lurking around, too."

Just as Doctor Hayes started for the door, he stopped. "Lizzy, my proposal of marriage is still good. I would love to care for you and the children. With your Pa living here, traveling the countryside with me wouldn't be a problem for you. You'd make me a fine nurse."

"Doctor Hayes, you're too kind, and I appreciate your sweet offer of marriage, but I hope to marry Pete Peterson. Once his father has recovered from surgery and we know what's in store for his care, we'll plan our future. I'm sure we'll be living here on the farm."

He shrugged. "Well, I had to ask again. I hope you know I care for you and the children. I'll always be as near as town. Pearl will be fine, and I'll be out to see her on my nearby rounds." He flopped his hat on his head and leaped in his black carriage.

Lizzy watched the doctor drive away and sat down in the porch rocker. "What now?" she thought as she watched the boys' race to her.

"We didn't get to visit with doctor," Jake said.

"He checked Pearl over, then he had to get back to town. The doctor will be back in a few days and you can talk with him then." Lizzy rocked faster staring out at the corral. Pete said that he would like to purchase young colts to raise. She sighed and prayed he would be living here soon.

After supper, she and Pa walked out to the corral. She conveyed Doctor Hayes's news about Sheriff Jackson to her father. He blew out a sigh of relief and smiled for the first time in a while. Just then, the young boy who worked at the telegraph office came riding up to the front porch.

"Here we are, young man," Pa called to him.

"I have a telegram for Miss Montgomery."

"Thank you so much for bringing it out so late. Pa, give this fine young man a half dollar." Lizzy looked to see who the message was from.

As Herman dug in his overalls for some change, the young man said the telegram was from that Peterson fellow."

Pa handed the money to the young man and said, "I guess you know what the message says, too." Pa wasn't pleased that the whole town would know a person's private business.

"Wow, thanks." He stuffed the coin in his pocket and smiled. "Not this time. Pa just told me who it was from and said Miss Montgomery would be happy to hear from this man." He turned his pony around and headed back toward town like a cat with a scalding tail.

Lizzy laughed at the expression on her Pa's face. "Let's go sit on the porch and read this very private message from Pete."

Chapter 32

"Pull your chair closer, Pa, and I'll open the envelope." She unfolded the message and smiled. "The boy was right. The message is from Pete. It says he needs me to come to Austin as soon as possible. He needs my help with his father."

"I thought Pete said he had two brothers living on his pa's farm." He scratched his head. "Wonder why Pete needs your help. Aren't his brothers married?"

"You're right. Pete has two older brothers who have been married for a while because they have children. I can't imagine why he needs me, but Pa, Pete would never request I come to him if it wasn't necessary."

"I know you're right. I can keep the boys, but Pearl is another thing. Can you take her with you?"

"Yes, I'll leave the boys with you because they can help you with the farm, and I'll take Pearl. I'll catch the afternoon train tomorrow. Pete will be happy if we arrive quickly. We'll be a happy family very soon."

~

The twins stood at the edge of the porch listening to Lizzy and their pa. "Lizzy is going away and she ain't taking us," Jake whispered to his twin. "She's taking Pearl and leaving us here with Pa. I can't believe she doesn't want us anymore."

"She's going to Pete. They're going to get married and

be happy . . . without us," Joshua said. "I thought Pete liked us."

"I always thought Lizzy loved us like a mama would, but I guess she never felt like we belonged to her. Now that Pa has returned, she's just giving us to him like we're leftovers." Jake and Joshua both wiped tears from their eyes.

~

The next morning, Lizzy cooked breakfast and called the boys to the table, she smiled at them. "Good morning. I made your favorite flapjacks. Now, eat while I check on Pearl. Your pa is in the barn preparing the wagon for a trip to town."

The boys glanced at each other. Both boys knew their sister was going to Austin and they weren't going. They turned to their full plates and picked at their food. "I wonder if Pa can cook. We'll probably starve to death," Jake whispered.

~

Lizzy stood over Pearl's bed. "Good morning. You look better today. Your red spots have healed, and you don't have any fever. So, I have a surprise for you. We're going on the train. What do you think about that?"

"Wow, that's super. The boys love the train." Pearl's excitement was too much for Lizzy. She hated to have to leave the boys, but with Pete needing her help, she had no idea what would be expected of her.

"The boys aren't going on this trip. Pete has asked me to come to his home and help him. The boys are going to stay home with Pa."

The little girl frowned. "Golly, maybe I should stay home, too."

"Well, that's sweet of you, but Pa and the boys can get along without your help. I'll need you to help me when arrive at Pete's home. Now, eat breakfast and then we'll pack your new dresses Mrs. Balding made for you."

She folded her arms across her chest. "But I want the boys to go, too. Why can't they go and help Pete?"

. "Pearl, I told you I want them to stay with Pa. It will be good for the three of them to bond together. Mr. Peterson really likes you, and I know having you with me will lift his spirits."

"I know. I like him too, but I ain't never been anywhere without the boys. They'll be sad when we leave them." Pearl said, her lower lip jutting out.

"They're big boys now, and they need their Pa more than they need me. Come on and don't make me sad that I'm leaving them behind."

Jake and Joshua leaned their ears close to the bedroom door and listened to the girls' conversation. The boys scooted away from the door. "She ain't even sad she's leaving us. I believe I'm beginning to hate her," Jake stomped back to the table.

~

Pa, Lizzy, and the children rode to the train station and purchased two tickets to Austin, Texas. Pearl cozied up to the boys in the back and told them she really wished they were going with her. "I'll tell Pete you want him to hurry and come back here."

Jake's brow knitted together. "Don't tell him anything. I don't care if Lizzy or Pete ever come back. You take care because our sister might just leave you there." Jake was fighting back tears, but his anger helped him control himself.

"That's a lie. Lizzy wouldn't come back without me." Pearl's smile vanished.

"Libby, I don't want to go. I'm going to stay here with Pa." Pearl moved close to Herman. He smiled down at her and patted her small back.

Lizzy glanced over her shoulder at her little sister. "Now, Pearl, we've talked about this. Of course, you're going with me. Let's go to the bakery and get a sweet to take with us and the boys and Pa can take some home with them. We don't have long to wait for the train."

Once the train was moving away from Crooksville, the sisters waved at the boys. Pa waved but Jake and Joshua stood like stone statues. Libby couldn't help but notice how sad her little brothers looked.

~

After the train was out of sight, Herman gave the boys a nickel. Now, you two run to the dry-goods store while I run an errand.

"What you going to do Pa? We can go with you," Joshua said.

"I won't be but a minute, so head on over to the store. When you finish your purchases, sit on the bench out front." Pa gave each boy a little shove and walked toward the dressmaker's little house at the end of the street.

He knocked and opened the door at the same time. The doorbell jingled and Miss Balding appeared. "Well, my goodness, Mr. Montgomery. Are you here to pick up the dresses I made Pearl? If so, you're a little late. Lizzy got them a few days ago."

Herman started to speak but first needed to clear his throat. He suddenly felt tongue-tied. "No, I thought I'd stop by to say hello." Leaning closer to her, he quizzed. "Do you have a customer in the backroom?"

Blushing bright red, she twisted her body and whispered back. "No, we're alone."

"Well, that's good. I didn't want to take you away from your business. I had to come into town this afternoon. Lizzy and Pearl went to Austin. The boys and I are home alone for a while." He gave her a playful grin.

"My goodness, I'll have to prepare you something good to eat. I enjoy cooking, but I haven't cooked much since Mr. Balding passed."

He lifted a palm. "Please don't put yourself out. I thought I might come into town day after tomorrow and take you to supper if I'm not being too forward?"

"Oh my, Mr. Montgomery, I would enjoy that. I normally close my shop at five. Will six o'clock be a good time for you to come by?"

"Six will be just fine. Well, I better go and collect my boys and head home. Until then, goodbye." Herman doffed his hat and strutted down the street whistling.

Later that day when Pa finally came in from the barn, he wondered what the boys were doing sitting at the kitchen table drumming their fingers.

"Hey, Pa. What's for supper? We're hungry," Jake said as he watched his Pa head to his bedroom.

"Listen to me, boys. You are both old enough to make a sandwich or heat up some leftovers. I'm tired, so I'm going to bed."

Jake and Joshua stared at each other. "I can't believe Pa wants us to use the stove. Lizzy would never let us cook unless it was outside over the fire pit."

"Let's make a sandwich, eat some cookies and drink milk." Suddenly, Jake jumped up. "We've got to milk and feed the livestock their dinner. Come on, we'll eat later." Jake pulled Joshua off his chair and hurried to the barn.

"Joshua, I don't want to stay here with Pa. I know he will make us do all the work while Lizzy is gone. All he has on his mind is that woman in town."

"Where do you want to go? We ain't got no other kin to go and stay with," Joshua said.

"I think we should go to Yuma at the Indian reservation. I bet he'll let us stay with him and Lizzy will never think to look there for us."

Joshua kicked at a stone. "When do you think we should go?"

"Well, let's go into town tomorrow and get two tickets on the train. We will get off the train like we did with Lizzy at the first water stop. Then, we'll travel the same path we took to the reservation. Yuma will be happy to see us."

"Train tickets cost money. I have less than a dollar in my box."

"We can use the egg and cheese money in the kitchen. Let's get it down and count it." The boys rushed back into the house. Jake moved a chair, stood on it and took the can down from the cabinet. He poured the money out and counted it. "Wow, there's twelve dollars here. We'll have a couple more dollars after we carry the eggs in tomorrow. This will be plenty for two train tickets. Let's use the old backpack that Pete left here and pack a change of clothes, food to eat, and water to drink while traveling. The food will keep our strength up while walking through the woods."

"Gosh, Jake, you think of everything. I'm ready to get away from here. Lizzy doesn't want us and Pa couldn't care less if we eat. We are practically grown men."

"Come on, little brother. Let's finish caring for the animals and go to bed. We have a lot to do tomorrow."

After the animals were fed and the fresh eggs washed and packed in the same basket Lizzy used, the boys saddled one of the plow horses and left for town. Their first stop was the Mayberry's dry goods store. "How are you youngsters doing this morning?" Mr. Mayberry asked.

"We're fine. We brought in some fresh eggs like Lizzy does. Can we have the money, instead of putting it in your book? We want to buy a present for Pearl to give her when she returns."

"Of course. What do you want to buy Pearl?"

"Well, we aren't going to get it today. We need more money, so we'll wait until we bring more eggs."

The boys rode the horse over to the stable. "Toby, will you keep our horse until Pa comes in town and gets it. He will pay you for board and keep."

"Sure thing. Where you two going?" Toby asked.

"Just off on an adventure for a few days. See you!"

Chapter 33

The Pacific Railroad pulled into the station in Austin, Texas, with Pete standing on the train platform. He waved when he saw Lizzy looking out of the passenger car. When the train stopped, he rushed to her. "Lizzy, I am so pleased you could come so quickly. And look who you brought with you, my sweet Pearl. My goodness, little Miss, you look like you have grown a foot."

"Oh, Mr. Pete, I ain't grown too much. Miss Balding said my dresses fit the same except she has to make them longer.

"Well, you sure have gotten prettier, if that's possible." Pete reached and picked her up into his arms. Then he squeezed Lizzy's hand and gave her a sweet smile.

Lizzy's heart was full. She could only look wordlessly into Pete's eyes. She was happy and tried to hold her emotions in check lest he could see the glimmer of tears in her eyes. It had been a short trip on the train, but she was sad she had to leave her little brothers home. She felt torn between her little family and the man she loved.

"How is your father? Is he adjusting to being in the hospital?" Lizzy quickly asked Pete, attempting to get her mind off her family at home.

"Yes. He's ready to get the surgery over. After we arrived, he had a fever so the doctors wanted him to be better before they performed the operation. We'll go to the hospital after I get you and Pearl settled at the house. My two sisters-in-laws' were at the house preparing the rooms when I left."

"I hope I'm not taking them away from their families," Lizzy said as she glanced around at the dirty city streets. The big-footed horses picked up speed as Pete led them onto a smooth dirt road out of the city. Hugh oak trees came into view and Pearl pointed at the birds perched on their branches.

"How far to your home?" Lizzy asked.

"It should still be daylight when we get there."

Hours later, a huge house came into view. A farmer was plowing with a team of big mules. The black rows lay like ribbons across the land. Lizzy pointed to the farmer and asked Pete if he was working on the Peterson's property.

"Yes, that's Tabby. He has lived and worked for us for years. A nice man with a big family. His wife and children all work on the farm. You might get a chance to meet his wife. I believe she works in the kitchen." Pete drove around a large curve and stopped at the foot of a long bridge. He pointed to the big house. "There's home," Pete said, "If you look behind the house, you can see one of my brothers' farmhouses and in the other direction is the other brother's nice place."

"So, for now, you still live with your father? I know he's happy you're home."

"Actually, my father has willed the home place and acres of land surrounding it to me. My sisters-in-law's are unhappy that he did that, but my brothers both each have a lovely home and many acres of land."

"How do your brothers feel about you owning your parent's place instead of one of them?"

"They have never said anything to me about it. My father can do whatever he wants. Besides, he helped build their houses and helped them acquire farm animals. He has been very generous to them."

Suddenly, Lizzy got the nerve to ask Pete what she wanted to know. "Do you plan to live in Austin?"

"Lizzy, you and I have to discuss our future after Father's surgery. We'll have to make plans before we marry, that is, if you are still willing to share your life with me?" He gave her a shy grin and squeezed her hand. "Giddy-up," Pete snapped the reins, and the animals moved across the long bridge onto the Peterson's land.

"Is that big house where you live, Mr. Pete?" Pearl's eyes were big as a saucer.

"For now, Princess. You'll have a big room upstairs and one of the maids will ensure you have everything you need while staying here."

"Golly, I will be treated like a Princess." Pearl said as she moved closer to her big sister. "What about Lizzy? Where will she sleep?"

"Lizzy can choose her own room. She won't need a maid to stay with her because she's a big girl." Pete patted Pearl's shoulder.

Pete opened the front door and led Lizzy and Pearl inside the massive farmhouse. Lizzy stood with her mouth open for a second. The foyer was large and double doors closed off another area of the house. Lovely chandeliers hung from the high ceilings, and the floors shined with fresh beeswax. The upholstered fabric chairs were colorful with matching pillows. This wasn't just a house, to Lizzy, it was a mansion. A painting of Mr. Peterson hung over the large fireplace and the hearth looked like it had never been used.

"Good, Marilyn, I'm so pleased you're still here. I want you to meet Miss Lizzy Montgomery and her sister Pearl. Lizzy, this is Marilyn, who is married to my brother Will. You'll meet Will at dinner tonight.

"It's so nice to meet you, Mrs. Peterson. This is a lovely home."

The woman's smile didn't reach her eyes. "I'm glad you like it. Evelyn and I try our best to keep it looking nice."

Lizzy noticed the cold greeting from Pete's sister-in-law, but Pete continued with his introduction. "Marilyn, will you please show Lizzy the rooms upstairs where she can choose one to stay in while she's here."

"Of course, I already have a room prepared for her.

The maids have made her room very comfortable. We didn't know she was bringing a . . . child with her, but she can sleep in the room with her sister. Will that be all right?" She lifted her chin and stared at Lizzy, waiting for her to disagree with the arrangements.

Pete frowned. "Pearl can have her own room, Marilyn. She's a big girl and one of the maids can attend to her needs. Lizzy will be busy with me," Pete said as he greeted the housemaid.

Lizzy lifted a hand. "No, Pete. I would rather Pearl share my room. She will feel better if she is with me at night." Lizzy's hand shook between sadness and anger as she poked loose strands of hair behind her ears. She knew she wasn't welcome, but she wouldn't allow this woman to make her leave.

Pete motioned toward a woman with graying hair. "Lizzy, please meet the lady that practically raised me, Hester."

Lizzy offered her hand. "How do you do? It's so nice to meet the lady that raised this find man."

She grinned, clearly relieved. "It's nice that you're here. Pete's father had told me about you and your brothers and little sister, and I'm guessing this is little Pearl?" Hester bent down and shook Pearl's small hand. "I bet you're hungry, little one. Would you like to go to my kitchen and get some milk and cookies that will hold you over to dinner?"

"Yes, Madam, if it's all right with Lizzy."

"Go ahead and run along with Miss Hester. I'll go to our room upstairs."

"I'll bring you some tea or would you rather have coffee, madam? And please call me Hester, not Miss."

"Tea will be lovely, but you don't have to wait on me. I can come to the kitchen and get it."

"That's not the way we do things here, Miss Montgomery. We have servants to take care of us. Please allow them to wait on you. You aren't in the 'sticks' here," Marilyn said.

Hester and Pearl turned and left the foyer. Marilyn walked toward the staircase and said, "You coming, Miss Montgomery. I'm sure Pete has things to do since he just arrived." She didn't wait for Lizzy as she marched up the stairs. Lizzy turned to Pete and saw his face filled with anger.

"I'm sorry, Sweetheart. I hope Evelyn is nicer to you. Please tell me if she isn't."

"Don't fret, Pete. I'm a big girl. I can take care of myself."

Before the dinner hour, Lizzy stood and coiled her long hair then ran a comb through Pearl's hair. Bracing herself, she left her bedroom and walked downstairs. She wanted to protect her emotions from the crushing behavior that she received from Marilyn.

The door opposite the dining room was open. Voices came from the kitchen. As she neared, she heard the rattle of pans and dishes. Hester was giving Pete orders. "If you and your lady go to the hospital, I'll care for Pearl. She can help me bake pies for tomorrow's meals."

Lizzy paused in the doorway. The aroma delighted her nose, making her aware of her hunger. She walked to the kitchen door and gave Pete a big smile. "Good evening, Pete, Hester. Are we ready for dinner?"

"You look lovely, Sweetheart. And Pearl, you look beautiful. Hester has volunteered to keep you while we visit Father at the hospital."

"Yes I heard her and I know Pearl will love making pies. She like to help me make dumplings." Lizzy smiled at Hester as she smoothed Pearl's hair.

"Come, let's take our seats at the table. Will, Marilyn, Jeff, and Evelyn and their children will join us."

"That'll be nice. I look forward to meeting the rest of your family."

Lizzy took the chair that Pete pulled out for her. "I have no idea what Hester has cooked but it sure smells wonderful and I'm hungry."

Will and his children entered the dining room and

continued to the kitchen. Lizzy noticed that Will came out by himself. In a few minutes, Jess and Evelyn entered the dining room and went straight to the kitchen with their daughter in tow. They came back into the dining room with Marilyn and took their seats. Pete introduced his brother Jeff and wife Evelyn to Lizzy and Pearl.

"Welcome to our home, Miss Montgomery. Any friend of Pete's is always welcome," Evelyn said with a sweet smile.

"This is Pearl, my little sister. Will your children be joining us?" Lizzy asked.

"No, children are not welcome at the grownup's table until they are older and have learned manners," Evelyn said, and smiled at Marilyn.

"How in the world will they learn anything while eating in the kitchen?" Pete asked. Lizzy's twin brothers and Pearl eat every meal in the dining room. They have manners, and if they do something incorrectly, Lizzy instructs them on the proper way."

"Pete, dear, things are done differently in the big city. Country folks have their own way, if you know what I mean," Marilyn said.

"Lizzy, what does that mean—country folks? Pearl quizzed.

"Children are to be seen and certainly not heard, little girl." Jeff, Pete's brother, spoke for the first time. Pete's brother was looking at Lizzy as if she didn't belong at the table either.

Lizzy bottom lip began to quiver, and silent tears leaked down her cheeks. Pete placed a firm hand on her shoulder. She had forgotten that he was sitting next to her. "Use your napkin and wipe your face. I'll handle these rude people." Pete stood and looked all around the table. "I want you four to listen to me. While I'm home, I'll not have you making rude remarks to my guests. And I want your children to eat at this table with grownups. If you don't want to do as I request, you can eat at home. This is my house, and I have different rules than you have."

"This is not your house yet," Marilyn spluttered. "Your father isn't dead."

"Marilyn, listen to me. In fact, you all need to hear this. Father signed over his deed to this house and surrounding land to me before I left months ago. You all have your share of his property. I can do whatever I like with this place, and I told Father to let you come and go as you please because I thought you were caring for him. But, now I know wouldn't dare sully your lily-white hands cleaning or cooking. You have been acting like ladies of a great mansion. Well, I hate to tell you this, while I'm here, you'll stay at your own homes without my servants. If you want servants, hire yourself some."

Lizzy didn't believe Pete had the spunk to speak to his sisters-in-law's like he just did. She could tell even his brothers were surprised at his words.

"Now, I would appreciate it very much if you would go into the kitchen and bring your children in here to have dinner with us. I haven't seen them since I returned, and I would enjoy their company." Pete waited. Finally, Evelyn and Jeff stood and walked into the kitchen. Their daughter carried her plate and took a seat next to Pearl. Marilyn and Will stepped into the kitchen but didn't return. Hester said they took their boys and went out the back door and they wouldn't be joining the family.

"Well, that's their choice." Pete looked sad but told Hester to please serve dinner. We're starving."

After dinner, Lizzy and Pearl departed to their room. With the train ride and meeting the family, they both were worn out. Pearl undressed and crawled in the big four-poster bed. She was fast asleep soon after saying her prayers.

Lizzy sat on the edge of the bed. Slumping forward, she braced her elbows on her knees and held her face in her hands until the pounding in her head creased. She replayed the scene at the dinner table in her mind. Pete hadn't said anything about a future marriage, but he did make an enemy out of Marilyn. She was a dangerous woman.

LINDA SEALY KNOWLES

Chapter 34

The following day, Hester had laid out fresh loaves of bread, a platter of ham and bacon, and scrambled as well as fried eggs on the dining room's sideboard. It was a breakfast feast fit for a king.

Lizzy entered the kitchen with Pearl on her coattail. "Good morning, Miss Hester," called Pearl, as she ran over and begged to be picked up.

The morning sunshine was lovely. Lizzy noticed Pete drinking coffee on the small back porch. "Hester, can we eat outside with Pete?"

"Honey child, you can do whatever you like, but fix your plate before going outside. I'll bring you a pot of fresh coffee."

"Pearl, you want to eat inside the kitchen with me?" Hester asked.

"I'd like that but may I have bread with butter and jam and a glass of milk. I don't like coffee." Pearl said.

~

Pete's two dogs were barking as Marilyn entered the foyer. William, the butler, took her bag and shawl. "Where is everyone?"

"They're on the back porch having breakfast Miss," William said.

"Sure they are, country hicks, for sure," she said under her breath.

Clipped footsteps sounded in the kitchen. Marilyn

walked out onto the back porch. In the depth of her eyes, Lizzy read contempt. Lizzy also noticed for the first time that Marilyn was a beautiful woman. She wore her golden hair coiled into a crown on the top of her head, and her eyes matched her lovely hair. Her eyes reflected her angry mood. Her skin was unmarked, but her beauty was only skin deep. She was an ugly, angry person.

"Well, I see you're an early riser, Miss Montgomery. I thought I might be able to catch Pete *dearest* alone for a private conversation," she said as she signaled William to bring her a cup of coffee. "Marilyn, dearest," Pete said sarcastically, still smiling, "if you wanted to speak to me privately, you could have said so."

Lizzy stood. "Yes, Marilyn, I'll happily leave you alone with Pete. I can have my breakfast in the kitchen with Pearl. If you excuse me." Lizzy smiled sweetly and hurried into the kitchen.

"Now that you have rudely interrupted Lizzy and me, what is so important that you must speak to me privately?" Pete's skin warmed up.

"Since you've been away on vacation, traveling to see the western part of the state, your brother is about to toss his hat into the ring and run for governor. Once he decides, he'll need your support and some of your funds. How do you feel about helping him with both?"

Pete stared at his sister-in-law with a frown on his face. "I'm surprised to hear that Will is interested in politics. He has never mentioned anything to me about running for office. I would think he would want to be mayor of Austin before attempting to be governor of the State. You can't get much higher as a politician except to be president. Does he have grand ideas of becoming the next President? Or do you simply want to be the first lady?"

She rolled her eyes. "Don't be ridiculous. Running for governor is Will's idea. I'm just his wife who will help and stand beside him. You're his brother and I'd think you would be willing to support and help him any way possible to get him elected. Your Father will be so proud of him."

"Father is already proud of Will. He doesn't have to do anything to impress him." Pete stood and poured himself another cup of coffee. "Marilyn, I cannot do anything at the present to help Will with his political future. I have Father to think about and make sure he has all the help I can give him while he's recovering. Regarding my money, I am planning a future with Lizzy and her siblings. I don't know where we're going to settle down."

Marilyn's eyes lit up for a moment. "If you aren't going to live here, you must give Will this house. He'll need it to impress other politicians. We'll need to give grand parties to gain their support." Marilyn waltzed around the room like she was in a dream.

"This is my house and property to do with as I like. If I'm not going to live here, Father won't be here either. I will sell this place-- lock, stock and barrel."

"You can't do that," Marilyn screamed. "I don't care if you or your old man aren't here. Will and I must have this place. Don't you see? With this grand mansion, we'll look successful, and voters will know Will can run the state."

"If Will is going to run for governor, he'll need more than a mansion. He will have to sell himself to the people, not show off his assets. People don't care about rich people. They want an honest, God-fearing man they can trust. That's the man I'd vote for," Pete said as he opened the door to go inside.

She posted her hands on her hips. "Don't walk away from me, Pete. We still need to finish our discussion. You haven't agreed to help your brother. He needs money and I know you have plenty. You would help him if you cared for him."

He turned to her. "Listen to me. I'm not going to help you and Will with his new career. Both of my brothers got the same inheritance I did from our mama. The difference is I saved my money. I have no idea what you and Will have done with yours over the years. It is not any of my business, but my personal finances are mine and they're staying that way. Now, excuse me. I have business to take care of at the hospital." He strode toward the door.

"Pete," Marilyn said, stopping him from walking away. "I hate you." She grabbed the tail of her skirt and rushed off the back porch.

Lizzy greeted Pete as he came into the kitchen. "I'm sorry we couldn't help but overhear some of your conversation with Marilyn, especially the last part." She lowered her face and said, "I'm sorry she feels that way toward you."

Chapter 35

With their tickets in hand, the twins sat out of sight behind the train station. They waited until the train arrived about an hour later and the conductor called 'all-aboard.' After giving the conductor their tickets, they took a seat in the rear passenger car, not wanting to be noticed.

The boys stood at the window and watched the scenery go by. The train traveled for miles and finally pulled to a stop at the first water station. Jake motioned for Joshua to follow him, and they got off the train, like so many other men to stretch their legs.

Once the conductor called 'all-aboard', the boys pretended to step on the train, but just as it began to move, the boys stepped off and watched until the train was out of sight.

Walking back toward the trail that led them to the reservation, they squeezed under the barbed-wire fence and began hiking along the way they remembered. It seemed like they had been walking for hours when six braves jumped out into their path, shirtless with war paint on their faces and chest. The Indians nearly scared the boys to death. Jake recognized one of the braves, so he attempted to say something in their language.

"We know you, paleface," the braves said, laughing. "Come, we take to Yuma."

"Thanks, we came to live with him, if he will let us," Jake said.

Three braves walked in front of the two boys while the others trailed behind. Joshua whispered to Jake, "I'm so glad they found us. I wasn't sure we were going in the right direction."

"Same here. Yuma will be happy to see us I'm sure," Jake said.

~

What in the world are you two doing this far away from home? Where is your sister and the man she's going to marry, Pete?" Yuma's face was red and his neck veins were popping. The boys had never seen him so mad.

Jake frowned. "Lizzy left us with Pa while she went to be with Pete. She took Pearl but she left us behind. Pa don't care about us either. We've been doing our own cooking and taking care of the farm. Pa is only interested in some old woman in town. He doesn't care if we eat, so we decided to come and live with you."

"You are telling me that your sister is in Austin and your Pa is courting some woman in town. Lizzy thinks you're home with your Pa, safe and sound?"

Joshua's face reflected his brother's. "She don't care about us. We heard her telling Pa that she couldn't take care of us, only Pearl. She's going to marry Mr. Pete and live somewhere with him." The boys kept stepping away from Yuma. Yuma looked like he wanted to throttle them.

~

"Maybe, we shouldn't have come here, Joshua," Jake whispered, but Yuma heard him. Yuma really wanted to blister their backsides, but he controlled his temper.

Yuma pasted on his scariest face. "Here comes Morning Flower. She'll help prepare a place for you to eat and sleep. While you're here, you'll have chores to do just like before. I better not hear any grumbling from you either. I still feel like tanning your hides. When Lizzy finds you have left the farm, she's going to be so upset. And don't tell me again she doesn't want you. I know better," Yuma said.

Yuma gave Morning Flower a shy smile. "We have visitors again, without their sister or little Pearl. Will you help me care for them while they're here? I'll have to plan to take them back to their farm. Maybe you can come with me," he said. "Lizzy will be happy to see you."

"That would be wonderful. I haven't been off the reservation since I was a child. It will be an adventure." Morning Flower placed her hand on Jake's shoulder. "Do you hear that? I am going to go home with you when Yuma takes you."

"Lizzy won't be at the farm. She went to Austin, Texas to marry Mr. Pete. She didn't want us anymore."

"Young man, if those words come out of your mouth again, I'm going to place you in a teepee all alone, do you understand me?" Yuma sighed and left the boys with Morning Flower.

"Come on little braves. Let me show you where you're going to sleep. Afterwards you can join the other braves and eat with them."

After supper Yuma spoke to his father, Viho. "The little white boys have returned. They want to live here but I have to take them home soon."

"Did the little girl come with them?"

"No, they said that their sister doesn't want them anymore, but when she left their farm she did take Pearl, the little girl.

"I liked Little one. She was smart," the old man pointed to the top of his head. "And she made me laugh."

"She's always with her brothers. I know she's missing them." Yuma walked out of his father's teepee and went to sit with the little braves to eat.

~

Early the next morning, a bunch of big braves went hunting and came back with a basket of dead snakes. Snake meat was a delicacy. The boys were so excited, and several chose a snake then prepared to cut off his head, making sure it was completely dead before skinning it.

One of the braves pointed at Joshua. "You, paleface, grab a snake, cut off his head and begin skinning it. You eat, you work." Joshua looked into the basket of snakes that was slithering around on top of each other.

"They aren't dead. I could get bit."

All the boys laughed. "Yes, but you better choose one before we place your head in the basket."

"You better not touch me. Yuma will beat you if you touch me."

"Is that right. Now you know what the big warrior will do to us if we touch you?" the tall brave remarked as he walked toward Joshua.

Joshua glanced all around and the other braves had formed a circle near the basket of dangerous snakes. He looked right, then left, and suddenly dove between a young man's legs to escape into the forest. He ran until he was out of breath with the others on his heels. He saw a large tree with many branches. He scooted up the tree as high as he could go and scrambled out onto a big limb.

Yuma appeared out of nowhere. "What's going on here?" he demanded.

All the braves were silent until Yuma demanded once more. "Speak up or all of you will be in trouble."

Finally, after dragging his foot into the dirt, a very young brave spoke. "TomTom was going to make paleface cut off a head of one of the snakes in the basket and then skin it. All the snakes aren't dead. Pale-face was afraid. TomTom was going to poke the boy's head in the basket, so he ran. He's hiding in the treetop, but we can see him."

"Jon," Yuma called. "Climb up and drop the boy straight down. We'll catch him."

"I ain't coming down, Yuma. Make them go away." Joshua yelled.

Jon reached Joshua as he held tight to a limb. "Paleface, I am going to toss you to the ground."

"Are you nuts? You could kill me. Get back before I

make you fall."

Jon continued to get closer to Joshua until he was able to grab his foot. He pulled Joshua close to him, while Joshua kicked with the other foot.

"Leave me alone!"

Jon dangled Joshua with one foot. "Here he comes," Jon called to the braves on the ground. Before Joshua knew what happened, he went flying through the air with leaves and small branches scratching his skin until he was caught by Yuma and two big Indian braves. The jar of the fall knocked the breath out of him. He was sure he was going to die when Jon pushed him from the tree.

Yuma stood Joshua on the ground and held him up straight. Come with me. The rest of you go about your chores and take care of those snakes. I'm not happy and we'll have a discussion in a little while." Yuma placed his hand on Joshua's shoulder and pushed him forward.

He walked him to the large teepee.

Morning Flower raced over to Joshua and said, "So you were the one in trouble?" Without waiting for an answer she said, "Let me clean all those scratches."

Yuma patted the boy's shoulder. "Joshua, I'm taking you and Jake home today. As soon as Morning Flower is ready for the trip, we'll leave. Try to stay clean."

Chapter 36

After breakfast a farmhand hitched the black surrey to a pretty brown bay horse. Pete and Lizzy drove to the hospital to check on the judge. Once they arrived, they were told to wait in the patients' waiting room. Pete's father was with the doctor and he was giving home-care instructions.

"Nurse, we need to be in that meeting, since we are the ones that will be attending to my father once he is released."

"Please wait here and I will tell the doctor that you're here. Your name is?"

"Pete Peterson, the judge's son, and this is Miss Lizzy Montgomery."

After a few minutes, the nurse returned and motioned for them to follow her. She led them to a small room where the doctor and judge were waiting for them. As they walked down the hall, the judge's laughter came from a room they approached. A lady's voice was heard giggling and saying, "Oh judge, I am still in love with your son. I regret many times we didn't marry."

Pete had a grin on his face a mile wide, while Lizzy froze in her tracks. Pete didn't notice Lizzy had stopped walking. He rushed into his father's room and grabbed the most beautiful girl Lizzy had even seen. She was dressed in a deep, green velvet dress with a matching hat covering her lovely midnight black hair. She wore as much make-up as an actress on the stage, but it was becoming. Pete whirled her around and around. Lizzy felt very out of place, so she backed out of the room and rushed down the hall, then out the front door.

The doctor offered his hand to Pete. "Hello, Mr. Peterson. Your father is all ready to be discharged. I was going over a list of do's and don'ts for him while he's recovering."

"Just a second," Pete held up his hand to stop the doctor from talking. He looked all around the room and peeped down the hall. "Where did Lizzy go, Father?"

The doctor glanced at his pocket watch. "Mr. Peterson, I don't have all day. I have other patients waiting so please let me go over these instructions," the doctor was running out of patience.

"Excuse me doctor, but there are two ladies here to see the patient. They say they're his daughters-in-law's."

"For goodness sakes, send them in and I won't have to go over this list but once," the doctor said with a frown.

"Marilyn and Evelyn marched in the small room like they were royalty. "Good day, Mr. Peterson," Evelyn said, as Marilyn nodded at the judge.

"Pete, we had no idea you and Miss Montgomery would be here this morning. We could have come at a different time," Marilyn commented.

"It's good you came because I'm going home in a little while. The doctor was going over my home care instructions. Go ahead, doc, and finish. I know that Pete and Lizzy have taken everything in you said earlier."

"Everything is written on this sheet of paper. My nurse has made duplicates of it." the doctor pointed at a white sheet of paper. "The main thing I want to tell you, Judge, is the operation was a success, so therefore, the other doctors and I feel in time you'll walk. Be patient, exercise every day, and rest. I don't need to see you again for three months. The nurse will schedule an appointment before you leave."

"What about my bill? Will I pay today or will I be sent a bill?'

"Your son can go see about your bill before you're

released. You have been a wonderful patient and I'm going to miss our checker games."

~

A large group of reporters were waiting at the entrance of the hospital to ask Mr. Peterson questions about his health and if he would be returning to the bench anytime soon.

Lizzy stood over in a corner of the waiting room, waiting for Pete to come out of his father's room. The two sisters-in-law's noticed her.

Evelyn motioned for her to stay put. "For goodness sakes, Miss Montgomery, stay in the background. You aren't dressed to be seen with the judge's family while in the presence of reporters. You look like a poor-relation in that pitiful outfit you're wearing. Go on outside and hide behind the surrey."

Lizzy looked down at her dress. It was the nicest one she owned, and she had worked hours making it. She couldn't believe her attire would embarrass the Peterson's family. Her face heated as she stared at the two women who were attempting to get the attention of a reporter. Marilyn wanted to say something about Will running for governor and Evelyn wanted to announce a big fall tea that she was hosting. Neither mentioned the judge.

Pete left Judith, his lovely friend, in the room with his father while he took care of the hospital bill. He continued to search around for Lizzy. Marilyn and Evelyn were standing at the front door, blocking it so the reporters couldn't leave.

"Girls," Pete called to his sisters-in-law's. "Where's Lizzy?" he said as he attempted to remove Judith's grip on his arm who'd follow him out.

Evelyn looked his way. ""I told her to take her ragtag self out to the surrey. She's an embarrassment to all of us with the way she's dressed. Now, excuse me, Pete, I'm trying to speak to a reporter."

"Pete, sweetheart, who's this ragtag girl Evelyn spoke about?" Judith wondered.

Pete sighed and tried to make Judith turn him loose.

"Judith, it has been wonderful seeing you again and I appreciate you visiting Father, but I'm engaged to be married to a young lady named Lizzy. I wanted to introduce you to her, but for some reason she has disappeared. I must get Father in the surrey and find my fiancée. I hope you'll come out to the house for dinner before I have to leave. Good day," Pete rushed over to his father, took the back of his wheelchair and pushed him out to the surrey.

Lizzy stepped out from behind the black surrey and reached for the judge's hand.

Pete blew out a breath. "Oh, there you are. Where did you go?"

She ignored Pete and turned to the judge. "It so good to be able to take you home. I know the hospital staff has been good to you, but your family will take excellent care of you." She opened the back door and picked up a soft blanket to lay over his legs once Pete and an orderly placed him in the backseat.

"Good day," the orderly closed the surrey door.

"Good day to you young man. Thank you for all of your help. The next time I see you, I pray I'll be walking." The judge tipped his hat.

Pete helped Lizzy into the front of the surrey and unhitched the reins. "Lizzy, where did you go? The doctor gave me instructions about Father's home-care, then you were gone from the room. I also wanted you to meet Judith, an old friend of mine."

She smirked. "She didn't look like an 'old friend' to me. It appeared to me she was an old lover of yours who had been waiting for your return."

"I have never seen this side of you, Lizzy. Jealousy?" Pete chuckled, but Lizzy didn't even smile at his comment.

She lifted her chin. "I have every right to be concerned. You looked like two long-life lovers."

He chuckled. "Believe me Judith, I mean Lizzy . . . I haven't thought about her in years."

"Really, she seemed to still be on your mind." Lizzy

looked forward, making plans to pack and leave on the first train to Crooksville. With Marilyn and Evelyn's resentment toward her and now, Pete's lover returning, she couldn't stay.

~

William, the butler and Hester, the housekeeper, rushed out the front door to welcome the judge home. "It so good to have you home. Now, you'll get well. William and I will care for you." Hester fussed over the judge.

"I have missed your cooking, Hester. Please fix me something special tonight. I'm starving for your food." The judge handed her the blanket that covered his legs.

"William, will you retrieve the wheelchair from the back and help me get Father settled into it. He can push himself around a little, but he'll need a lot of help. We need to settle him in a downstairs bedroom."

William nodded. "Hester and I have prepared the front room for him. We moved furniture in the room so his visitors can sit and have refreshments. He can look out the two big windows that oversee the front of the house." William took the judge's right arm and leg while Pete took his other side, then they settled him in the wheelchair.

"That wasn't too hard, now, was it men?" The judge laughed as William pushed him into the house. All the other maids were standing in the foyer and clapped when the men entered. The judge smiled at each one. He gave a little wave toward them and said, "Thank you. Now, get back to your chores."

When the judge was tucked in bed, he stretched his arms. "It feels so good to be home," he said to Lizzy as she smoothed the blanket over his feet. "And it's wonderful having you here. I'm surprised my grandchildren didn't drop in today to see me. I really love my little boys. Has Pearl been playing with them?"

"No I'm sorry to say. They met her at dinner the first night we arrived, but I haven't seen them since. That's all right. Hester has kept her busy in the kitchen. As far as them coming to visit you today, their mamas knew you'd need to rest. I'm sure they will come tomorrow." Lizzy tucked his covers under his arms and leaned down and kissed him on the forehead. She had learned to love this old man and she was sad she wouldn't see him again.

Pete entered the door and gave Lizzy a big smile. "It's so sweet of you to help Father."

Lizzy said good night to the judge and walked past Pete and closed the bedroom door without a word.

~

"Well, Father, how do you feel? I bet you are worn out from the long trip home and eating the delicious meal Hester prepared for you," Pete chuckled as he took his father's hand.

"Yes, son, I'm happy to be home, but I am sorry to say Lizzy is not happy here. You need to talk with her and start making plans for your future. If you marry, you'll have to decide where you're going to live. If you decide to stay here, well that will be just fine. I believe the boys would love living in this big house and having a lot of help with the chores. But, Pete, if you make plans to move back to Lizzy's place, I'd be willing to move with you, that is, if you would allow me to live with you."

"Father, believe me. I'll never leave you alone. Lizzy and I will talk tonight. So, please close your eyes and get some rest."

Pete closed the door and noticed his father's eyes were already closed. He walked upstairs and knocked on Lizzy's bedroom door but she didn't answer. He knocked softly once again, but she didn't answer. He put his ear against the door but it was silent inside. Maybe she'd retired early.

Pete awoke early and headed downstairs to have coffee. He lifted the lids on the food and smelled the wonderful food on the sideboard. "Good morning, Hester. Has Lizzy and Pearl come down for breakfast?"

"Not yet. Soon, I'm sure, because Miss Lizzy is not one to lay about."

"She is an early riser. I'm too hungry to wait for them, but I will join them for coffee when they arrive."

Hester brought Pete a handful of unopened correspondence once he completed his meal. She poured him coffee while he began looking through the stack of letters. "Hester, would you mind checking on the girls? I have a lot of things to take care of today and I really need to speak with Lizzy before I have to go see Father's lawyer.

"Maybe Miss Lizzy is having trouble with Pearl this morning. We'll be down in a minute." Hester knocked on Lizzy's door but when she didn't answer, she opened the door and called her name. In one quick glance, Hester knew the room was empty and all of Lizzy's personal items were gone. She rushed down the staircase, stopping to catch her breath before entering the dining room.

"Lizzy has gone. She took Pearl and all of their belongings."

Pete leaped from the dining table and rushed out the front door. He saw a field hand and questioned him about the whereabouts of Miss Montgomery. "William drove her away about thirty minutes ago. Can I help you with something?"

"No, thank you. Would you please saddle my big bay? I need to change clothes and I'll be right out."

~

Lizzy and Pearl stood on the back platform of the passenger car and waved bye to William. He had been a good friend to her while she had stayed at the mansion. She would miss Hester and William. They had been kind and helpful to Pearl and her since they arrived at Pete's home. She wished she could say the same about his two brothers and their wives. They treated her like scum.

Lizzy took Pearl's hand and a porter led them to a large seat next to a window. "May I get you some refreshments, madam? Water or coffee?"

"Mercy, I had no idea we would get such grand treatment."

"Well, madam, a gentleman in the first car told me to get you whatever you desired."

"A gentleman? Who?" Lizzy asked, because she didn't know anyone traveling.

"Can't say, but he's a nice man and he travels a lot on this train. I don't think he means any harm, but I will be watching over you and the little one while you are in my section. Don't you worry, you hear?"

"Thank you, sir. What's your name?"

"Henry madam, just Henry." He tipped his hat and walked up the aisle to help some other passengers.

Lizzy made Pearl and herself comfortable. She felt better knowing the porter would be watching over them. She wasn't afraid, but she had not traveled on a train by herself before.

After the six- hour trip to Crooksville, the train arrived before dark. Lizzy led Pearl off the train, and they walked to the livery stable. She waved at a few people on the boardwalk, but she didn't stop to make small talk. She wanted to get to the livery before it closed for the night. Toby was watering some horses when she entered.

"Hello Toby," Lizzy called to him.

"Well, hello to you to Miss Montgomery. What are you doing in town this late in the evening?" Toby had noticed that she had luggage when she entered the wide double doors. He didn't see any means of transportation for her.

It felt so good to be welcomed home by someone. "We just arrived on the train from Austin, and I need to rent a horse and carriage. Do you have something I could use to drive home until tomorrow morning?"

"If you wait just a few minutes, I'll drive you and Pearl home. My pa would skin me alive if I let you travel home alone when it will be dark soon." Toby gave his last charge a bucket of water and dried his hands.

"I won't be but just a moment. I'll hitch the horse to the carriage, and we'll be ready to go. Do you need to fetch anything from town before we leave?"

"That's nice of you, but no. We're tired and ready to be home. I know my little brothers will be happy to see us."

~

Toby glanced at Miss Montgomery but didn't say anything. She had no idea that her two brothers had ran away while she was gone. He didn't think he should be the one to tell her. Pa wouldn't like for him to stir up trouble when he didn't have all the answers. Miss Montgomery was going to be very upset because everyone knew she was more of a mama to those boys than a sister.

Chapter 37

Lizzy questioned Toby about what had been happening in town while she had been gone. Unfortunately, Toby didn't offer much information as he continued to look forward. Lizzy was surprised he was so quiet, but he must be tired from working a long day.

When Toby drove into the yard of Lizzy's farm, she noticed construction on the new house had begun. The flooring of the house had been laid and two sides of the house stood. Lizzy couldn't believe that so much had been built while she was gone. She wasn't sure if Pete or her papa had hired the men to help with the construction. Although she remembered speaking with Pete about the design of the house, but nothing had been confirmed.

Toby pulled up to the door and jumped down to help Lizzy and Pearl down close to the porch. The front door opened, and Herman stepped out and gave Lizzy a big smile. "Well, I wasn't expecting you home so soon," Herman said. "Come here, Pearl, and give your old pa a big hug."

Lizzy head was on a swivel as she looked around for her little brothers. She was disappointed they had not come running outside to greet her and Pearl.

"I best get on home, Miss Montgomery," Toby said.

"Wait," Lizzy reached into her bag and took out a dollar. "I can't thank you enough, Toby. I will thank your father when I see him. He has raised a wonderful young man."

"Aww shucks, Miss Montgomery. I'm glad you're home. See you soon." Toby jumped back on the wagon and drove toward town.

"Pa, where are the boys?" Lizzy had walked up on the porch and looked toward the barn.

"Lizzy, after you left, while I was in town, the boys ran off. The deputy and many men in town have looked everywhere for them. I have no idea why they decided to run away."

Lizzy nearly fell down. She couldn't believe her brothers were out somewhere all alone. She had no idea why they would leave home.

Lizzy took Pearl inside and cooked some bacon and eggs with buttered toast for supper. Afterwards she helped dress her for bed. Once the kitchen was cleaned, she sought her pa out. "Pa, what were you doing in town without the boys?"

"Are you blaming me for the boys running away?" He frowned.

"No, I'm just asking why you left them at home. I never go in town alone without an adult watching over my siblings. They're too young to be left by themselves."

"Well, they were busy doing their chores and I wanted to go see Miss Balding. I wanted to ask her to have supper with me. I wasn't gone but a couple of hours."

She sighed. "It's all my fault. They wanted to go with me, but I had no idea they were so upset. I really thought they knew I went to help take care of Pete's father. I guess I forgot they are still very young." Lizzy walked across the room and asked her Pa, "How are we going to find them?"

"I thought we could contact Yuma. I believe he could track them."

"But, Pa, how can he track them when they have been gone for days?"

He shrugged. "I still think we should reach out to him. I know he'd come and help." Herman had looked the countryside over and questioned many farmers.

"I will go into town tomorrow and asked Mr. Mayberry if he knows a young man who will go to the reservation with a note to Yuma. I don't know anything else to do but try to go myself." Lizzy wiped tears from her eyes and walked toward her bedroom where Pearl was already sleeping. "I will take a look at the construction on the new house in the morning. Did you or Pete contact the men to come and start building?"

"Pete did that before you two left. It was to be a surprise. He said he wanted a new house for you and the kids, even if you didn't move to Austin."

"So, he plans to stay in Austin?"

"Now, don't go putting words in my mouth. I don't know what the man is planning. I thought you would know that." Herman said as he closed his bedroom door.

Pearl said at the breakfast table early the next morning. "Lizzy where are my bratty brothers? Are they hiding from us?"

"Pearl, I believe the boys were upset I left them home when we went on the train."

"I told Pa and you the boys would want to go with us. He said they would be in your way. I think they heard him say that, because Joshua said to me I was your favorite. I told him I didn't know what that meant and he said you loved me more than you loved Jake and him."

"Oh, my goodness. I wish you'd told me that. I had no idea they were so upset with me." Lizzy sat down and held her face in her hands. She just wanted to scream and cry her heart out. She hardly slept last night thinking about all the things that could happen to her little brothers.

Pearl, please go get dressed. You and I are going into town and see if we can get some help to find the boys." Lizzy stood, "Listen I heard a wagon pull into the yard. Let's go see who it is."

Lizzy couldn't believe her eyes. Sitting on the bench seat of a large wagon was Yuma and Morning Flower. In the back, her brothers peeked around them.

"Thank God, Yuma. You found my brothers."

"Wrong, Lizzy. They found me a few days ago." Yuma said as he helped Morning Flower to the ground.

Jake and Joshua leaped down and raced to Lizzy. "We're sorry we worried you but Yuma took good care of us. We knew you wouldn't care if we visited with him while you were gone."

Yuma stood firm, staring down at the two young boys, "Jake, you know you weren't visiting. Don't cover up your bad actions. I won't go along with your tale. You know you did wrong."

Lizzy looked at Jake and shook her head. "Let's go inside and get something to eat. You've traveled many hours. And Morning Flower, it is wonderful you came with Yuma. I'm so happy to have you here."

Morning Flower stepped forward and hugged Lizzy. "I'll help you prepare a meal. May I go to your outhouse first?"

Yuma took Morning Flower's hand and pointed to the side of the house. "I have got to put the horses in the barn and feed them."

Herman came from the barn and smiled at Yuma. "I see you have the boys. Lizzy was going to go to town and get someone to travel to your reservation and ask for your help."

"The boys arrived at my village a few days ago. I had things to do before I could bring them home. I scolded them good and put them to work while they were there. They knew I was very angry with them for running away from home."

Herman tapped his hat on his knee. "I'm sure happy to see them, safe and sound. Lizzy has nearly cried her heart out when she discovered they were missing, and we'd done everything we could do to find them."

"I'm happy to have brought them home and that Lizzy is home." Yuma walked the two horses into a separate stall. He gave them both feed and pitched hay in front of them. He filled two buckets of water and placed them in the stalls.

Walking back to the house, he headed over to the new

construction and climbed up on the floor foundation. He stomped on the floor as he walked across to look at the newly erected wall frames. As he was looking at the window frame, a wagon of men drove up and parked their wagon next to the barn.

Yuma jumped down off the new floor and greeted the men. "Hello," Wilbur Barnes, the foreman of the job, reached a hand out to Yuma. "You must be the new man that Mr. Peterson hired."

"Sorry, I'm not. My name is Yuma and I live on the Indian reservation north of here. I brought Miss Montgomery's boys home."

"Oh, that's great news. Some of my men joined the search for them a few days ago. I'm sure happy you found them."

"Thanks. Your men are doing a good job on the new house. The floor is very strong." Yuma said, as he walked to the house and entered the door. He smelled bacon which caused his stomach to growl.

The boys and Pearl were sitting at the table waiting to be served by Lizzy. She offered her Pa, Morning Flower and Yuma a plate of food before the children. Once the grown people had their coffee, Lizzy placed pancakes, her brothers' favorite, and bacon on a plate. She poured them a glass of milk. Lizzy offered the grace while everyone bowed their heads. Lizzy praised the Lord for bringing her siblings home and gave thanks for their friendship with Yuma and Morning Flower. Everyone said 'amen' when she finished.

After the adults completed their meal, Yuma softly asked Lizzy where Pete was and how was the judge doing after his surgery. She smiled, and said Pete was still in Austin with his childhood sweetheart. And as for as the judge was doing, he would be able to walk in the future if he exercised and tried to walk each day. She was very hopeful for his recovery."

"Lizzy, I don't believe Pete is staying in Austin with someone else. He loves you and the children, and I know you have misunderstood his reasons for remaining in Austin."

"Yuma, you weren't there. Besides, I could never live in Pete's world in Austin. I don't fit in there. His brothers and sisters-in-law's have not accepted me as Pete's bride-to-be. They think I'm poor white trash."

"What?" he shook his head and sighed really big. "I don't believe it."

"Well, like I said, you weren't there. I couldn't do anything right. I wanted to take care of myself. Their servants had enough work to do without waiting on Pearl and I. My clothes were unfit to wear out in public. They wouldn't take care of the judge, but he didn't care, He only wanted me, which they resented. Like I said, if Pete wants to marry me, he will have to live here."

"I believe that is his plan. Why else would he be building a big house?"

"I had no idea he was planning this house while we were gone. We had only talked about it and I did look over a few designs." Lizzy circled Yuma as she spoke. "I have to admit I was more than stunned when I discovered Pete wrapped in the arms of his old, beautiful sweetheart. I 'm sure they didn't see me. I was in shock. I couldn't stand to watch them any longer so I had to leave." She wiped tears from her eyes. "Pete has to decide what he wants out of life."

Yuma frowned. "This doesn't sound like the man I know. The man that you nursed back to health and the man who loves you and the children. Something is very wrong. I'm sure he will come soon, if he's not already on his way."

"I'm beginning to believe I chose the wrong man to fall in love. You are so gentle and kind." Lizzy said, as Morning Flower entered the room.

"Yes, he is and he has always been that way. That's two reason I love him." Morning Flower quickly rushed over to Yuma and placed her arm around his waist. "He's my big strong warrior," she said, making sure Lizzy knew who Yuma belonged to.

Lizzy nodded. "Those are the features I learned about

him very quickly. I also saw the love he had for you whenever he looked into your big brown eyes. I wish I saw the same love from Pete."

"Lizzy, Yuma tells me your Pete loves you very much." When Lizzy didn't respond to Morning Flower Yuma immediately jumped into the conversation.

"He does love her and she'll learn this very soon. I'm sure he is on his way here," Yuma said.

Lizzy smiled and said it was time for all of them to get some rest. "I know you've had a long trip."

Chapter 38

Early the next morning Herman was working on the new house. He was bent over and drove nails into two-by-four boards when he grabbed his chest. The pain nearly tumbled him to the ground.

"Hey old man, are you all right?" Mr. Barnes dropped his hammer on a table and walked over to Herman.

"Sure, I'm fine." Herman stood and wiped his mouth with a hanky.

"You better go in the house and get some coffee and rest a while. You're white as a sheet."

"I could use some coffee. You want me to bring you a cup?"

"No, just take care of yourself." The day was nice and sunny, but not too hot.

Just as Herman stepped down from the floor, he fell flat on his face. Mr. Barnes yelled for the men to help Herman. "Go get Miss Peterson and one of you ride into town and bring the doctor back."

~

At the sound of a man's shouts, Yuma stepped out of the barn and saw a cluster of men gathered around another person that lay stretched out on the ground. He hurried over to the group of men. Herman was lying as still as death. He knelt beside him and placed his vest under the old man's head. "Herman, can you hear me?"

Lizzy rushed to her father's side. "Pa, oh Pa, can you hear me?" She told the men to make a stretcher and carry her pa into the house."

The foreman said, "Miss Peterson, I sent for the doctor. Hopefully, he'll be here soon."

"What happened? Did he fall off a ladder or something?"

"No, madam. He was pounding nails into lumber, and he nearly fell over. I told him to stop and go into the house to get some rest. Thought a little rest and coffee would make him feel better. He was already white as a sheet. After he got up from the floor, and started to the house, he fell over. The men stretched him out, but he hasn't said a word."

Several men came carrying a homemade stretcher. Yuma and three others picked Herman off the ground and placed him on the stretcher and followed Lizzy in the bedroom. The men placed Herman onto the bed, then one man helped to remove his work boots.

Lizzy rushed into the kitchen and filled a pan with water. She grabbed a rag and hurried back to her pa's bedside. She bathed his face and neck and spoke softly to her pa but he didn't respond. "Mr. Barnes, Yuma, I'm worried that Pa can't hear me or make any movement. Perhaps he had a heart attack, but he has never said anything about hurting before."

"Now, Lizzy, wait until the doctor arrives. Just keep your pa comfortable. Remember sometimes people can hear others talking even though they can't make any responses." Yuma motion for Morning Flower to come into the room and sit with Lizzy.

"I'm going into the kitchen and make the children a sandwich for lunch. They are very worried about their pa." Yuma told the children to take a seat at the kitchen table while he prepared them some food. "Your pa is still asleep, but the doctor will be here soon." He took bread and cheese out to make sandwiches. It was the best he could do.

A furrow formed between Joshua's eyebrows. "That woman in town probably did this to Pa."

"What woman? There wasn't a woman here."

"Well, he went into town and stayed real late. He was spending a lot of time with her. She's really the reason Jake and I went to your place."

Yuma set the sandwiches before the children. "Now, how did she make you leave home?"

Jake piped up. "Pa only wanted to go to town and be with her. He didn't do any chores or cook us any food to eat. All he had on his mind was hugging and kissing that woman. I bet he was thinking about her when he became ill."

Yuma shook his head as he set glasses of milk before them. "If he has a lady friend, that doesn't mean it was her fault that he's not well. Be careful about blaming someone."

"All right, if you say so." Joshua said, rolling his eyes at Jake.

"Do ya' think that pa might marry and get us a new mama?" Pearl said.

"Hey, dummy, we have a mama. Lizzy has been our mama for years and we don't need an old woman coming here telling us what to do," Jake shouted. *"Go wash your hands and your face. Clean your feet before coming inside."* Jake shook his finger at the other kids while mimicking Miss Balding.

"Jake, you don't need to shout. Your pa is not well, so settle down." Yuma scolded.

"Yuma, the doctor just drove up the lane." Mr. Barnes came into the kitchen and poured himself a cup of coffee.

Yuma hurried to the front door and guided Doctor Hayes to the front bedroom. Let me know if I can help you," Yuma said.

Lizzy and Morning Flower stood as Doctor Hayes came into the room. "Doctor Hayes, thank goodness you weren't out on call. Pa fell over and he hasn't woken up. I tried to wake him and get him to speak, but he hasn't opened his eyes or said a word."

"Stand aside and let me examine him, Lizzy," Doctor Hayes said.

~

Lizzy moved slowly away from the bed. She eased only a few feet from her pa, afraid that his heart had given way and the doctor wouldn't be able to help him. She watched Doctor Hayes listen to her pa's heart. He checked his pulse on his wrist and at his neck. He checked his eyes and spoke to Herman, but he didn't get a response.

"Lizzy," the doctor said softly, "your pa's heart is very weak. I can hardly hear or feel a heartbeat. He's in a bad way, and I don't think he has long to live. I'm so sorry there isn't anything I can do to help him." He placed his instruments in his black bag and snapped it shut.

Lizzy eased down on her knees next to her pa's frail body. He appeared so lifeless and frail. Reaching for the pan of water, she dipped a clean rag into it and squeezed it out. She placed it on her pa's face and wiped his forehead. Then she leaned her head down on her pa's chest and prayed.

Suddenly, Herman took in a deep breath and his body felt limp. "Doctor Hayes, come quickly." Lizzy called and stood up.

Doctor Hayes listened to Herman's heart, lifted his eyes and felt the veins in his neck. He reached down and pulled up the quilt and covered his face.

"I'm sorry Lizzy. Your Pa has gone." He peered around at the others in the room. "Let's move into the front room and give Lizzy a few minutes alone."

Lizzy fell over her pa's covered body and cried her heart out. Li, her brothers joining her and bowing their heads. "Oh Lord, this isn't fair. Pa has only been back in our lives for a few months. He suffered at the hands of bad people for years and finally got freed to make it back to us. Pa has brought joy and laughter into our lives. How am I going to handle his loss, on top of me losing the man I love? I just don't know if I can go on."

When she said she couldn't go on, both boys hugged their sister. "You have to go on, Lizzy mama. We love and need you so much." Tears were streaming down the boys' faces. "Please don't leave us. What would Pearl do without you?"

Lizzy took her little brothers in a tight grip. "I'm sorry babies. I will never leave. Pa couldn't help leaving us. His heart just gave out. And I only went to Austin to help Pete with his father. I never wanted you to think that I was going away and not coming back. I knew that I couldn't take care of you while taking care of Mr. Peterson. Pa wanted me to take Pearl. He said she was too much for him to handle but you would help him and you could take care of yourselves."

"We're sorry. We can't say anything bad about pa now that he died, but Lizzy he didn't take care of us. That's the reason we went to be with Yuma. Honest!"

She patted their shoulders. "Well, let's put this all this behind us. We have a lot to do now. The cemetery needs to be raked and cleaned. I'm going to prepare Pa for burial." Lizzy burst out crying again and the boys grabbed her around the legs and sobbed. She patted the boys on their backs. "I'm all right now. It's just hard to believe he's gone. I really loved him."

Morning Flower entered the bedroom. She had heard Lizzy say that she was going to prepare the body for burial. "Lizzy, I help you bathe and dress your pa. Yuma said the foreman is going to build a box coffin built. He and his men have started on it in the barn.

~

The death of Lizzy's Montgomery's papa had spread like wildfire. Wagons of families pulled into the front yard. The ladies carried big bowls of food while their husband unpacked shovels and picks.

Yuma stood on the porch and welcomed everyone. He guided the women folk into the kitchen while the men huddled together outside. Mrs. Mayberry introduced herself to him and asked where was Lizzy?"

Yuma led Mrs. Mayberry to the bedroom and stood at the door. Mrs. Mayberry entered the bedroom and saw Lizzy and her little brothers standing at the foot of the bed, where their Pa was covered with a lovely quilt.

"Lizzy, I took it on myself to bring some nice white material to line the coffin. Once it is built, several ladies will help me prepare the inside. If you will, please lay out the clothes you want to dress Herman in. If you want him to have a suit, I will go back to town and get one for you at the store."

Lizzy looked up at her through her tears. "No, Mrs. Mayberry. Pa never worn a suit. I'll dress him in his nice overalls and a new plaid shirt that I bought him weeks ago. He never wore them. I want him to look like himself. You do understand, don't you?"

"Of course, dear. I think he'll look fine. Do you want some help with bathing his body? I'll help you, if you like."

"Thank you, but I would like to spend this private time with him alone." Lizzy could smell delicious food coming from the kitchen. "It's so nice of the community to bring food. I know the children will appreciate it."

"Several ladies have volunteered to sit up with you tonight. I can too."

"Oh, I forgot about that. Do you know if Preacher Booker has been notified? I need him to perform the service over Pa.

"Yes, he's here. I believe I saw him in the kitchen with a plate of food." Mrs. Mayberry smiled. "You know his wife told me, the only thing he liked about burying people was the food." Mrs. Mayberry left the room, leaving Lizzy alone with her father.

After Lizzy bathed and dressed her pa for burial, she went to the closet and pulled down one of her nice day dresses. She would like to look nice as she greeted everyone that had come to help her. Lizzy pulled out a lovely black dress that she had made to wear to one of her neighbors' burial a year ago. She would try to make herself a black veil this evening when everyone had gone home.

After feeling presentable, she left the bedroom and

greeted many of the ladies who had come to help and offer their condolences.

Mr. Barnes, the foreman of the construction crew, rushed to Lizzy and took both of her hands in his. "Miss Montgomery," he said softly. while looking over his shoulder at the other women watching him, "if I can do anything for you, please call on me. I'm heartbroken for you. Your Pa was a nice man and I feel so sorry this happened to him while working for me. Please call on me if you need even the smallest thing. I'm here for you."

"Well," one of the ladies said. "You would think he wants to take charge of your life, Miss Lizzy. How long have you known this man?"

"Please, he was only trying to be nice. I don't know him at all." Lizzy went into the kitchen where one of the ladies poured her a cup of coffee.

From the window, she watched the ladies direct the bigger boys to place boards together to make several large tables. After sheets were spread over the boards, the women filled the tables with platters of food. By the barn, the men gathered at the outside pump and washed their faces and hands then joined the women. Lizzy headed outside to join everyone at the tables.

After Reverend Booker said grace, the ladies served the men's plates. The men sat on the end of the porch, several benches had been taken out of the back of wagons, and many sat on quilts on the ground.

Lizzy tried to eat, but her appetite was gone. She placed her fork in her plate and massaged her temple. The throbbing headache reminded her that she needed to eat. She would need strength to get through the night and all day tomorrow. *Tomorrow.* What a sad day that would be for her and the children. She took a bite of food, chewed it slowly and forced herself to swallow.

As she walked over to the children who sat on the porch, she heard one man say that the burial box was ready. The *burial box.* Hearing the words bought reality pouring down on her. Her legs wobbly as she reached the porch and the whole porch felt like it was swaying.

"Are you alright," Yuma ran over. He took Lizzy's arm and moved her to the porch swing. "I'll get you some coffee. Don't move from this spot," he ordered.

Chapter 39

The eulogy was short. Not much had happened in Pa's life. The pastor talked about his marriage to his lovely wife Marie and the four children he'd sired. He was a nice man, not really a Christian man, but kind to everyone. Lizzy stood at the gravesite with her three siblings. They stood like little soldiers with tear-stained cheeks. Lizzy wept as friends sang "We Shall Gather at the River". The coffin was lowered as everyone sang *Nearer My God to Thee*.

The faces of the mourners were solemn, and a few of the ladies squeezed out a tear or too, but Lizzy knew she was the only true mourner. She felt as if her heart had gone down in the grave with her pa.

After the service, many of the people shook her hand or gave her a light hug. As she was preparing to place the flowers she had been holding on her pa's grave, a voice that she had longed to hear said, "Lizzy, I'm here and I'm so sorry."

She was pulled into Pete's sweet embrace and held tight. Over the man's shoulder, she saw Judge Peterson surrounded by her siblings. Pearl had climbed in his lap in the wheelchair. Pushing away from Pete, she looked into his eyes. "Pete, I was expecting you to return, but not so soon. Did you learn of Pa's death?"

"We can't talk here, but I had to come to you. I brought Father with me. And no, we only learned about the burial when we got off the train in town. Toby, the stable owner's son, told me about the service while I rented a carriage. Father and I stood over to the side, watched and listened to the service. I didn't want to interrupt or cause a scene.

Pete stood close by as people passed Lizzy, offering their condolences as she stood by the grave. He took the flowers she held and knelt down on one knee. Smoothing the dirt into a mound, he laid the lovely wildflowers on the dirt. Pete stood, brushed the dirt off his pants, and smiled at Lizzy. "I'll have a marker made for him soon."

"Pa will like that. I had always wanted to get one for Mama, but . . . oh well, when we order Pa's, we can get mama a nice one too."

Pete took a firm hold onto Lizzy's elbow and led her over to his father. "Hello, Judge," Lizzy said. "Pearl, please get off Judge Peterson's lap." As Pearl slid off, he said, "Lizzy, I'm sorry about your Pa. I was looking forward to spending time with him."

His eyes trailed after Pearl who took Hester's hand.

"I hope you are going to stay here with us, Miss Hester," Pearl said.

"Hello, Miss, I hope you don't care but the judge wouldn't leave Austin if William and I didn't come along." Hester smiled at Pearl, but was speaking to Lizzy.

"My goodness. Of course, you and William are very welcome." Lizzy turned to Pete and smiled. "We're going to have to make a few arrangements in the house."

We need to talk. My father and I packed nearly all of our belongings. We both want to stay here in Crooksville with you and the kids." Pete pushed his father toward the house as Lizzy walked beside him. "Father wouldn't come here without Hester and William. They've been with him for many years, and they're like family."

Lizzy smiled down at the judge. Absolutely. We'll talk about this later.

As they passed the new house construction, Pete was surprised how much the carpenter and his crew had accomplished in just a couple of weeks. "The house is coming along real nice."

"Miss Lizzy, may I help the ladies serve the food? I didn't come here to stand around," Hester said as she walked inside the house.

"Come with me, Hester. I'll introduce you to the ladies. I don't know what I would have done without their help." Lizzy led Hester into the kitchen and told the ladies that Hester had come with Mr. Peterson from Austin, and they will be living with her and the children for a while."

"Hester, would you like to slice the ham and place the meat on this large tray? The men all love ham." Mrs. Brown, one of Lizzy's neighbors, handed her a sharp knife.

"Be happy to help in any way I can," Hester replied.

Lizzy walked to the porch and saw Pete pushing his father to the outhouse. She waited a few minutes and we they returned, she instructed Pete to take his father to the back porch and use the pans of water and hand towels to freshen up. There're plenty of tables to push his chair up to. The ladies will be serving the food as soon as everything is warmed."

~

Lizzy helped spread tablecloths on the makeshift tables. One of the older ladies came over to her. "You go and sit down, Lizzy. You have many hands to help with this work. This is a very sad day."

Lizzy thanked the older lady and turned to Pete. "I didn't expect so many people." She turned and scanned the wagons parked on the road leading into the farm, near the barn and close to the corral.

"I happened to know you're well thought of and the community is mourning your lost." Pete said as Lizzy blinked back tears.

Wiping her eyes, she said, "I better go into the house and check on the food and the ladies. Please make sure William feels welcome. We will have to find him something to do, like Hester."

"I saw him spreading quilts on the ground and

instructing children to take a seat. The old man is a jewel. I couldn't believe he was willing to leave Austin and come here with Father."

"I hate all of you came on such a sad day, but I'm so happy you're here. I do want to tell you later why I left without telling you. I just couldn't stay any longer where I wasn't welcome."

Pete hugged Lizzy and said, "I was upset at first, but I soon realized that you felt you had to leave. You don't need to offer me an explanation. I just want us to make plans for our future.

Hours later, Lizzy, Pete and the children stood together at the edge of the porch and waved goodbye to all their friends and neighbors. The sun was setting, and the children were yawning.

Pete and William had insisted earlier that the judge lie down. He was resting in Jake's bed while Pearl was sleeping on Joshua's bunk. Once everyone had left the farm, Lizzy told Hester that they would need to make pallets for the men in the boy's room. "Pearl can sleep on a pallet in my room and Hester can bed down with me."

"Lordy, Miss, I ain't never slept with a white woman," Hester shook her head side to side.

"Well, there's always a first time for everything." Lizzy turned to see what the boys wanted. They were practically jumping up and down with excitement.

"Lizzy, can we sleep in the barn with Yuma and Morning Flower? Yuma said we could if you agreed." Jake reached for the blanket Lizzy was holding.

"If you think it will be warm enough and they don't mind?"

"Morning Flower said for us to come and ask you. We have plenty of hay bales to lie on."

"All right, but you have to behave and go to sleep. Yuma and Morning Flower will be going back to the reservation tomorrow so they need their sleep.

The boys raced outside with Blue on their heels. Yuma

came in the house and walked straight to Pete and Lizzy. "I will be leaving soon to go home but I want to take the children on a fishing picnic tomorrow."

"Will you care if we all went on this outing?" Pete asked. "I know father would enjoy fishing."

"You know, Miss Lizzy, we have a lot of leftovers that would make a nice picnic lunch. I will be happy to pack the food after breakfast in the morning," Hester said.

"Great," Yuma smiled. "Let's have a big breakfast and head to the river after everyone is ready. The boys can dig worms and Pete and I will make sure the fishing poles are ready. See you at breakfast."

~

After the picnic lunch was packed and the boys had a bucket of fresh worms, Pete and Yuma placed two long boards from the ground to the back of the wagon in order to roll the judge in his wheelchair onto the back. They blocked the wheels so they wouldn't move. The rest of the family climbed in the bed of the wagon. William and the twins rode one of the corral horses behind the wagon.

When they arrived at the river, everyone jumped down and grabbed quilts, food and fishing poles. Pete and Yuma placed the boards on the back of the wagon and rolled the judge to the ground, then Pete instructed Pearl to stand beside his father until he could come back and roll him to the river.

Pete hurried down to the river and instructed the boys where they could fish, but no swimming. "The water is too cold to get soaked."

~

"Oh, look at those pretty flowers. I'm going to pick you some." Pearl hurried away from the judge and started picking flowers.

"Okay, don't go too far, little one." The judge turned his chair so he could watch Pearl. As he rocked his chair to make it turn, the wheels started moving down the slope. It moved slowly at first, and the judge tried to make it stop to no avail. The wheels picked up speed as the chair careened down the hill.

Pearl screamed came from behind as he hurtled toward the river.

Pete and Yuma came running up the hill, but just as they reached him, the wheels hit tall grass on an uneven path. As Pete reached to control the chair, it flipped over and tossed him onto the ground.

The judge immediately sat up and he moved his right leg. Pete reached to help his father. "No, don't touch me. Look, I moved my leg and then the other leg." The judge scooted his bottom away from the chair and lifted his hand to Yuma. "Pull me to my feet," he laughed.

Once the judge was standing straight, he offered his other hand to Pete. "Just help me keep my balance while I take a step or two," he said chuckling. Everyone crowded him, and William began to pray.

"Look son, I can move my feet. I am walking!"

Pete hugged his father. "Bless the good Lord, Father, we thought you were going to do more damage to your legs when you started down that hill. It's a miracle!"

"God did this!" Jake yelled, "You can walk!"

"Mercy, Jake, you sound just like Preacher Booker," Pearl said, as she rushed over to the judge and wrapped her little arms around his waist. "I'm so sorry. I didn't mean for the chair to start rolling. You could have gone into the river, and we might never have seen you again."

She tossed her flowers on the ground and began wiping the dirt off his clothes.

"I'm fine child, let's go fishing." Pete and Yuma walked beside the judge to the river's edge. The boys pushed the wheelchair down the slope and parked it near the river.

"If you get tired, Judge, you can have a seat," Joshua said, as he picked up his fishing pole.

"Do you want me to bait your hook, Judge?" Jake asked.

"Son, I've been fishing long before you were born. I don't need any help."

~

Once everyone had baited their poles and was busy fishing, Pete took Lizzy by the arm and led her away from the river into a small clearing in the woods. He wrapped his arms around her and kissed her. His lips had never felt more right. Wrapping her arms around his neck, she kissed him back.

Pete scooped her into his arms.

"Where are you taking me?"

"I am taking you away into the woods, so we can have privacy and talk without being overheard." Pete's thoughts and desires grew stronger as he sat Lizzy down on a log and he sat beside her. She was a beautiful woman. He said a silent prayer that she would agree to his plan. She had already agreed to be his wife, the love of his life forever.

Pete grinned. I can't wait to show you how much I love you. You're the perfect woman for me. You have more goodness inside your little finger than anyone I have ever met. That is only one of the things I love about you."

"It's one of the things I love about you, too," Lizzy commented. "I would never have imagined I could love the cowboy that rode into my yard half dead. It's amazing and I cannot stop smiling when I think about you." She scooted closer to him. "You, Pete Peterson are the love of my life."

Pete grinned. "I can't wait to show you how amazing I am."

Lizzy's face reflected joy. "I am deeply in love. You are a real man behind the rough exterior—good, sweet, and kindhearted."

Pete flashed her a shy grin. His voice was raw with emotions when he attempted to speak. "Lizzy, sweetheart, I don't want to wait until the house is completed to marry you. It may take months instead of weeks. We can make sleeping arrangements while we are building. I have supplies ordered with a large number of men coming to help. Also, Father has shipped many pieces of furniture from the mansion to your farm. Please say that we can marry very soon. I will need to tell Yuma so he can plan to return for the wedding to be my best man."

"Yes, I would like to get married soon. Please give me time to have a dress made for myself and Pearl and suits for the boys."

"I believe I can wait that long," he said as he pulled her into his arm to give her a kiss. "You're supposed to close your eyes," teasing her as he held her tight.

"If I close my eyes, I won't be able to look at you. And looking at you is one of the things I enjoy most," Lizzy said.

Chapter 40

Yuma and Morning Flower stood on the caboose of the train and waved goodbye to Pete. The train started moving as Pete ran long side of it, yelling at the top of his lungs.

"Remember you promised to be my best man at our wedding."

Yuma smiled and nodded. "We'll be there," he yelled.

Pete laughed, then untied his horse and rode to the telegram office.

He leaped on his horse and rode to the telegram office. He was expecting to hear from the foreman, Mr. Thornton, about when he would arrive. Thankfully, he wasn't disappointed. He had a telegram from the man stating they would be arriving tomorrow to help complete the house. Pete walked his horse to the hotel and reserved five rooms for the construction crew. Before he left town, he went to the dry goods store and had Mr. Mayberry fill his list of supplies needed at the farm. Pete couldn't hold in the good news. "Lizzy has agreed to marry me as soon as the dressmaker completes her wedding dress. Lizzy doesn't want a large wedding with her still mourning for her papa. But, of course, we could never marry without your presence."

Mr. and Mrs. Mayberry rushed from around the counter and gave him a great big hug. Mrs. Mayberry said, "Oh, we're so happy. You know we'll be there with bells on. Just let us know when."

~

Judge Peterson was eagerly waiting for his son to return from town. He wanted to inform Pete that he had decided to make a trip back to Austin. William will go with me," he said.

"But Father, don't you want to wait until your legs are stronger? Lizzy and I can't get married if you aren't here." Pete ran his hand through his hair.

"I'm only going to be away for a few days. I need to see the doctor and go to the courthouse and get approval to be the judge in Crooksville." He limped over to the swing on the front porch and sat. "I want to see my sons and grandchildren, too. Perhaps Will has changed his mind about running for governor. If not, I will speak my mind and try to sway him otherwise."

"You know you'll upset Marilyn," Pete grinned. "She'll never forgive me for putting your mansion up for sale."

"*Your* house and land. And I don't care about Marilyn. She doesn't like me anyway." The judge frowned. "I also want my grandchildren to know they can visit in the summer. Those little rascals of Lizzy's can teach them to be real boys. You know, Will's sons are scared of their own shadows."

"Of course, they will be welcome. I hope my brothers and their families will come to my wedding. I'll write out an invitation for you to give to them. Later I'll send a telegram with the date of the ceremony."

"I believe the boys will come, but who can say about the women they married?" The judge shook his head.

~

Lizzy whirled around in the kitchen. "Pete, I have been trying to make sleeping arrangements for everyone. I was thinking about this house once the new one is ready for us to move in." Lizzy said as she walked around in the kitchen. "I don't want it to be used like a barn or storage building. I love my little home."

"Well, I was thinking we could allow Hester and William to live here."

"I would love that, but Pete, they can't stay here alone.

They aren't married."

"Let me call William, and you get Hester. Let's talk about this problem," Pete said.

After the four of them sat around the kitchen table, Lizzy told the couple they wanted them to live in the farmhouse once they had moved into the new one.

"It wouldn't look good to have you living here without marriage. What do you think?" Pete said, stumbling over his words.

"Marriage?" Hester replied, smiling at William. "Pete, I thought you knew. William and I jumped the broom many a year ago. Shoot, I must have been sixteen, and he was only a youngster." Hester glanced at William.

William, being a very quiet man listened to Hester's words. "Now, Hester, I was old enough to work in the fields and take a woman. On a big plantation near Austin, where we were slaves, I was chosen to be a coach driver, and then I was brought into the house to take care of the plantation owner's old man. Later, after he passed, I was trained to be the butler. Soon, Hester and I fell in love and, like she said, jumped the broom. Years later, we were freed, the judge visited the plantation and asked me if I would like to work for his family. He had three little boys, and his wife was desperate for help. He offered a good salary that I couldn't refuse. It wasn't a problem leaving the plantation because the owner had already told me they needed to reduce their house servants. Everything worked out, and Hester and I were happy we worked for the judge."

Pete shook his head and smiled. "Hester, I had no idea you two were a married couple. Of course, I was a child, but I never paid any attention to what you did after we were put to bed. You always helped us dress for school, packed our lunches, and were home when we returned."

"I guess William and I were so busy with children, the kitchen, stables, and overseeing the other servants, we didn't have time to show any affection in front of others." She grinned and looked at her man.

"It looks like we don't have a problem with you two living in this house. I would like the children to stay with you, here when we have guests, which won't be often, if that's all right with you. Lizzy looked at the two wonderful people who would be a wonderful addition to their family.

~

Early the following morning, laughter and loud voices were heard coming into the farmyard. Pete rushed to the front door and saw four wagons loaded with lumber and big, bushy-faced men. Mr. Thornton leaped off the lead wagon and joined him on the porch.

"Come in, Mr. Thornton, and meet my future wife, Lizzy Montgomery. She will have a lot to say about how she wants the house to look. I'm sure she will be easy to work with."

"It's so nice to meet you, Mr. Thornton. I'm eager to see the walls go up and the fireplaces being built. I'll have some coffee in a few minutes."

"Thank you, Miss Montgomery, but I had plenty of coffee at the hotel this morning. I need to show the men where they can unload the materials, especially the large pieces of stone and rock. Would you, Mr. Peterson, come and help me determine the best place to put the lumber and rocks?"

"Absolutely." He turned to his future bride. "Lizzy, please tell the children to avoid the construction site. The men will not have time to watch out for them."

Chapter 41

For many days after the funeral of Herman Montgomery, people filled the house, bringing comfort and food. Lizzy always dreamed of having a big, beautiful wedding, but she felt it was wrong to have a celebration soon after her papa's death. She wanted to have her close friends and Pete's family in attendance, but not a large church wedding. She knew many people would understand her feelings.

Lizzy had ridden into town to have her last fitting. Miss Balding was making her a simple but lovely white dress, although the seamstress wasn't her usual sweet self. Lizzy remember the boys had told her that *Pa only had the dressmaker on his mind,* but she didn't know he had planned to take her to dinner. Lizzy expressed her sympathies to Miss Balding. "I am sorry Pa was taken from us so soon after he arrived home. I'm pleased he had made a good friend in you."

Tears formed in the dressmakers' eyes, but she didn't say anything.

"I can't tell you how much I appreciate you. My dress is lovely, and I hope you'll come to the wedding. We plan to wed Sunday, after the church service."

~

Everything was in place, Pete thought. Yuma and Morning Flower, Will, and Jeff, along with Jeff's wife, Evelyn, and daughter, had arrived for the big day. Pete's father was asked to be Lizzy Papa's stand-in and walk her down the aisle. Lizzy asked Mrs. Mayberry to be her matron of honor.

Pete had settled everyone into the Grand Hotel. He had arranged for the hotel to provide a small buffet lunch for the family and close friends. He didn't want Hester to have to do anything before the service, and he wanted Lizzy to have privacy while she packed her things to take to the church.

Pete had never been so antsy before. He couldn't stop cracking his knuckles as he paced around the small room in the back of the church's sanctuary. Pete couldn't believe Lizzy would soon be his wife. He could look far and wide and never find a more beautiful, wonderful woman. As his thoughts flowed to his future wife, the door busted open, and the twins rushed to him.

"How do we look, Mr. Pete?" Jake asked as he turned around. Both boys wore new black suits identical to his. They had on new shoes which Joshua complained pinched his big toe. Pete laughed and told Joshua he wouldn't have to wear the new shoes very long, but not say anything more about it because it would upset his sister.

"Where is Pearl?" Pete asked.

"She's with Lizzy. She looks pretty for a girl. She's holding a basket of flowers. Hester called her a flower girl," Jake said.

Pete and the boys heard Preacher Booker say amen. That was a clue the service was over, and the wedding was beginning soon. As Pete cracked the door, Yuma pushed it open and entered. He was dressed like an Indian Chief. A woman would say he was beautiful, but Pete walked around and looked Yuma up one side and down another. "You didn't have a white man's dark suit?"

"I am no white man. These are proper clothes for a ceremony. I can always leave if you dislike what I wear."

"No, I am joking with you. I'm proud you are here, to stand beside me, no matter what you wear," Pete smiled at Yuma.

"I am pleased you like my dress because I will be

wearing it when I speak for the Sioux Indians in front of Congress in many moons," Yuma said, as he strutted around the room.

"Is Morning Flower with Lizzy? I bet she's lovely today."

"She is lovely every day," Yuma said. "We will come together soon."

Jake pulled on Pete's new suit. "It looks like everyone stayed to watch you marry Lizzy. The Preacher is asking everyone to be quiet because he wants to start the wedding."

"Oh, my goodness," Pete whispered to Yuma, "I hope there's enough food to feed everyone."

Yuma smiled. "It's too late to worry about that now. You should have known country folks always attend everything-- weddings, funerals, births."

Preacher Booker knocked softly on the door before he opened it. "Let's get started. Boys, go to the front and help some of the ladies take a seat."

"What do you mean?" the boys looked at the preacher like he had lost his mind.

"Well, you take their arm and guide them to a pew. Can you do that?"

"Sure," commented Jake. "Come on, Joshua, we got this."

The pianist began to play a sweet melody. The preacher, Yuma, and Pete stood in front of the church. Many ladies whispered about how handsome the men were.

Mrs. Wilson, a ninety-year-old woman, played the Wedding March. The boys had taken seats on the front pew next to Hester. Mrs. Mayberry stood in the back and kept Pearl still until it was time for her to walk down the aisle.

When it was her turn, Pearl strolled confidently down the aisle, glancing side to side at the wedding guests, as she threw flowers on the floor. After Pearl stood in front of Yuma, Mrs. Mayberry smiled and walked to the front standing opposite the men. Lizzy took the judge's arm, and they walked slowly, one step at a time. She couldn't hold in the tears that flowed down her lovely face as she thought of her mama and her papa. This was a day that they would have loved.

Once they arrived at the altar, Lizzy gave Mrs. Mayberry her lovely bouquet of flowers. Mrs. Mayberry had cried when Lizzy asked her to stand up with her. The judge kissed Lizzy on her cheek and shook his son's hand. He placed Lizzy's hand in Pete's. Turning at the same time, they faced the preacher.

"Who gives this woman to be married to this man?"

"I do," Judge Peterson said, and sat beside Hester.

Tall and powerful, Pete stood dressed in his newly acquired black suit. The smartly cut jacket hugged his shoulders and lean hips. The ivory shirt collar was a perfect contrast to his suntanned skin. It was hard for Lizzy to keep her eyes off him.

~

Pete took in the vision before him. She was a beauty. He still couldn't believe this lovely creator could love him as much as he adored her.

Time stood still as they were moved through the marriage ceremony. Lizzy listened intently as Pete responded to the preacher's question.

"I, Peter Lane Peterson, take Elizabeth Marie Montgomery to be my lawful wedded wife." Thankfully, Lizzy spoke the same words, pledging herself to this man in tearful tones.

Pete slid a small lovely, gold band upon her finger. They bowed their heads as Preacher Booker said the closing prayer.

"I now pronounce you husband and wife."

Pete and Lizzy stood like two statues, gazing into each other's eyes. "I believe it is customary for the groom to kiss his bride." Reverend Booker chuckled.

Pete smiled as he crushed Lizzy to him in a fierce embrace. He turned her loose when the guests laughed and clapped their hands. Yuma pushed Pete away from Lizzy as he lowered his head and kissed her on her tear-stained cheek. "I pray you will always be as happy as you are today."

"Thank you, sweet friend. I want you and Morning Flower to be happy, too.

Lizzy's twin brothers raced to Lizzy and wrapped their arms around her waist. Pearl stood eyeing Pete and said, "Mr. Pete, when Lizzy gets old and ugly, you can marry me."

"Pete stooped down and lifted Pearl into his arms. "Is that a promise?"

"Yep, but she might never get ugly because she is so beautiful today."

Morning Flower smiled and wiped tears as she hugged her new friend, Lizzy. "You made a lovely bride."

Pete shook the preacher's hand and slipped him an envelope while asking that he and his wife join them at the hotel for a nice lunch. Once all the hugs were over, Pete announced that everyone join them at the Grand Hotel for refreshments.

Pete and Lizzy accepted many toasts and good wishes. The foreman of the construction crew said his men would work double-time and complete the house. Many friends brought homemade gifts that Hester and William loaded in the wagon to take home.

Everyone agreed that the wedding was beautiful and extra precious since the children were involved. Pete's father made the final toast and announced that it was time to allow the love birds to go up to the bridal suite. Everyone laughed, gathered up their things and left for home.

Chapter 42

"Come on, William. Let's gather the children and head home." William eased closer to Hester, dressed in a dark green dress with a string of white pearls entwined in her black curls. "Hmm," he said, whispering softly into her ear. "We need to get home and spend some time alone. I would like to suck your face off."

"Oh, you old fool," Hester laughed, giving William a little shove. "You'd better behave and let Pete do things like that to Lizzy." Giggling, she took her old husband's hand.

Back in the hallway, the couple looked up and down. "Where in the world did those young'uns get off to?" Hester asked.

"The boys were playing hide and seek up here with little Sarah. They like Jeff's girl."

After the boys and Sarah were found, Pearl was still missing.

~

Pete pulled Lizzy behind him as he rushed up the large hotel staircase to the bridal suite. He used his shiny, black shoe to shut the door, then pranced to his bride, resembling a great big panther. His kiss was like a greedy animal who might eat her alive.

Her lips opened and were smothered, taking in the invasion of his tongue.

Mercy thought Lizzy, never having been so intimate

with a man. She suspected Pete was having a hard time controlling himself until she was ready.

It was a short walk to the big four-poster bed with a wedding ring quilt.

"Pete, slow down and help me get my gown off."

Sighing, he turned her back to him, "Goodness, how many buttons does this dress have?"

Before Lizzy answered, there was a knock on the door. A soft voice called out, "Room service."

"Go away, we don't need anything," Pete yelled.

"I have a gift for you from your father, Mr. Peterson," the soft voice replied.

Pete walked to the door and opened it. A young man held a bucket with a bottle of champagne and a tray with two glasses. "May I place this on the table, sir?"

"Please," Pete said as he reached into his pants and pulled a few coins. "Thank you," Pete said as he locked the door.

After the young man left, he gave Lizzy a shy grin and returned to her. He slipped off his shoes, jacket, and vest and proceeded to attack the buttons on her dress again. He snuggled her neck as he fumbled with her covered buttons. She laughed as another knock sounded on the door.

"Now what?" Pete straightened and marched to the door. Unlocking the door, he practically yelled, "What?"

"Oh, Pete, we're sorry." Hester looked embarrassed, "But we can't find Pearl. She had been playing with the other children, but now that we're ready to leave, she is nowhere to be found."

Lizzy, holding her gown onto her shoulders, rushed to the door. "I'm sure she will show up. Please keep looking."

"She's going to get a good tongue lashing when I find her," Hester said. "Sorry to have bothered you but we had to make sure she wasn't with you. Good night."

Pete sighed and turned to Lizzy. "Now, where were we?" he grinned, suddenly scooping up his lovely bride in his arms and carrying her back to the four-poster bed.

Standing Lizzy on her feet, he continued with the buttons. Lizzy laughed and quickly stopped. Something was moving under the lovely quilt on the bed. Lizzy placed her fingers over her lips, touched Pete to get his attention, and pointed to the bed.

Pete bent over the bed and jerked back the wedding ring quilt. In the center of the bed lay Pearl. Being discovered, she sprang up on her knees with eyes as large as a saucer.

"What are you doing in our bed, darling?" Lizzy asked, very surprised to find her baby sister under the covers.

"Darling, my foot." Pete was angrier than Lizzy had ever see him. "Pearl, don't you know that everyone is looking for you? They are ready to go home."

"I had to come and protect Lizzy from you." Looking down at her hands, she finally glanced up, and screamed, "I couldn't let you suck her face off!"

"What?" Both Pete and Lizzy said at the same time.

"Pearl, where did you hear something like that?" Lizzy asked.

Someone banged on the door again. Hester's voice sounded from outside the door "Pete, is everything all right?"

Pete unlocked the door and allowed Hester and William in the room.

"Him! I heard it from him. He said Pete would suck Lizzy's face off," Pearl shouted as she pointed at William."

"My Lord," Hester said as she reached for Pearl, dragging her off the bed into her arms. Along with William, they rushed out of the room. Pete glanced at his lovely bride as she held her white dress to her breasts. He sat down on the edge of the bed and ran his hand through his hair. "Man that was a mood killer."

Lizzy couldn't hold in her laughter any longer. "This is a night we'll always remember. By the way, how does one go about sucking off someone's face?"

Pete reached for Lizzy, and both fell back on the bed." Let me show you."

Epilogue

Lizzy and the children drove the old flatbed wagon under the new archway that read, *Montgomery and Peterson's Farm*. They had gone to town to meet the new schoolteacher, Mr. Walter McCabe and his lovely wife, Angela. The children liked the tall, blond man immediately, who laughed as he greeted each child. The school board was pleased to have found a good Christian man who seriously enjoyed teaching children.

William held the reins of Libby's two new black horses as she and the children jumped upon on the porch. Yuma and Morning Flower had arrived for Christmas and stood waiting for them to return.

Morning Flower hugged everyone. "Lizzy, your home is beautiful. Pete showed us all around.

"Speaking of beautiful, you are the perfect picture of an expectant mother. Will the child be here this spring?" Lizzy asked.

"Yes, hopefully by April." Morning Flower ran her hand across her large stomach.

Pete, Yuma and the judge carried piles of packages into the house. "It looks like you bought out the Mayberry's store," Pete said.

"I also have a list of supplies their delivery boy will bring out later. By the way I have invited Mr. and Mrs. Mayberry to have Christmas dinner with us tomorrow.

Early Christmas morning, Hester and Morning Flower

cooked a big breakfast. The children helped clean the kitchen before sitting in the big room to wait to open presents. Pete asked Pearl to help him pass out the gifts.

Lizzy had knitted everyone mittens with scarves to match. Morning Flower had made Pete and the boys' deer hide Indian vests and Pearl and Lizzy an Indian shift decorated with beads circling the neckline.

Pete asked everyone to dress warm and come outside with him. The judge hurried behind the barn as Pete led the twins to the corral. Pete instructed them to close their eyes while the judge brought two pinto ponies to the gate of the corral. "Boys, you can open your eyes, now," Pete said.

The twins were overjoyed with their ponies.

"Now boys, you're old enough to take care of your own animal. You'll be able to ride to school, but you'll have to take turns carrying Pearl behind you."

The twins reached for the reins of their new ponies. "Thank you, Grandpa," Jake said.

Before Joshua led his pony into the corral, he gave the judge a big hug. "Thanks, Grandpa."

He stood with tears in his eyes as he looked at his son. "That's the nicest present I could have received from those little fellows."

Pete tilted his head. "What present?"

"They called me *grandpa* for the first time." He took his hanky from his jacket and wiped his eyes. Pete was pleased the children had accepted his father as their grandpa.

"All right, Lizzy, it's your turn to close your eyes." Pete instructed.

"Me? But Pete, you have already given me a beautiful gift." She flashed her ring finger to show the others a lovely diamond ring.

"Hurry now and close those big eyes of yours." She did as instructed as Yuma drove a large black two-seater carriage with fringe surrounding the edges from the double doors of the barn.

Lizzy opened her eyes and screamed. "This is for me?"

"Well, yes, but you'll have to allow us to ride in it." Pete grinned as everyone laughed.

Pearl hugged Lizzy and asked if she could get in it. Pete smiled and said, "First little lady, I have one more surprise for someone special to me."

"Who are you talking about?" Pearl asked, glancing at the others.

"You silly. Now close your eyes like Lizzy did."

Pearl looked around and finally shut one eye. "No," said Pete. Both eyes now, or no surprise."

Pearl sighed and closed her eyes. William came out of the barn carrying a small, fluffy rabbit with pink eyes and sat it down in front of Pearl.

"Open your eyes, sweetheart." Pete stepped closer to Lizzy and smiled.

"Oh my. This pretty little thing is all mine?" She looked at Pete and Lizzy.

"Yes, it's all yours to love and take care of. William has built a cage for it to sleep in at night and while you're not around to watch it."

"Oh, Mr. Pete, I love you so much." Pearl said as the boys chimed in, "We love you too, Mr. Pete."

Yuma, Morning Flower, Judge Peterson, and William all walked back to the porch as Hester held the door open for them to come into the warm house.

Morning Flower and Hester tied an apron around William and the judge's waist. "You, William, peel the potatoes and Judge, you start setting the big table." Hester grinned at Morning flower.

The men looked at each other. The judge whispered to William. "We sure know some bossy women."

~

Before returning to the house, Pete led Lizzy to the small, fenced cemetery behind the house. Tears filled Lizzy's eyes once she saw the new headstones for her parents. Large rocks surrounded and outlined each grave.

"My folks would be so proud. I can't express my love for your thoughtfulness" Lizzy closed her eyes and placed her hand across each marker as she said a silent prayer. She snuggled close to her husband and thought about the blessing God had sent her way--a wounded cowboy. Because of this wonderful man, she and her siblings were loved and cherished.

As the couple strolled toward their warm haven, Lizzy realized her little farm was a place where love happened.

The end.

With over sixteen historical romance novels, Linda Sealy Knowles enchants her faithful readers with her intriguing stories. She is grateful for the gift that God has given her to write. Linda was raised in Saraland/Satsuma area of Mobile, Alabama